MURDER, SCAMS AND
GRAVY TRAINS

Also by John Henderson

A Blind Eye
Anchor Man
Musgrave Solution
Taipan Club

MURDER, SCAMS AND GRAVY TRAINS

Simon Webster's third fiasco

JOHN HENDERSON

Murder, Scams And Gravy Trains

ISBN eBook: 978-0-9875769-2-7

ISBN Paperback: 978-0-9875769-3-4

Publisher: J. Henderson, Canberra, Australia

For Fergus

Chapter 1

After several minutes gazing at a map of Sydney's eastern suburbs stuck to the wall of his office, Ralph Glover rose from his chair, extracted a map pin from one position and relocated it to another position on the map. Ralph, a short stocky man in his mid thirties and desperately trying to maintain a trendy youthful appearance, was vain. His hair, shaggy and pulled back into a ponytail clipped with a rubber band, fell over the collar of his white, tieless shirt that looked like it was worn as a wash and wear item that wasn't. While in the office Ralph always rolled his shirt sleeves to a position halfway between the wrist and the elbow as he believed it gave his staff the impression he was getting on with the job.

Ralph headed a small property enterprise, Glover Property Development, located in the Sydney eastern suburb of Bondi Junction and, through no fault of his own, was finding the lucrative government tenders being called for property development harder and harder to bring to the contract stage. To keep the company solvent, Glover Property Development had resorted to the purchase of dilapidated real estate and, after demolition and rebuilding on the site, selling the property at a profit, sometimes. The administrative costs involved in such a process were ever increasing with many local councils imposing mandatory construction ordinances, along with a never-ending list of bureaucratic approvals required as each brick is laid. Countless people within the redevelopment business regarded these costs, and the associated ridiculously imposed red tape, as nothing more than bureaucratic extortion with stupidity running rampant. Ralph saw it as a case of out and out money-making piracy and legalised banditry.

That Ralph was now head of GPD, as it was more frequently referred, was brought about by a simple case of murder; that of Bruce Glover, one of Ralph's two older brothers. The murder of Bruce had been a simple case of fratricide perpetrated by the eldest brother of the Glover clan, Paul, and Andrew Glover, uncle of the three brothers and, at the time, head of GPD. Paul and Andrew were now incarcerated in the Long Bay Correction Centre where they should, all things being equal, remain for the next ten years. However, as all things are not always equal and, in spite of the sentence handed down by a crotchety old judge, the legal fraternity had, in its own inimitable way, provided Paul and Andrew good reason to anticipate a release from prison within the next few months. While civil rights do-gooders were chaffed at the prospect of the men's release, there were those people disgusted with the thought that the Glovers would serve a mere eighteen months of a ten year sentence for the brutal bashing to death of a beloved younger brother and a nephew.

Ralph Glover's office was not neat due to the fact that

there was limited storage furniture provided for the countless rolls of suburban maps and building plans that littered the office. Notwithstanding the limited space for business related records, Ralph's desk was clear, save for an empty McDonald's paper bag, an empty coffee mug and an ash tray with a smouldering cigarette butt. He now stood with one hand in a pocket of his navy blue trousers, unmindful of the ash falling from his cigarette held in the other, while he continued his scrutiny of the map. 'Henry, I need you,' he called without turning.

'Yes, you have a problem?' Henry, in a tone that suggested he hoped Ralph did, asked as he entered the office. In his forties, Henry Haynes was a tall, strong man with broad shoulders and bulging biceps. Quite apart from his dark brown hair and matching dark brown eyes, which added to his intimidating physical appearance, Ralph considered Henry a cantankerous sod at the best of times and a right real bastard at the worst. Other members of the GPD staff shared Ralph's feelings towards Henry who had failed to display any amiable qualities, steadfastly refusing to participate in any office social function since joining GPD some twelve months earlier.

It was ironical that Henry, who had previously worked for the property development company Dayman Brothers, had taken a job at GPD following the financial collapse of Daymans. While the collapse had been considered by many to have been the result of poor management decisions, those in the know were well aware that bureaucratic bungling was the mitigating factor. To be more accurate, the frequent changes of mind to decisions already made by officials, from the lowest level of bureaucratic local councils to the highest echelons of parliament, and specifically within those areas relating to major development schemes, had prompted the fall of the Company. The end result was that Dayman Brothers had gone broke only to be subsequently purchased by GPD at a very attractive price.

'If I have a problem, then you've got one too so just shut up and listen,' Ralph snapped as he sat behind his desk and folded his arms. 'As you know, or might not know, I have two older brothers, Paul and Bruce, and one uncle that I know of, Andrew. Bruce is dead and Paul and Andrew are in Long Bay for having done away with Bruce. Before Uncle Andy and Paul were incarcerated, they were involved in a deal to redevelop a property over at Elizabeth Bay that had been willed to Paul and Bruce. Nothing came of it because brother Paul and Uncle Andrew both became totally deranged one night and bashed brother Bruce over the head killing the poor bugger.

'Both Bruce and Paul had received the inheritance after mumsie kicked off; Paul wanted to redevelop, Bruce wanted to keep it, for his own good reasons, so brother Paul and Uncle Andy bashed him to death. Seeing I had never got along with the family and held no expectations of anything from mumsie, I was quite happy and surprised with what she did leave me. Anyway, the point is I don't know what the legal position is at the moment, but the place over at Elizabeth Bay is still standing.'

'Yeah. So what? I wouldn't touch the place with a barge pole. I know a few of the bureaucrats in the area's local government and, so help me, they change their mind as often as they change their knickers. If by some very remote chance they make a decision, don't count on that decision lasting for too long.'

'Look, Henry, Andrew had already received council approval to redevelop the building. The only thing that prevented the work to commence was a glitch in mumsie's will that left the place to Bruce and Paul. They could do whatever they liked with the mansion as long as both agreed, and they didn't. Now we have Brucie dead and Paul banged up for his murder, along with Uncle Andy. I want you to get over to Long Bay and have a chat with our two homicidal maniacs and find out where we're at. Oh yeah, and get yourself over to the local council and see what the position is with the redevelopment application,' Ralph added as an afterthought. 'I think it might be an idea if you did that. If I came across that little pipsqueak Boswell, I'd ring his bloody neck. And sure as hell, if I didn't run into him, I'd run into some other bureaucratic halfwit.'

Having issued his brief but succinct orders, Ralph unfolded one of his folded arms to hold his chin while in deep concentration. 'I don't know who in local council is making all the money, but between them and the politicians up in Macquarie Street, I reckon the kickbacks being taken could pay off the national debt. I know Andrew and Paul received approval to knock down the existing building and put up some town houses. However, this approval was dependent on certain conditions, one being that any demolition or construction work had to be carried out by the council's own appointed sub-contractors. And as we're the bunnies who get the bill, you can bet they don't come cheap.'

'Yeah, but with so many shonkies going on, I can't see the attraction in this Elizabeth Bay property,' replied Henry, showing a gross lack of enthusiasm.

'The attraction is money, you surly bugger, even if we do have to comply with the council's conditions. We could still make quite a bundle on the place. Anyway, what is it with you? Ever since you joined GPD you've been a bad tempered, ill mannered and thoroughly obnoxious individual. So just what is your beef with life?'

Henry sighed and flopped down into a chair, a look of bored resignation on his face. 'It's a long story but the short version is the company I last worked for, Dayman Brothers, went bust, as you well know seeing it was GPD that bought us out. Everything was rosy with a large residential development planned for Rose Bay. We had all the approvals from the planning authorities and local council had rezoned the area from low density residential to high density residential. After coming to an agreement with a bank for additional capital, we had even gone so far as to start buying up properties to make way for the development.

'It wasn't until after we had spent bucket loads of money that some bloody tree-hugger mob started jumping up and down saying it would be an environmental catastrophe. Well, that's the story we were told. They said the trees in the area were home for the green spotted tree frog which, according to the tree-huggers, is an endangered species that only live in the specific trees we wanted to chop down. Some trumped up politician thought it would mean a few extra votes so he took their whingeing onboard and started jumping up and down himself. As no-one else in parliament knew what he was talking about, and cared even less, he was able to have the whole deal quashed. That's when the company fell apart.'

Ralph lent forward, his elbow on the desk and rested his chin on his hand, the other hand on his hip. 'Well Henry, it seems we all have a cross to bear. I have some idea of what goes on as far as kickbacks to politicians go, but never been involved myself. Uncle Andy was the boss here and I didn't ask questions or dispute his decisions. However, it's obvious he and Paul couldn't be that bright as they had themselves thrown in the jug just when they were getting the redevelopment of this Elizabeth Bay property organised. We were counting on that scheme to make a bit of money then along comes this bloody copper investigating Bruce's murder and took an interest in the place. It seems Brucie was using the place to cultivate a bit of marijuana, and anyone with half a brain who knew Bruce would have expected something of that nature would have been going on. Obviously the police had bigger fish to fry as they couldn't have cared less about finding a pot plot in the middle of their investigation. Then this overzealous plod, who according to Andy likes sprouting Shakespeare, hauls both my brother and uncle off to the clink.'

Henry frowned. 'Hey, hang about. You say this copper likes to quote Shakespeare?'

'Yeah. I believe he goes by the name of Simon Webster, is a detective chief inspector and believes Hamlet is a story about a small country village. If I'm right and he is the bloke, he's known to be pally with a polly and some gangster bloke. I think the polly is that egomaniac Mr Porter, MP. But then again, all politicians are nothing more than egos on legs.'

'Holy hell,' swore Henry. I knew some bloody rozzer with a bent for showing off his thespian ability, or lack thereof, was chummy with Porter although I didn't know who it was. Small world ain't it?'

'What do you mean?' replied Ralph, mystified.

'Well, you'd expect a detective would need to know some gangsters pretty well, so I can excuse this Webster character for being friendly with a crim. But friendly with a politician, and the one who sent our company broke? Hell, that's really scraping the bottom of the barrel.' Henry shook his head in wonderment of the mysteries of life.

'Seems we both have a couple of things in common and that's this copper Webster and a politician named Porter.'

Ralph shrugged. 'Yeah, as I said, he's the one who busted Paul and Andy. I don't know the man, but if he's as bad a copper as he is at reciting Shakespeare, society is in one hell of a mess.'

'So, I don't like Porter and there's no love lost between you and this Webster character either?' Henry asked before realizing it was a stupid question in the first place.

'Well, what would you expect if he'd put your brother and uncle away. Sure, I might have an axe to grind, even if he was just doing his job. But somehow I think you may have more of a reason to plant the dirk in this bloke Porter's back than I have for doin' Webster in.' Ralph smirked a cynical smirk. 'Problem there is that it's probably a bloody waste of time trying to plant the dirk in any politician. They're so used to being dirked, usually by a political colleague, they've become immune to the occasional stab in the back. It comes with the job.'

'Bloody hell. I didn't think of that. But you're right, of course,' responded Henry. 'So, if anybody is thinking of doing away with a politician, literally that is, how do you suggest they go about it?'

'Cripes, I've never given it any serious thought. Well, not until lately. Look, I've no real beef apart from the same complaint everyone has with any politician. I can't think of the last honest polly we had, if we've ever had one. I suppose the success of a politician is governed by the ability to convince the electorate of his alleged altruistic motivation for being elected in the first place. Once he has himself elected, all he has to do is have the ability to tell untruths with a bit more sincerity than a used car salesman. And if there is a truthful politician, one who doesn't tell porkies, you can bet he's up to some shonky activity to line his pockets, like on the take from some developer or council bureaucrat. No, if I have a beef at all it's with this bloke, Detective Super Constable, or whatever, Webster. Here he is carting my brother off to the slammer, along with my uncle, while at the same time he's out hobnobbing with a gangster and a crooked politician. Sorry, I think crooked is a pleonasm, but you get the message.'

'Yeah, okay. But what's a pleonasm?' Henry asked in total ignorance.

'Don't worry about it. You go and fix up your politician, and I'll go and stick pins in my copper. That should make us both a lot happier than we are just at the moment.'

Chapter 2

Andy Crawford sat back, hands resting together on his lap with thumbs arched, his legs crossed at the knee. Standing over six feet tall, Crawford was thin but not skinny, with long blond hair and blue eyes. And he was wealthy, very wealthy, and wasn't backward in coming forward to let everybody know. As could be expected, his Giorgio Armani suit fitted perfectly and his Rolex was just visible under the cuff of his shirt. He drove a new red Ferrari, an essential acquisition necessitated by the fact that his previous car, a red Ferrari, had been written off after it had been torched, presumably by some disgruntled gambler. Whatever impediment his height created in driving his new acquisition, if indeed an impediment ever existed, it was dispelled by the thought that no-one could be uncomfortable behind the wheel of a Ferrari.

Sitting opposite Andy Crawford and half hidden behind a large wooden office desk was Paul Stack. Paul was a short, portly man and, if you were polite, would describe him as having a receding hair line. Truth be known, Paul

Stack was bald as a badger. His clothes were a mixture of flamboyance and drabness, his plain dark grey trousers set against an orange shirt and an iridescent green tie. It was unfortunate for Andy, a non-smoker, that Paul was in the process of enjoying a cigar, as was his norm. The remains of a butt, still smoldering in an ashtray, only added to the fetid, eye-stinging office air that clearly attested to the expense Paul would not go to satisfy his addiction; Paul did not smoke Cuban cigars. Quite apart from the physical differences between the two men, they did have one thing in common; they were both gangsters operating illegal casinos, Andrew, The Red Ruby and Paul, The Spinning Wheel where the two men were now engaged in conversation.

'So, you reckon it's only a matter of time?' Paul asked as he tried to raise himself higher in his chair to view Andy over the desk. Wish he'd bloody well sit further back or I gotta get myself a lower table he thought, annoyed that his mind was preoccupied with getting a glimpse of his visitor.

'If I was a betting man, I'd put the house on it,' replied Andy with certainty. 'This polly pillock has put his bill to legalise gambling to parliament twice before and had it defeated. With society's attitude towards most things changing, he's gaining more support and the next time he presents it, it could get through.'

'Okay, but what's the motive behind it? Is he trying to establish legal casinos or abolish the illegal ones that now exist? The police know all about us but don't close us down because they think, and rightly so, that if they come down on us we'd just pack up and start somewhere else.'

'Harrumph,' Andy exclaimed. 'Doesn't matter one way or the other as it means the same thing; it's the end for us. But who is this political twerp who wants his name in lights? Some bloody do-gooder who doesn't even bet on the Melbourne Cup, I bet.'

Paul leaned back in his chair and disappeared from Andy's view. The desk started to speak. 'This do-gooder is Robert Porter. He's been in the Legislative Assembly for a few years and is ambitious. He currently holds a couple of port-folios, including that of the Minister for Planning and Infrastructure. I think the other is the Environment port-folio, but don't quote me. The thing that really gets up my nose is the fact that this Porter bloke used to be friendly with that Lee character. Recent indications are that the two are not so pally now and are at logger heads over something or other.'

'Not the Lee who owns The Taipan Club?' Andy asked the desk.

'That's the bloke,' the desk replied before a head slowly reappeared. 'He's got his bread buttered on both sides. The police are quite happy for him to run The Taipan Club while he provides the police with information on the drug scene. If Porter gets his dream of legal casinos, I heard Lee will be looked after by Porter with a position within a legal casino, a sort of payback for his work for the police. Maybe that was true once but I certainly don't believe it now, and if Lee believes it then he probably believes pigs can fly.'

There was one point Andy couldn't quite work out. 'Okay, so Porter wants to close down the illegal casinos and open up a legitimate one. But what's in it for himself. He can't be doing this out of the goodness of his heart.'

'Aah yes,' replied the desk as Paul disappeared – again. 'Porter is an ambitious man who sees himself as premier, if not higher office. He has this damn-fool idea that by shut-ting us down the government will reap bags of money in gambling taxes and make him popular with the majority of the electorate. And no-one will ever know just how much he'll pocket from expenses and the kickbacks that will be generated.'

Andy looked thoughtful for a moment. 'So, Porter is really just another pain in the bum. Hey, isn't his lady shacked up with this Lee character now?'

'Yep. They've been an item for a while now and it's getting pretty serious, so the rumor goes. I believe her bust-up with Porter was amicable, a sort of mutual decision. Trouble now is that while Porter is out to make life as miserable as hell for Lee with his hankering to shut The Taipan Club down, and us along with it, he's also out to make life pretty miserable for his ex as well'

Andy shrugged in acceptance of the inevitable. 'I s'pose there isn't much we can do about it unless someone has a quiet word with Porter, you know, something that might encourage him to reconsider his bill, so to speak. You have a big bloke out the front, why don't you tell him to go and whisper in Porter's ear?'

The head disappeared again. 'What, you mean Jacko? No way. Jacko wouldn't know what to whisper, and apart from that, he wouldn't hurt a fly let alone do a job on someone. He's a good doorman as long as everything is quiet, which it always is with him standing there. No, Jacko's good at intimidation as long as he doesn't have to say or do anything, and that's about it. But I like him and he's a good bloke, all the same.'

Andy sighed and folded his arms. 'Well, the last things we need are legal casinos popping up around the place. Instead on us making squillions of dollars, it would be the government raking in all the money. It might be okay if they knew how to spend it, but it's more likely some bureaucrat would arrange to have it squirreled away in a Swiss bank account.'

'Gee, you think so?'

'No, I think I was only joking. But I need the money more than the bloody government does. And at least I know how to spend it. With our options running out, there may be only one way to get this problem sorted.'

Paul's head lurched forward so he could look Andy in the eye. 'Oh no. I know what you're driving at. Look, I've already had some bloody detective inspector asking questions about someone's body being fished out of the harbour. If you're thinking what I think you're thinking, forget it; I don't want to know anythin' about it.'

'Okay, okay. Keep your knickers on. It was just a thought.'

Chapter 3

'Come on, sir, you have to be joking. It's not five o'clock yet and it's still dark. Whatever it is can surely wait until the sun comes up.'

'Yeah, okay. So it's dark. Be bloody odd if it wasn't. And don't go thinking I'd ring at this unearthly hour just to bugger up your day. But now that I have, I suggest you give your sergeant a ring so you won't be the only one inconvenienced. Come to think of it, I was woken up earlier than you, so you can suffer along with the rest of us.'

'Can I ask just who the rest of us might consist of, sir?'

'Well, there's a report of a body on Bondi Beach, of all places. Graham Gallymore from forensics is on his way, and the local uniform boys have created a crime scene, which would have been a bit tricky.'

'Sounds like a problem for the Eastern Suburbs Local Area Command. Okay, sir, thanks for the call, but seeing it has nothing to do with us, I'll get back to sleep.'

'Look, Chief Inspector, I don't know what this is all about either and I've given you all the details I have. All I've been told is that someone's reportedly found a body, well, they think it's a body, and the inspector at the scene wants you there. There is some urgency, if you must know, as time and tide waits for no-one, and the bloody tide is on the way in. So grab your bucket and spade and get over there. There's a police car on its way to pick up Sergeant Elliott before collecting you. I'd therefore suggest you contact your sergeant ASP as the car should be at his place in about ten minutes.'

Simon Webster replaced the receiver of the bedside phone and heaved a sigh. 'Bugger. Sorry to have woken you, sweetie, but that was Fisher. Seems they have a bit of a problem over at Bondi and they've requested our presence, for some stupid reason.'

'Yeah well, hurry up and give Noel a ring so I can go back to sleep. And you can get your own breakfast 'cause stuffed if I'm getting up at this hour of the morning.'

THE POLICE CAR, detached from the Northern Beaches LAC located at Dee Why, had picked up a very disgruntled Detective Sergeant Noel Elliott from his Mona Vale home before arriving at number 24 West Bank Lane, Collaroy. The phone call that had interrupted the peaceful slumber of both Noel and his wife, Sue, had been received with the same indignant and disgruntled reception as a similar call that had awoken both Detective Chief Inspector Simon Webster and his lovely lady, Georgie, a few minutes earlier.

Once Simon had settled himself into the back seat of the Holden with the flashing blue light on the roof, Noel gave Simon what information he had managed to elicit from the responsive but uninformed driver, Constable Flanders, during the trip from Mona Vale to Collaroy. 'That's about it, isn't it, Constable?'

'Yes, Sarge. The boss just directed me to pick you and the DCI up and get you over to Bondi ASP. I heard on the police radio net that someone found a dead body on the beach and they're waiting for you and forensics to have a look. Apparently the tide is on the way in hence some degree of urgency.'

'Well, bugger me and beware the tides of March. And you haven't heard who the body belongs to?' Simon asked, careful to refrain to comment on the tautology of describing the body as a dead body. It was Simon's view that a body had to be dead otherwise the body continued to remain being a person until all life was extinct, hence only then becoming a body.

'No, not a whisper, sir,' replied Constable Flanders. 'It does seem a bit funny that you should be involved in what-ever there is to get involved with, my apologies if that sounds a trifle insubordinate, sir. I believe both you gentlemen work out of Day Street which is in the City Central LAC. Now, with Bondi being in the Eastern Suburbs LAC and Dee Why in the Northern Beaches LAC, I get the idea there aren't that many LACs around that aren't involved in what's going on. Whatever it is must be big as Bondi's a bit out of your bailiwick. Sounds interesting.'

'Well, obviously there's something rotten in the state of Bondi. Anyway, Noel, how did Sue respond to being woken up in the middle of the night?'

'No problems. She jumped out of bed and went and cooked my breakfast.'

'Humph. Lucky you. I didn't get anything while I suppose you had eggs and bacon?'

'Not quite. Corn flakes.'

The conversation ceased, both detectives happy to watch the lights of the suburbs flash by as the constable took advantage of the deserted streets to display his high-speed driving skills. The first tinges of pink touching the eastern skies heralded another perfect autumn day; a perfect day marred only by the fact that some goose had chosen the celebrated Bondi Beach to give up his existence on planet Earth. However, with the two detectives having had their presence specifically requested, it was quite plausible that whoever it was who had passed on had done so with the not insignificant assistance of person, or persons, unknown.

'Hey, Constable, have you any idea as to the name of the inspector we're about to meet?' asked Simon as a matter of interest.

'Yes. I think it's Inspector Francis from Waverly as he's the one who rang your boss before ringing us at Dee Why. Anyway, I'd say you're about to find out as we're nearly there.' The car sped down the hill into Campbell Drive before making the right hand turn in to Queen Elizabeth Drive, the thoroughfare running the length and within spitting distance, of Bondi Beach. Constable Flanders announced their arrival with a screech of breaks amid a conglomeration of vehicles, all displaying flashing blue lights. 'Looks like all the action is down this end of the beach, gentlemen, so I'll drop you off here,' said the Constable as he brought the car to a standstill.

Chief Inspector Webster and Sergeant Elliott alighted from the vehicle that had come to a stop at the southern end of the beach. The first thing Simon took stock of was the condition of the surf which, to the bronzed, blond and blue-eyed part time Collaroy surf life-saver, looked miniscule, almost a mill pond with an occasional wave breaking on a sandbar about thirty metres from shore. The second point he noticed was that the tide appeared to be on the way in; about two hours after the low tide had been reached and with another four hours before the next high tide.

The two detectives dressed in mufti, their shoes squeaking on the golden sand, headed towards a small group of people partly obscured by a hastily constructed fence of plastic sheeting. It was clear the fence had been erected with an aim of restricting the view around something considered unsuitable for general exhibition. For Noel, it probably obscured the scene totally as Noel was not tall. In fact, Noel was at the minimum height for a policeman, his short stature compensated by a muscular frame. With black hair, an olive complexion and a nose broken on the football field more than once, Noel was pugnacious with a body to back up his pugnaciousness.

'I somehow get the feeling I'm overdressed on this particular occasion. Shorts and flip-flops seem much more appropriate,' Noel remarked.

Simon ignored the comment as he approached a gentleman dressed in something like a white boiler suit fitted with a hood. 'Hi Gally. And just what's this all about?'

'Simon, good to see you again,' responded Graham Gallymore. 'Before we get into it, I'd best introduce you to Detective Inspector Ian Francis. He seems to be the head honcho at this little soiree.' Graham Gallymore approached a tall, thin man, somewhere in his mid forties, casually dressed in civilian garb and in earnest conversation with a uniformed, overweight police sergeant. 'Excuse me Ian, you have a visitor,' interrupted Gally.

Detective Inspector Ian Francis turned and smiled. 'Ah,

DCI Webster and DS Elliott. Sorry to have got you out of bed so early, but it will be a beautiful sunrise, eventually.' The sun had risen but was currently masked by a line of pink and golden edged clouds that stretched along the horizon. 'Best you come along with us, Mr Gallymore. You can explain things better than I can.' With that, Francis led the three other men through a gap in the fence where they positioned themselves to view the cause of the early morning excitement.

'Holy hell,' remarked Noel. 'Someone really had it in for the poor bugger. He looks like he's got more holes in him than a golf course. I take it it's not suicide?'

'I very much doubt it,' responded DI Francis. 'I've never seen a case of suicide where someone tries to stab themselves to death. If you weren't successful after the first couple of goes, I think you'd be better off to give up and go blow your brains out with a shotgun. Gally, have you any thoughts?'

'None at the moment, apart from the fact that the body is definitely dead. I won't be able to establish cause of death until I get him back to the office and have had a poke around. Seeing he's dressed in nothing but a pair of swimmers, I'd say he'd been down for his early morning run along the beach before taking a swim. At least I can say with some certainty the bloke was fit when he got himself hacked up. He's big boned but no fat.'

'And who found him?' Simon asked DI Francis.

'Aah yes, there he is, the bloke over there,' he said nodding to where the uniformed sergeant was now in conversation with another fitness fanatic while jotting down notes into his notebook. 'He said he usually gets down here for his run and a paddle around four thirty, summer and winter. He doesn't know the name of our body although he says he was a regular and might say "gidday" as they passed.'

'And what's going on up there?' Simon asked, nodding to where an inordinate number of cars for such an early time of day were parked near the Bondi Surf Clubhouse.

'Oh that,' DI Frances replied, 'they'd be the people for the aerobic classes, mostly women with a few blokes brave enough to attend.'

Simon grunted and returned his attention back to the body lying on the beach. 'Hang on a moment,' said Simon with a look of concern, 'I think I've seen this codger somewhere before. Noel, come and take a closer look at this bloke. Tell me if you think you can recognize him.'

Although not overly excited by the prospect of taking a closer look at the very pale and sickly looking cadaver lying supine on the sand, Noel bent down for a closer inspection.

'Bloody hell. It's that politician. You know, the one married to Louisa. We met him up in Macquarie Street and later on Graham Lee's boat.'

Simon squatted on the sand and peered at the body. 'Alas, poor Porter. I knew him well, and yes, Noel, you're right. This is, or was, the honourable member Robert Porter, the high-flying politician who was married to the lovely Louisa.'

'Well, I don't suppose he's married to anyone now. No wonder I didn't recognize the poor bugger. He's not looking all that healthy right at the moment.' said Noel as he pulled a bit of seaweed from behind Robert Porter's ear.

Simon looked at DI Ian Francis who shrugged and pursed his lips, a display that conveyed his somewhat ambivalent attitude towards the condition of the late Mr Robert Porter. 'Just a stab in the dark, but I don't suppose there were any witnesses, or suspicious characters seen in the vicinity?

DI Francis, being in charge of the crime scene, spoke briefly to the uniformed sergeant before returning to Simon's questions. 'Well, until Gally can come up with a time and cause of death, the answers to your rather indelicate "stab in the dark" questions are; probably not and taken for granted.'

'Would you care to elucidate?' replied Simon.

'Well, the actual murder must have taken place pretty early, too early for the majority of fitness freaks. It's just lucky there was someone else out for his morning constitutional before the body was washed away with the tide. Despite the beach being fairly well illuminated, the finder of the body said he saw no-one else until he tripped over Mr Porter. As it stands, we have no witnesses to the stabbing. As for suspicious characters, the night spots don't close until after the sun comes up so you're likely to find suspicious characters wandering around at any hour, and anywhere in the city.'

Simon nodded his head in agreement. 'Sorry, Ian, but it's too damn early in the morning for me. I take it you'll be the investigating officer?'

'Maybe. One of the first officers on the scene thought he recognized the body, well, the face on the body, as that of Porter. As you probably know, most of the Force is aware that your familiarity with Mr Porter is on a first name basis. Thinking you may be able to contribute something, I rang and asked Superintendent Fisher if he wouldn't mind you attending this morning's little debacle. Quite apart from the information angle, I thought you might like to have a look and give us a tentative ID, you being friendly with Mr Porter.'

'Yeah, thanks. Noel and I both met Porter nearly two years ago when he and his wife were having some problems, not that their problems had anything to do with us or the police. Our association just happened to overlap an investigation we were conducting,' replied Simon in an effort to disassociate himself with the now very dead Mr Porter. 'You still haven't answered my question. Will you be doing the investigation?'

DI Francis shrugged. 'I know the body is within my LAC and I expect that's a good enough reason for me to be the poor sod landed with it. By the same token, you already have a head start on me by knowing the bloke. If I am investigating the case, I hope you don't mind if I draw on your knowledge of Porter?'

'No, no problems at all, not that I've spoken to him for well over twelve months now,' replied Simon. 'I can't say I'd like to be in your shoes though. Porter was quite an entity in the political arena and once the press gets a hold of this there'll be an uproar. They'll be baying for someone's blood, and if you don't arrest someone pretty quick smart, that blood will be yours.'

'Gee thanks. You wouldn't like to volunteer to it take on, would you, please?' implored Inspector Francis.

Simon shook his head and held his hands up in horror. 'Hell, no. Right now I haven't a clue as to if this is a murder or an assassination. Believe me, this is one case that could prove to be either a career limiting exercise or the perfect opportunity to make a name for yourself. Find the culprit and your career's assured. And as I don't suppose there's anything Noel or I can do to contribute right now, we'll let you get on with your examination of the scene. Oh, yes. I take it someone has broken the news to his wife, even if she hasn't been living with hubby?'

DI Frances lowered his head and looked at Simon with raised eyebrows. 'I'll lend you a car and a driver. And it would be appreciated.'

'Oh great. Come on Noel. Let's get this over with so we can set about trying to figure out how a politician can get themselves into so much of a mess.' As the two detectives left Bondi Beach, Simon muttered, 'A hearse, a hearse. My kingdom for a hearse.'

Chapter 4

It was with some reluctance Simon rang the doorbell to the exclusive Point Piper home and settled down to an anticipated extended wait. Knowing that both Graham Lee and Louisa Porter would have been at work at Graham's casino, The Taipan Club, until the wee hours of the morning, neither Simon nor Noel expected an immediate response to their early hour intrusion. The Taipan Club, an illegal gambling venue, tended to cater to the upper middle class clientele all eager to lose their money in fashionable surroundings. The majority of other casinos in Sydney were considered dives in comparison, the only common feature being that they were all operated by criminals or gangsters, not that Graham Lee wasn't a criminal, albeit a gentleman criminal. However, the police had come to the conclusion that it was far better the devil they knew and were therefore happy for the Taipan Club to operate, provided there was no trouble. And the patronage of the Club just happened to include many influential members of Sydney society, including senior police officers.

It wasn't until after about ten minutes of impatient waiting, and a lot of doorbell ringing, that lights started to go on within the building. Eventually, the door was finally opened to reveal a bleary-eyed, and not surprisingly, a cantankerous Graham Lee, bare footed and wrapped in a black satin dressing gown. Simon had half hoped nobody would be home as he deplored being the bearer of bad news, especially when it related to a fatality.

'Okay, who's dead? The "Gemini" has been stolen. The casino's on fire. Whatever it is, it's going to be pretty important or someone will definitely be dead, and that someone will be you, Simon. What is it that's so earth shattering that you have to get me up at this God unearthly hour of the morning?'

Simon shrugged and gestured in a placatory manner. 'Sorry Graham, but you were right the first time; we have a body, and yes I know, a body isn't a body until it's dead.'

Graham, tall, dark complexion, and black hair, screwed his dark eyes shut and shook his head in annoyance. 'Bugger. Then you'd better come in and tell me the story.'

Graham led the two detectives into a lounge room that offered panoramic views across Sydney Harbour, the early morning sun's reflection off the water heralding another beautiful day in paradise. Despite the opulent décor and a baby Steinway in a corner, the room exuded a comfortable and cosy atmosphere. The thought lingered in Noel's mind that here was the place to sit back with a Hennessy cognac, relax and watch the world go by. 'Please, take a seat,' Graham said, indicating. 'Coffee for anyone because I have to have my morning brew to kick-start my brain?'

'Love one,' replied Simon, Noel nodded his acceptance, 'but before we go any further, it might be an idea if Louisa was present as I think she might like to know just what's going on.'

Simon's call for Louisa's presence had an immediate effect; Graham Lee was wide awake. 'Why, what's Louisa got to do with a dead body?'

'Look, just get Louisa down here and all will be explained,' replied Simon, trying to be as sensitive as the situation demanded. After all, he was just about to advise the lovely Louisa that her ever-loving husband had been stabbed to death. Who was it; Brutus? If you have tears, be ready to shed them now, he thought.

Graham disappeared into the household to dig Louisa out of bed and to make the coffees. After looking around the lounge room Noel said, 'I think I'm in the wrong job. I should have taken up being a gangster as it looks like it pays pretty well.'

Simon grunted. 'We've already been down that road and decided being on the baddies' side wasn't for us.' The decision not to be on the baddies' side was made after their policing careers appeared destined for ruin. As a consequence, they had decided to view life from the other sides' perspective and, with the aid of Georgie and Sue, the four-some had robbed a bank in the middle of Sydney.

'Yeah, okay. Doesn't mean I wouldn't like to make the money Graham is obviously making. Ah, here's the lovely Louisa.'

Louisa was a tall brunette with shoulder length hair and hazel eyes. Although her hair looked like she had just got out of bed, which she had, Louisa still manage to exuded sensuality. With a light blue chenille dressing gown wrapped around her very well proportioned body, and wearing a pair of white fluffy slippers, she entered the lounge room with her arms folded against the early morning chill. 'Hi Noel,

Simon. I must look like the wreck of the Hesperus, but that's your fault, calling at this time of the day.'

'Sorry, but the circumstances demanded we call on you as a matter of some urgency. As soon as Graham's back with the coffee, we'll give you the details.'

It wasn't long before Graham Lee returned with four mugs of coffee, which he placed on a glass topped coffee table. 'Okay, Simon, now, what's this all about?' Graham asked as he settled himself into a leather lounge next to Louisa.

'First off, I'd like to ask Louisa a couple of questions. Louisa, when's the last time you saw your husband, Robert Porter?'

'Before I even try to answer that, I think it appropriate to set the record straight,' she replied, somewhat miffed by Simon's question. 'I know how finicky you are, Simon, especially when it comes to the English language. But I have now been married for several years to the same person, in fact, my one and only marriage to anyone. I am therefore perfectly aware of my husband's name.'

'Okay, sorry. But when is the last time you saw your husband?'

'God knows. Both Graham and I have approached him, both independently and together, seeking a divorce as we feel our relationship has reached the point where we would like to make at least something in our life legal. Problem is, I have this stupid imbecile of a husband who's just completed his metamorphosis; from human to politician to brainless troglodyte. Mind you, it's just one teeny quantum step from politician to troglodyte. He's under the impression a divorce would do his political aspirations no end of harm. If Graham wasn't such a moralistic gangster, I'd ask him to put the illustrious Robert Porter, MP, away permanently.'

Simon pursed his lips and looked at Noel with eyebrows raised. 'And Graham, you feel the same way about Mr Porter?'

Graham Lee didn't hesitate in answering. 'Hell, yes. I used to think he was alright, well, as alright as a politician can be. But I suppose if the opportunity presented itself, I'd nudge him over a cliff, and I certainly wouldn't throw him a lifeline if he was drowning.'

Simon took a sip of his coffee before continuing, a look of disappointment etched across his face. As his two good friends appeared anxious for some terrible fate to befall Robert Porter, maybe, just maybe, they were somehow involved in the heinous crime. 'So, as you both seem to prefer Robert Porter dead, I presume it would come as good news if I were to tell you Robert Porter's very dead body was found on Bondi Beach this morning.'

Louisa smiled and gazed at Simon in hopeful expectation. 'Come on, Simon, don't get our hopes up. Has someone really done us such a favour?'

'Yep,' replied Simon simply. 'There's either someone out there with a dislike for politicians far greater than mine, or someone who harboured a very personal grudge against the late Robert Porter. So, I'm terribly sorry Louisa, we would offer our condolences but I have this vague idea his death could be looked upon as somewhat serendipitous and cause for celebration. We will need you to confirm the identity of the body, being next of kin to whom we think the body belongs to. Naturally, we'd like you to do that sooner than later as the forensic boys are waiting to have a closer look at whoever it was. We will get back to you in this regard, but we're pretty sure you'll no longer have to wheedle a divorce out of your husband.'

Silent during the discourse between Simon and Louisa, Graham Lee asked the unasked question. 'And have you any idea as to who the killer is?'

'Good grief, Graham, the body's not cold yet. We've just found the bugger. And let's face it,' interjected Noel, 'once we start our investigation, if we are appointed, that is, and given the popularity of his vocation, I think we'll find there was a bloody lot of people queued up to do him in. The only profession we can discount the perpetrator coming from is the public service as the most exciting thing they get up to is the drive home on a Friday afternoon, if they haven't flexed off on the Thursday.'

Graham Lee nodded in agreement. 'Well, if I can be of any help please let me know. I'll keep my ear to the ground as you often hear snippets of information at the club you would prefer not to hear. The one thing I do know is that Porter had it in mind to legalise the gaming industry by introducing legal casinos. There must be a few casino owners, including myself, who would be sorry to see such legislation passed.'

'That would include people like Paul Stack and Andy Crawford?' Noel asked.

'Certainly,' Graham replied.

'Simon, I have just one question,' Louisa said as she took Graham's hand. 'Robert has some personal documents of mine that I need to have, stuff like marriage and birth certificates. There's no problem if I drop over to his place sometime to pick them up?'

Simon frowned. 'Sounds simple, but in this case it can be somewhat complicated. If Porter had a solicitor we'll need to approach him for the documents. If he didn't, an application will have to be made to a magistrate for approval for you to enter the building and remove specifically named items. Sorry, Louisa, but it can be a real pain in the proverbial.'

'Bugger,' Louisa exclaimed in annoyance.

Chapter 5

Following his graduation from Police College, Simon's initial posting was to The Rocks precinct in Sydney before being posted to another city precinct, Day Street. It was here he was reacquainted with his former colleague, Sergeant Noel Elliott who, after serving with Simon at The Rocks, had been transferred to Day Street a couple of years before Simon's arrival.

Quite apart from the professional rapport between the two men, a strong social friendship had developed between the Websters and the Elliotts. On most weekends, when the weather permitted, it was likely you would find the two couples at Collaroy sipping beer or wine on Simon's back lawn and engrossed in amiable discussions. It was not surprising that these discussions were usually drawn to the unscrupulous illegal activities perpetrated by certain elements within the community. Both Simon and Noel had been quick to learn that an individual's standing in society, or a person's particular station on the socio-economic scale, had little bearing as to the perpetrator of a macabre or revolting act; a gruesome murder just as likely to be carried out by a pillar of society as by someone from the lower end of the social scale. To Noel's way of thinking, the assassination of a member of parliament could have been a random act committed by some flee brained young thug, boozed to the eyeballs after a night at a local disco. On the other hand, a disgruntled company executive or entrepreneur, finding Porter not as compliant as they may have wished, could just as easily have eliminated the politician.

'Okay, boss, just where do we start?' Noel asked as he rocked back and forward on his Day Street office chair, arms folded.

Simon rested his chin on his left hand, elbow on the desk, while the fingers of his other hand tapped out an annoying non-rhythmic beat. 'Not quite sure, yet. I believe there was a meeting up in Chief Superintendent Paxton's office earlier this morning and, from what I hear, it was attended by half the senior officers in the Force. But then again, I suppose it's not every day they get something as exciting as a homicide case involving a prominent politician to talk about. Anyway, Superintendent Fisher wants us in Paxton's office at eleven. No doubt we'll get all the news then.'

'And I thought you'd think a "prominent politician" was an oxymoron,' quipped Noel. 'With your love of politicians, I didn't think any politician would be prominent.'

'Ah yes, but many a good murder prevents a bad marriage, even if it is a politician's.'

'Sorry boss, but I think Mr Shakespeare said it's a good hanging, not a good murder, but I s'pose you still get the same result.'

. . .

CHIEF SUPERINTENDENT PAXTON was dressed in uniform; the other four men seated around the office, in mufti. Considering the serious nature of the morning's events, the atmosphere within the office was quite relaxed, almost frivolous. CS Paxton sat behind his lavish wood-grained desk swiveling his large leather chair from side to side, his arms folded. The four seated in front of the desk were Simon, Noel, Detective Superintendent Nigel Fisher and Ron Lange.

Ron Lange was not a policeman. In his forties, rather short, balding and, while not obese, at least portly, Ron had established himself as a reliable police informant. Quite apart from the fact that he had once been a criminal himself, Ron had chosen to change sides after his wife had been killed in a bungled robbery of a hotel in Brisbane. Because of the nature of his work, it wasn't long after his arrival in Sydney that Ron had developed a friendly relationship with the Websters and the Elliotts, and had established cordial ties with Graham Lee and Louisa Porter.

Detective Superintendent Nigel Fisher, who now held the same position he held at Day Street some two years previously, was a different kettle of fish. When his womanizing, and a case of blackmail, were uncovered, CS Paxton had given Fisher a choice; a prison term in Long Bay Jail, or volunteer his services and go undercover in the fight against the increasing illegal drug trade. Fisher reasoned his longevity as an inmate of Long Bay Jail, especially being a cop, was problematic. As a consequence, and despite the risks involved in a highly dangerous environment, he chose the latter option. Now, having survived his time in purgatory without getting himself killed, Nigel had returned with unbridled elation to the comparative safety of Day Street.

CS Paxton stopped his swiveling, lent back on his chair

and clasped his hands behind his head. 'Alright, gentlemen, we had better make a start. I have no doubts you all have better things to do than sit around and talk about the footy, although I suspect some of you may consider the footy more important than the assassination of a politician. The meeting of the hierarchy earlier this morning came to the conclusion that the investigation into the Porter assassination should be conducted from here with you, Simon, being the investigating officer. Needless to say, Eastern Suburbs LAC ducked and weaved and gave all the excuses you could think of not to do it, as did every other LAC. With the press already jumping up and down, and the Premier reported to be cutting short his fact-finding mission overseas, it seems everyone is out for someone's blood.'

'And we end up doing the investigation just because we happen to know the bloke, well, knew him. And that was a couple of years ago,' Simon said without trying to conceal his annoyance.

CS Paxton pursed his lips and shrugged, his hands displaying the inevitability of the situation. 'Well, it's not like you're the only one who knew him. Everyone here has spent the odd day or two in Robert Porter's company. Nigel, a lot of water has passed under the bridge during your stint of undercover work. I'm therefore leaving it to Simon and Noel, with Ron's assistance, to do the investigation. I want you available for press conferences and to function as liaison officer. I expect we will be inundated with stupid bloody questions from a host of bureaucrats and politicians, quite apart from members of the press who will be trying to give us hell. I therefore want someone who can display some tact and diplomacy.'

'No problems. I'm happy with that,' replied the Superintendent. 'The only question I have is one for Simon, if I may, sir.'

'No, be my guest,' replied CS Paxton.

'Simon, knowing you as I do, I can't help thinking that politicians may not be on your Christmas mailing list. If this theory is correct, do you believe you will be able to approach the investigation with the same enthusiasm and diligence expected of a detective chief inspector?'

'Well,' replied Simon, as he locked his fingers together on his stomach, steepled his thumbs and looked thoughtful, 'yes sir. Irrespective of any prejudice I may harbour against politicians, we have a body that certainly looks like a case of murder, and my professional interest has been piqued. To be honest, I would rather be investigating a murder of the Jack the Ripper ilk, although our Mr Porter did display some of the gruesome characteristics of a Ripper victim. Trouble is, when we find the perpetrator of the deed, do we prosecute or give him a medal?'

'Now, that's what I call devotion to duty,' chimed in CS Paxton. 'Noel, you've been very quiet on the subject. Have you anything to add?'

'Now that you've mentioned it, sir,' Noel replied, 'we're all aware of the fact DCI Webster isn't overly chummy with politicians, irrespective of their political persuasion. But I agree with him as far as our interest in the case goes. I somehow think that once we start looking, we'll have more suspects than you can point a stick at. It's unfortunate, but a lot of people regard it as a fact of life; politicians aren't the most reputable or virtuous members of society.'

Chief Superintendent Paxton frowned. 'Now, look you lot. I don't give a stuff as to your personal opinions. Everyone on the planet will be watching us like a hawk to ensure a timely and successful outcome to this investigation.

I therefore suggest you find some enthusiasm and get started, now.'

RON PERCHED himself on one of the two drawer security safes located in Simon's office while Simon and Noel sat behind their respective desks. The detectives' office was located on the third floor of the Day Street Police Station, an office that Simon and Noel had shared now for several years. With his promotion to chief inspector, Simon, having been offered an office more in keeping with the rank, had rejected the offer for no obvious reason apart from the fact that he felt comfortable where he was.

In the forty years of existence, the Day Street Police Station represented a ringing tribute to classical art deco architecture. Having been constructed in the 1930's and, along with a host of other infrastructure facilities in the city, had been built with the expectation that it would one day rival the longevity of the pyramids. The office occupied by Simon and Noel was just as art decoey and could not be considered in any way opulent by modern 1980 standards. The original green linoleum floor had faded to a sickly shade of greenish yellow, the original white walls now a shade of dirty beige. The one window that had once provided a view of the adjacent building's brick façade now provided a view of a construction site that had advance no further since the original building had been demolished some eighteen months previously. Whatever panoramic view the window may have afforded the two detectives was irrelevant as the window was fitted with a pull-down venetian blind that failed to operate in its designed manner. To ease anger and frustration, the blind was permanently pulled down to its extremity. Light to the office was provided by one fluorescent light tube operated by a cord hanging from the ceiling. As if trying to enhance the drab office's trendy art deco style décor, the furnishings were even drabbier, although adequate.

Noel sat at a desk fitted with a standard reading lamp at one end of the office and Simon, with similar furnishings, at the other. Both men were provided with a swivel chair fitted with arm rests although Simon's, dilapidated as it was, was more of an occupational health hazard than a chair. There was the standard number of four drawer metal filing containers provided, together with the standard number of bookcases, a hat stand and whiteboard, all in compliance with the administrative instructions relating to office entitlement according to the officer's seniority and rank. Obviously, art deco was in vogue when the instructions had been written.

Noel rested his elbow on his desk and supported his head by his hand. 'As I was saying, boss, where do we start?'

'Well, Louisa has positively identified the body so Mr Gallymore will be able to do his thing,' replied Simon. 'A good starting point will be the forensic report which should be able to establish a time and cause of death, not that I think there's any doubt about how he died. Before we start hunting down the culprit, we need to establish a motive for doing away with Mr Porter. Okay, I know, but we need a real motive, something worth killing for and not just someone saying "I could have killed the bugger" which we all say from time to time.'

Ron shifted his position from sitting on the safe to leaning against it, his legs crossed at the ankles, his arms folded. 'I suppose we can discount it being a family affair as I think Robert was an only child. Crikey, I didn't think of that. Louisa isn't shy of kicking a bloke where it hurts most if she thinks he deserves it, and from what I hear Robert deserved it.'

'Yes, the thought has crossed my mind,' replied Simon. 'She does extract her kilo of flesh.'

'Pound,' interjected Noel.

'What pound?' queried Simon, somewhat at a loss. Noel didn't bother to reply.

'How about the professional side of things?' Ron suggested. 'I can make some inquiries into his private life but I think it more appropriate if you chase up his Macquarie Street activities. It wouldn't be the first time a politician has trodden on someone's toes and Porter was about to tread on a lot of toes with his casino idea.'

'Good thinking, Ron. I very much doubt this was a random execution as there would have been easier targets around the Bondi night spots. The bloke who found the body says Porter was a regular on the beach, so the murderer probably knew where to find him. If it wasn't so serious you could even see the funny side of it, some bloke charging along after Porter with a bloody great meat cleaver. It would make some sense for the perpetrator to be a physical fitness freak and be exercising on the beach at the same time. Noel, have you any observations?'

Noel folded his arms and lent back on his chair. 'No, not at this stage, but I'm looking forward to Gally's report. I've never seen a stabbing victim so messed up. Sure, there were a few cuts to his arms which suggests he tried to ward off his attacker. But whoever killed him really had it in for the poor bugger; chopped him up something chronic in what could be described as a savage, sadistic ritual killing.'

'Struth!' exclaimed Simon, and looked at Ron with a look of profound consternation. 'So, we've got some deranged homicidal maniac who's a member of a satanic cult running rampant.'

'Come on, boss. That's not what I meant at all, and you know it,' replied Noel, a little miffed. 'I'm just anxious to see Gally's report.'

Simon raised his hands in submission. Okay, Noel, don't get you knickers in a knot. Look, it's been a long day so let's start what we need to do tomorrow.'

Chapter 6

Simon threw his coat onto the sofa before he collapsed into his favourite lounge chair, removed his tie and loosened the top button of his shirt. 'I suppose you know what's going on?' he called as Georgie disappeared into the kitchen for the wine.

'No, but I heard on the news someone's body had been found on Bondi Beach. I take it that was what got you up so early,' she replied as she entered the lounge room and handed Simon his glass. 'It must have been someone important to get both you and Noel out at that hour of the day,' she added as she relaxed onto the sofa, tucking her legs under herself after having relocated Simon's coat to the back of an unoccupied lounge chair.

'Well, "important" is subjective,' replied Simon after savouring a sip of the cold Chardonnay. 'I suppose some people might have considered him important, but irrespective of whether he was important or not is beside the point; murder is murder. Someone had an obvious profound dislike for Robert Porter and decided society would be better off without him.'

'You're kidding. Not *the* Robert Porter?'

'Wish I was. Seems he was out for his daily exercise routine as he was wearing a pair of budgie smugglers. Someone took a knife to him and made a real mess of the poor bloke.'

'And does Louisa know?' Georgie asked with some dismay.

'Yeah. We called around to Graham's place and told them the good news.'

'What do you mean "good news"?'

Simon yawned and rubbed his eyes with the balls of his hands. 'Good grief, you should know. Robert Porter has been denying Louisa a divorce for yonks now. With Robert out of the way there's nothing to stop her from getting remarried.'

'Well, you're right on that score. Talk about déjà vous. Remember Louisa asking Graham for the going price of doing away with the wife of that police Superintendent, Fisher, Nigel Fisher. What was her name? Oh, yes, Agnes, the wish I were high class Agnes. Anyway, we used to talk about what Louisa could do to entice Robert into divorcing her, and what she could do if he didn't.'

Georgie didn't have to explain who the "we" she was talking about were. A very close-knit group consisting of Georgie, Sue Elliott, Louisa and a new girl on the block, Judy Kemp, had established a friendly coterie with many similar interests, including the occasional glass of wine. 'You don't think for one moment that Graham and Louisa are responsible, do you?' Georgie asked.

'Good grief, no. Well, they sure as hell had motive, means and opportunity,' replied Simon as he gazed in contemplation into the depths of his wine glass. 'No. If they were going to bump him off it would have been very clinical and done with some class about it. The way he'd been put away was very tatty, very low class. And even if they had contracted out the job, you can bet they would have paid for some professional assassin who would do a nice neat job of it. Although we're yet to see the forensic report, the state of the body suggests the murderer must be either a learner on his first solo mission or Antonio out after his bucket of flesh.'

'Shylock.'

'Shylock who,' Simon asked.

Georgie frowned. 'Doesn't matter, sweetie. Another wine?'

'Yes please. And what's going on next door?'

'Well, I don't care what you say, but I have my doubts about those people. Okay, so they've just moved in, but they don't appear to have regular jobs and the visitors who have called in appear to be a really scungy lot. I think his name's Jason something or other. I haven't a clue as to what her name is. They still get around on the big black Harleys they drove around on when looking over the place and they still wear black clothes. Their T shirts have the words "Krims Noir" printed on the back which shows that they must be either illiterate or just can't spell. I'm sure it's supposed to mean something about criminals and crime. The girl looks like she could be attractive if she didn't have tattoos all over her and rings in her nose. But I suppose appearances can be deceptive. As I said, she looks like a bikie's moll and he looks a real dero just out of Pentridge, though I wouldn't tell him that to his face.'

'And just what is a fugitive from Pentridge Jail s'posed to look like?' Simon asked, intrigued.

'You know. Someone you wouldn't take home to meet your mother.'

'Crikey, I think the lady protests too much. Georgie, just because they wear black and ride a Harley doesn't mean they're members of an outlaw motorcycle gang. And what's in a name? What if they had "Pinky Panseys" scrawled on their T-shirts? Would that make them any more appealing to you?'

'God, I don't know. Anyway, we can blame Judy for the quality of our neighbours.'

Simon frowned. 'Now hang on a minute. We've had no trouble from next door for years and even if a couple of murders have been committed there, it doesn't say the new neighbours are into killing off the local inhabitants, well, not that we're aware of. You can't choose your neighbours, sweetie. And I don't think Judy ever considered to vet potential renters to assess the most appropriate for the neighbourhood. Come to think of it, the last little old lady who lived there you had to do away with.'

'You know damn well I didn't do away with any little old lady, and that includes Dorothy. She died as a result of poor health. Even the coroner found she had a bad heart.' In truth, Dorothy was the neighbour from hell who just happened to suffer from arachnophobia. That Georgia had exploited this affliction by placing an almost dead huntsman spider in Dorothy's peg basket was totally irrelevant to the death of poor Dorothy, at least to Georgie's way of thinking. In fact, Georgie's denial of having in any way contributed to the death was supported by the coroner's report that clearly stated Dorothy had suffered a fatal cardio infarction while hanging out the washing; end of story.

Simon, recognizing he had raised a sensitive issue, changed the subject. 'So, what's Judy up to now?'

'Now, there's one girl who has landed on her feet. She won the inheritance for the place next door and now gets a hefty rent for it. On top of that, she has a new job in the city and is comfortably shacked up with Ron. They make a good couple so good luck to them.'

Simon nodded. 'Yes, those two are as thick as Cleo and Brutus.'

'Anthony,' corrected Georgie.

'What, Brutus and Anthony? I didn't think they were that way inclined.' Georgie refrained from comment, her response limited to a shake of the head in wonder.

Simon gulped the last dregs of his wine and handed the empty glass to Georgie. 'Yes thanks, I will have another while you're asking.'

'Well, I wasn't but I will.' Georgie placed the empty glasses on the table, rose from the lounge and disappeared into the kitchen from where she soon reappeared with a four litre cask of rough red wine. 'I bet those yahoos are part of a bikie gang, you know, Harleys, gang wars, tattoo shops,' she said as she filled the glasses from the cask.

Simon, having decided the conversation called for a modicum of tact, and not wishing to convey his thoughts on the goings on next door, simply said, 'And yes dear, you're probably right. Our neighbours do appear to be members of a bikie gang.'

'Okay Simon, getting back to your murder case now we have that sorted. Just how do you propose to go about finding out who murdered Robert?'

'Come on, Georgie, does anyone really care who did him in?' Simon asked, not expecting an answer. 'So many politicians get knifed in the back metaphorically, it's a change to see someone get it literally.'

'Yes, but it would be interesting to know who did do it.'

Simon shrugged. 'Okay, let's look at the reasons someone gets done in. There's jealousy, and that could be professional or personal, greed, revenge, money. Who knows? There are countless reasons. Politicians, by their very nature of imposing their decisions on the community, lend themselves to being deleted from the How to Vote Card. I have no doubt the honourable Robert Porter MP, RIP, didn't always endear himself to everyone in his elec-torate. And then again, he could've been bonking the wife of the honourable member for Bondi. As I said, there must be so many reasons for killing someone off we could sit here and speculate all night.

'No, we'll start the real investigation tomorrow by arranging some interviews with his political colleagues. Hell, I didn't think of that. How much time do you need to interview a politician before you can decide if they've answered the question? Be that as it may, it will be good to have a real murder to investigate. And you're right, I've no doubt it will be an interesting case. But to more important things; what's for dinner?'

'Left-over tuna bake, broccoli and a potato, and we only have the red left,' Georgie replied as she absently ran a finger around the rim of her empty wine glass. 'You know, I think it might be an idea if we girls got together and had a bit of a chat regarding the new occupants of the house next door. I don't wish to appear stuck-up or prejudiced against others who might move in different circles of society, but right at the moment we don't know just what circles these two thugs circulate in.'

'Cripes, I think you might be jumping the gun just a

tad. And who knows, they might be a perfectly respectable couple,' replied Simon, a trifle surprised that Georgie had already arrived at the conclusion that the new neighbours were going to be the next neighbours from Satin's fiery underworld .

Chapter 7

'Right, boss, now the dust has settled and you've had a good think about it, where do you want to start?' Noel asked without any display of enthusiasm. While he was pleased to have a potentially interesting case to investigate, he felt that whatever forthcoming investigative procedures the two detectives were to embark upon, it would be subject to close scrutiny by members of the police force and the press.

To make matters worse, the politician's murder would produce a host of do-gooders hell bent on making sure to point out that it was the victim's fault for getting himself killed and that the killer should be exonerated of the crime. These would-be do-gooders would argue that the perpetrator of the deed, whoever it may be, had had a terrible childhood, his father an alcoholic and his mother forced to work long hours at two jobs including a nightlong shift in a factory somewhere around Kings Cross. No doubt there would also be those who appeared to be absolutely outraged by the event and be screaming that the murder of a politician was an offence against truth, justice and the

Australian way. Needless to say, the Australian way was generally accepted as taking the adversary out the back of a pub and punching his lights out in a fair fisticuff, not hacking him to death with a sharp instrument on Bondi Beach. Yes, Noel had no allusions as to what may be expected.

Simon had just entered the office at Day Street, Noel's question posed before Simon had even removed his coat. 'Yeah, well hang on a tick,' he replied as he placed his coat on the coat stand behind the door then dropped onto his battered swivel chair. 'We have a meeting with one of his party members later this morning. It's a bit ironical, but we'll meet him at the same coffee shop where we had the pleasure of our initial meeting with Robert Porter; the one on Macquarie Street.'

'That'll be cosy,' replied Noel as he scratched the back of his head. 'Pardon my ignorance, boss, but which party did Porter belong, the mob that's in government or the mob in opposition, not that it makes any difference, I suppose, and not that I really care?'

'I looked him up in the front of the telephone book. He's in government at the moment, or was, and was the Minister for Planning and Infrastructure and maybe one or two other ministries. If that imbecilic bureaucrat Boswell at the local council is an example of what we may expect, we may be in for a hard time trying to get a straight answer from a polly. By the same token, it may give us some indication as to if the murder was politically or personally motivated. I really don't care who we end up investigating, some puritanical, moralistic, prissy politi-cian or Jack the bloody Ripper. And if the murder was politically motivated, there'll be money behind it some-where, and when the mega bucks are being thrown around, no-one, not even a politician, can keep their dirty mitts off.'

'And who's this party member we're going to see?' Noel enquired.

'His name's Gavin Buckmaster, but I haven't a clue as to his position. When I rang I was put through to his office. I had asked to speak to the Premier or his deputy, but the Premier is not due back for another few days and the Deputy is out of the country on an extensive fact finding mission. Seems like a good time to call for a no confidence vote. Anyway, we'll go and have a chat to this Buckmaster bloke,' replied Simon without too much confidence. 'When we meet him, I want you to be conscious of the questions I ask and the responses. It might be a learning curve for you.'

Noel pursed his lips and frowned. 'Why? It sounds like you're expecting some difficulty.'

Simon harrumphed. 'Come on, Noel, get real. If you think talking to Boswell was tricky, and he was only a public servant, wait till you meet a politician. They wrote the book on how not to answer a question by waffling on about something they'd prefer to waffle on about. So, whatever happens and however frustrating it gets, keep your cool.'

NEITHER DETECTIVE HAD EVER MET Gavin Buckmaster, MP. However, the tall, thin man with a head of thick grey wavy hair set in a brush-back style of the 60's and sitting at a table on the footpath outside the coffee shop, had to be Gavin Buckmaster, MP. This conclusion had been arrived at independently by both Simon and Noel using intuitive detective work; the bored looking gentleman relaxing in the sun was the only patron of the coffee shop not sharing a table and, without any obvious effort, managed to exude all the charisma of a used car salesman. No, there was no doubt; here sat Gavin Buckmaster, MP.

'Sorry we kept you waiting,' said Simon as Mr Buckmaster stood to greet the two detectives. 'I'm Detective Chief Inspector Simon Webster and this is my associate, Detective Sergeant Noel Elliott.' After cordial greetings had been exchanged, the three men sat down and Simon nodded across to a waiter for orders to be taken.

'I suppose you want to have a chat about Robert Porter's death?' enquired Mr Buckmaster.

Simon nodded. 'Yes. I'm sorry to impose upon you, but I did try to speak to the Premier or his deputy.'

'Aah yes, well, both of them are out of the country on fact finding missions at the moment, although I believe the Premier has decided to cut it short and is said to be on his way home right now. The Deputy and his wife left about a week ago for the UK, Europe and Brazil. As politicians, it is essential we maintain close links with our trading partners. Naturally we avail ourselves of every opportunity to promote and develop new trading and cultural ties with other countries.'

'Yes, totally agree,' responded Noel, not really taking any notice with what he was agreeing to.

Without pause, Buckmaster continued. 'History has graphically shown that we can only achieve and promote these objectives by personal contact in the form of such fact finding missions. Unfortunately, there are many skeptics who fail to appreciate the time and effort that goes into such missions, or the benefits to be derived by establishing closer cooperation with many countries. And yes I know, many people regard such arduous missions as nothing more than junkets.'

'Yes, but it's the tax payer who pays the bill. It's a good

thing they don't take the family along with them,' quipped Noel. The coffees arrived just as Mr Buckmaster was about to respond to Noel's remark, which was a good thing because, despite Simon's suggestion, Noel was beginning to lose his cool already and the reason for the meeting hadn't even been broached.

'See, there you go,' said Mr Buckmaster, shaking his head as he leaned back and folded his arms, 'you have absolutely no idea the benefits that can be achieved in taking the family along. Many societies regard the family unit as the foundation of a happy, secure and successful life. It's a cultural thing. They like to see that the visiting politician is reliable and secure in a happy marriage. Naturally that can only be achieved by taking the family overseas with us, whether that be on a fact finding mission, a conference, an educational study tour, or whatever. Mind you, it's no picnic for the family members as some of the countries we go to are not quite like living here in Australia.'

'And just where have our illustrious Premier and his deputy gone to promote the miraculous mutual benefits to be derived by entering into complex long-term face to face negotiations?' Noel asked before Simon could terminate the direction the conversation had taken.

'Well, the Premier, his wife and two young sons have gone to Anaheim, which is in an impoverished part of the United States. He's trying to develop a new trade agreement while promoting the tourist industry, two programs that would prove beneficial to both states. The Deputy Premier and his wife are currently in the UK before they go on to Europe then South America for a cultural fact finding mission. Right at the moment they should be in London before going on to Paris.'

'I take it you were talking about the Anaheim in California. Pity the poor kids as there's not much for them to do there, apart from Disneyland. And no doubt we've sent dozens of fact finding missions to the UK?'

'Yes,' replied Mr Buckmaster, 'but our Deputy Premier is there to evaluate a new ticketing system for the underground railway. After that he and his wife go on to Paris for talks with the administrators of The Metro and a five day recuperation break before flying on to Manaus in Brazil.'

'You don't mean the Manaus halfway up the bloody Amazon River, do you?' Simon asked, somewhat surprised that the Amazon Basin should hold possibilities for future cultural and commercial development advantages for New South Wales.

'Yes, that's the place. Absolutely wonderful mission they're on, truly very significant, both culturally and commercially. Could be of real benefit to the State.'

'Yeah, well that's all very nice but we're not here to debate the merits of politician's fact finding missions. What we want is information on Robert Porter,' Simon stated, a touch annoyed with himself that he had allowed so much time to be wasted without achieving anything.

Mr Buckmaster finished off the last of his coffee and pushed the cup and saucer into the middle of the table. 'Okay, gentlemen, what is it you want to know?'

Simon shrugged. 'As I haven't spoken to Mr Porter for at least the last twelve months and, with any luck won't be able to speak to him anytime in the near future, I would like to know just who might want him dead. To start with, did Mr Porter have any enemies that you are aware of?'

'No, none apart from the general animosity that permeates through political ranks. You never know who your enemies are until it's too late and you're left with a knife sticking out of your back, metaphorically speaking, of course. As far as Robert Porter goes, it's sure as hell someone didn't like the man and decided to take things to the extreme.'

Mr Buckmaster lent back and clasped his hands behind his head and adopted a very serious look before he continued. 'Now, as to who would want to take things to the extreme is a very difficult question, Chief Inspector. To begin with, you have to look at the psychological profiling of suspects to ascertain just who might be likely to murder a person of such integrity and so highly regarded in the community. A person doesn't vote for a politician and then stab them to death; even the thought is just too horrendous to consider.'

'But it's happened and you can leave the profiling to us,' Noel interjected. 'And when did the community start regarding politicians as the bastions of social behaviour?'

'Look, let's cut all the crap and get to the point,' snarled Simon. 'Mr Buckmaster, we're here to ask you if you know of any reason why someone would want to kill Robert Porter.'

'Well, everyone knew Robert was not living with his wife. That situation sort of disabused him from any shenanigans he might have got up to, and probably did. After she left him I think he felt the world was his oyster and he was going to enjoy it.'

'You mean he was carrying on with women?' Noel asked in anticipation.

'Oh, he was carrying on alright but as far as I know, Sergeant, he wasn't carrying on with other men. Although not divorced, his marriage situation presented no impediment to his nocturnal activity which, if it is to be believed, he pursued with gusto and enthusiasm. No. Robert made it quite clear he didn't want to get seriously involved with any one particular woman. He set his eyes on the women of other men, as simple as that. To put it bluntly, he carried on with any married woman he could lay his hands on, and every married man in parliament hoped it wasn't his wife he was doing the carrying on with. As I said, everyone knew about it and some husbands probably suspected their wife had been involved. That would have provided motive enough for some enraged husband to kill him.' Simon couldn't help thinking Mr Buckmaster's reply was quite succinct and direct. Quite astonishing.

'Okay. I take it you can give me a list of those members' wives who may have been involved? Of course, confidentiality is assured,' Simon added as an afterthought.

'Yeah, no problems,' replied Mr Buckmaster. 'I can't say the list will be inclusive of everyone involved, only those I'm aware of.'

'Of course. And are you aware if Robert Porter gave anyone motive to murder him for political reasons? I suppose there will have to be a by-election for his seat and maybe someone couldn't wait for the next general election.'

'No, no-one. He had a clear majority. Look, I don't know if I should open my mouth but Robert, in his role of Minister for Planning and Infrastructure, did not endear himself to a lot of people,' ventured Mr Buckmaster.

Simon raised his eyebrows. 'Oh?'

'It's really quite simple. As politicians, we know what's best for the constituents whether they know it or not. It is because of our assiduous attention to detail that it comes as no surprise that, so far, we have never made an incorrect decision. Of course, I would be the first to say there is always the possibility there may be some brainless plebs out there who don't agree with us. Despite the common perception, we are not deaf to the demands of the community.

You'll find it's common practice for politicians of any persuasion to give the voters of the electorate their complete and undivided attention before ignoring them.

'I'll admit that on rare occasions an approval granted by a local authority may be abrogated by the Minister for Planning following representation. This occasionally happens in regards to environmental considerations where a minority group may try to promote their own agenda, usually aimed at evoking the "cute and cuddly" perception. This tactic endeavours to gain the support of witless people in the community who never stop to think and also to try and gain the support of the minor parties. After a cordial exchange of dialogue and consultation with experts in the related field, we usually find we can work around problems raised by the constituents and come to an amicable agreement. This is generally achieved by just doing whatever we wanted to do in the first place.'

'You mean you ignore them?' Noel asked, any esteem in which he may have held for politicians being rapidly washed away by a flood of cynical conviction.

'That's not the word I'd use, but yes, I suppose we do,' replied Buckmaster. 'However, regarding Mr Porter. According to my limited knowledge on the subject, an approval for a redevelopment scheme amounting to millions of dollars, and in the Minister's own electorate, mind you, had been reversed by the Minister, Mr Porter, following representation, ostensibly from a group of tree-huggers, maybe. This was after local council had already granted approval and the developer had outlaid a fortune to procure the site. As there is no provision for compensation in such cases, I would say there's one developer who's pretty upset, especially as the scheme eventually got the go-ahead but with the granting of the contract to another developer.

No, our Mr Porter was a nice enough bloke but I reckon there's quite a few people out there who couldn't care less he's pushing up daisies.'

'And the name of the developer, the one that lost the contract?'

'Oh yes. That was Daymen Brothers. But don't try too hard to find them 'cause they don't exist anymore; they went bust. They were taken over by a company named Glover Property Development. It's over at Bondi Junction.'

Chapter 8

It wasn't often all the girls got together on a weekday. Georgie and Sue were the exception, living as close to each other as they did in northern seaside suburbs. It was not uncommon for them, depending on the weather, to either meet at the beach or go for a coffee and a mooch around one of the burgeoning shopping malls in the district. Georgie often rang Sue so they could meet to discuss Georgie's plot. Georgie was into writing crime novels, well, one novel and, having once worked in a solicitor's office and having a detective chief inspector for a husband, she felt suitably qualified to undertake such a diversion.

Georgie, Sue, Louisa and Judy were seated around a table in the 1115 Coffee Shop at Collaroy on a bright sunny morning. It was the same Judy who had just rented the bungalow located at 26 West Bank Lane to two bikie gang members. She was an attractive lady, in her early forties with long curly red hair and freckles on her nose and under her eyes. By a strange twist of fate, she had acquired the house next door to the Elliotts following the deaths of the previous two owners of the property, dear old dead Dorothy and an even deader Roger Beaton with whom Judy had been in a de facto relationship. It was during these difficult times at West Bank Lane that Georgie had befriended Judy and it was here, while sipping wine at a very informal get together on the Elliott's back lawn, that Judy had met Ron Lange and prompting the start of a happy and burgeoning relationship.

Linda, the owner of the shop, had served the teas and coffees and the girls were now ready to get down to tin tacks. 'Louisa, we're all so sorry to hear about Robert. Who'd ever thought such a thing could happen to such a nice man,' remarked Georgie, not quite sure if she had displayed sufficient remorse in her expression of grief.

Louisa withdrew a small crocheted handkerchief that had been tucked into the sleeve of her blouse and dabbed the corner of her eye with all the rectitude expected of the grieving widow. 'Yes, it came as such a surprise to both Graham and myself. We never expected anything like this to happen. God knows, we'd been praying for such an event for what seems like years, and it's only now someone has been decent enough to hear our pleas.'

'Louisa, you don't really mean that, do you?' exclaimed Judy, shocked by the revelation.

'Oh yes, my dear, I'm so glad he's dead,' Louisa replied with a bright smile and without a trace of a tear in her eye. 'Even when I had to go to the morgue to identify the body, I was praying it was Robert. You see, Robert and I started out okay but it wasn't long before I found out the real purpose of our marriage, at least as far as he was concerned. All he wanted me for was to be his fashion accessory. Some women obviously love being dragged out to cocktail parties hosted by some witless politician. You'd think a politician, of all people, would learn to keep his mouth shut and have you think he's an idiot than rave on and confirm he's as brainless as the rest of his colleagues.

'You know, it never ceases to amaze me that a politician can be the State Treasurer while having no more experience in economics than breaking into his piggy bank. Robert was like that. He was Minister for Planning and Infrastructure and thought that meant planning social events for parliamentarians. I have no idea of what he thought he had to do with the infrastructure bit. Anyway, don't get me going. Now Georgie, what is the reason for this little get together?'

'Well, I'm glad you got that off your chest, Louisa,' replied Georgie. 'Now the problem is, and Judy, please don't take any offence as it's way out of your control, but the problem is our new neighbours. They're a young couple and, as I didn't see a ring on her finger, they're probably just shacked up together. And no, that's not the problem. Simon thinks I'm nutty but these two are up to something. At least they look like they're up to something but they're going out of their way to make sure they don't breech their lease conditions. We had a pretty quiet neighbourhood and we would prefer the contented ambience and quietness of West Bank Lane to continue.'

'So, are they noisy or play loud music? Just what is it that makes you think they're a problem?' Sue asked, unable to see what justification Georgie had to regard the neighbours as a problem.

Georgie frowned and shook her head. 'Look, I'm a pretty good judge of character and these two have done absolutely nothing to suggest they will fit into our lifestyle – I mean a beachside suburb lifestyle. Good grief, their T-shirts announce that they're criminals and they dress like reprobates from a motorcycle gang.'

'I take it you haven't spoken to them yet?' Louisa asked, knowing the answer.

'Good gracious no. They're not the sort of people you go out of your way to converse with,' Georgie replied, shocked that anyone would consider even approaching the two bikie gang members.

Louisa, Judy and Sue all looked at each other with the same quizzical look on their faces. 'Okay,' said Judy, 'we're not sure there is a problem and if there is, we don't know what it is so we can't help fix the problem that may or may not exist in the first place. If the problem constituted a breach of the tenancy agreement, I could have them evicted.'

'Right,' Georgie replied, 'there is one thing I haven't told you, and Simon is unaware of it. They're growing marijuana.'

Silence prevailed as the three other women again looked at each other. 'And how do you know that?' Louisa, gobsmacked by the revelation, asked.

'Look, I'm not into horticulture or anything like that. But I did see a movie once where this woman was growing marijuana plants using hydroponics inside her house. The one thing you need to do this is to have at least twelve hours of good lighting. She had the lighting rigged up in such a way everyone in the town used to watch the glow when she turned the lights on. That's what's happening next door. The buggers are growing pot and selling it off to these yahoos who come around at all hours of the night on their motor bikes.'

'If you're sure this is going on it's illegal for you not to tell the police,' Judy broke in somewhat surprised.

'Oh, great,' replied Georgie with more than a hint of sarcasm. 'Telling the police isn't going to get rid of them, permanently, is it? Even if they were charged and found guilty, the judge would most likely say "tut, tut" and send them home with a merit award for creating their own business. No, we have to confirm what I think is going on and then do something about it. But whatever we do do, it has to be done on the quiet without Simon's knowledge. Simon thinks I'm jumping the gun as they've only been in the place five minutes. However, the last thing I want to do is sit back, do nothing and then find 26 West Bank Lane accommodates the northern beaches chapter of some motorcycle gang.'

'So, what do you have in mind?' Louisa asked cautiously. 'I've no doubt Graham could send a couple of his associates around to have a chat.'

'No, too blatant,' replied Georgie. Our neighbours wouldn't need a degree in rocket science to work out who set the hounds onto them, and that could make for a very unhappy situation. Who knows? As they are from a motorcycle gang, they could be out to establish The Collaroy Chapter. That would prove just dandy, wouldn't it? A motorcycle club next door with its own drug factory, pot plants, tattoo parlor and God knows what. Cripes, we may even be in the middle of a turf war between two gangs.'

'Gotcha,' declared Sue. 'We create another bikie gang and muscle our way into the place. How exciting. I've always fantasized what it would be like to be a bikie's moll.'

Georgie rolled her eyes to the ceiling as other patrons in the coffee shop looked to see just who wanted to be a bikie's moll. 'Sue, you are not now and never will be a bikie's whatever. Judy, Ron knows a few people who do odd jobs around the place. It's for damn sure I'm not going to rock up on their doorstep and ask to buy some whoopie-weed. Now, it would be far more appropriate if we could find some derelict and have him arrive on a Harley and try to buy some. At least he would have more credibility and would look just like a normal visitor to the place.'

Judy raised her eyes questioningly, her forehead furrowed. 'Have anyone in mind?'

Georgie shook her head. 'No, not really. But as Ron has a vested interest in your activities, it might be an idea if you let him know what the problem is, together with our thoughts on the matter. If these two imbeciles do belong to a gang, as I'm sure they do, I thought it might not be too difficult to intimidate them in such a way that they may like to consider their options.'

Judy pondered the solution for a few moments before replying. 'Yes, that might work. We would need to find a volunteer willing to impersonate someone from one of the established gangs, and who has the nerve to go and buy a load of marijuana from our two neighbourly misfits.'

'That's why I thought of Ron. He must know people who would do anything for a few dollars,' replied Georgie. 'So, everyone agrees that we are living next door to an obvious drug cartel and need to do something about it?'

While both Sue and Louisa had reservations, specifically Georgie's belief in the existence of a "drug cartel" operation, if an operation should exist at all, there were no voiced objections, just a conspicuous lack of enthusiasm. According to Georgie's philosophy, a vast cultural divergence existed between those who liked the beach and go surfing, and those who never found it hot enough to shed the black leather jacket and preferred to ride around on a Harley Davidson. Maybe Georgie has a point, Judy mused.

Chapter 9

'Now, come on boss, that wasn't too bad, was it?' Noel remarked, more as an observation than a question. 'It's not as though we're investigating the ethics of a politician, although I don't think I could rort the system as blatantly as they apparently do. And that bloke Buckmaster, he seemed to give a straight answer, provided you kept him on the subject.'

Simon buried his face in his hands and rocked slowly from side to side on his chair. Simon was a disgruntled detective chief inspector. 'Somehow I thought we had seen the last of the Glover family and now we have another brother of the dead Bruce Glover, along with Paul Glover who's in Long Bay jail, popping up. And, to be honest, I'm not really enthusiastic over the prospect of having to interview a host of women Robert Porter was playing around with.'

'No, but I bet the girls would. They love a bit of a scandal,' said Noel as he withdrew his notebook and started to copy out the names Mr Buckmaster had provided. 'And just how do you propose to set up these little interrogations? It might be a bit tricky to ring the husband at his parliamentary office and ask him if you could have a confidential chat to his wife about her reported infidelity.'

'Good point, Noel, but that isn't my problem. While I go and have a chat with Mr Ralph Glover at Bondi Junction, you can find out just where we can meet these women with some degree of discretion. I'm sure they would like to keep everything on the hush-hush, especially if Buckmaster is right. By the way, just how many names did Buckmaster give us?'

'Well, it's not as though Robert Porter had so many women lined up that he was into having sex on his office desk in Parliament House. Hell, now that would be a sight, flagrante delicto on the Speaker's chair,' Noel said with a grin. 'Anyway, Buckmaster gave me the impression Porter had oodles of women, not just the four he gave us the names of.'

Simon shrugged, folded his arms and lent back on his chair. 'Yes, but don't forget, these are four names he believed were definitely involved with Porter. There may be others. Still, it should take you all of five minutes to find out how we can contact these women.'

Noel folded the list, placed it in his coat pocket and then asked, 'And while I'm being diplomatic, you're off to see Mr Glover?'

'Yes. I rang his office earlier to arrange an appointment, which was not a good move. I very much doubt Mr Glover is overly enthusiastic about my visit, especially as we were the ones to have his brother and uncle locked away for brother Bruce's murder. All in all, it will make my little chat interesting, to say the least.'

. . .

IT WAS Henry who ushered Simon into Ralph Glover's office and it was Henry who chose not to leave preferring to take a seat in a corner of the room. Ralph, sitting behind his desk with both elbows on the table, his chin resting on his clasped hands, was quite unperturbed by Henry's presence. While Simon had introduced himself to Henry on entering GPD, Henry had made no effort to introduce Simon to Ralph.

'And I suppose you're the policeman I spoke to earlier this morning which would make you Constable Whatsaname?' snarled Ralph, changing his position by folding his arms and adopting an aggressive posture.

Simon accepted the cynical remark with a nod. 'No, not quite. I'm Chief Inspector Simon Webster and I would like to have a confidential chat, if you have no objections?' he asked, his eyes falling on Henry sitting in the corner of the room looking grouchy.

'I have absolutely no idea what this is all about, so Henry stays. Whatever it is you want with me, don't expect too much in the way of cooperation as I know all about you. You're the copper who sent both my uncle and brother down for murder, is real pally with known criminals and is on friendly terms with politicians. And while we're at it, one of your polly mates just happens to be the bloke who sent Henry's previous company broke, so don't expect any favours from him either.'

'Well, that is interesting. You don't mind if I take a seat, do you?' Simon asked and seated himself on a collapsible metal chair before Ralph had time to reply. 'It's probably a good thing Henry is here as he may be able to answer some questions.'

'Yeah, well don't count on it, even if he does know the answers. As I said, Henry's pretty pissed off with politicians at the moment,' replied Ralph, his aggression softening with the realization that the Chief Inspector wanted something that he or Henry might possess; information.

'Okay, but if you can't accept that if it hadn't have been me who arrested your family members, it would have been someone else. And if you should think otherwise you must be as brainless as your brother. And while we're at it, Bruce's death doesn't appear to have upset you one iota. Have you no remorse for brother Bruce?' Simon asked, a little surprised at Ralph's attitude towards a case of fratricide.

'None whatsoever. Bruce was on a different planet and was making things very difficult for Paul and Andrew. Although I'm the black sheep of the family, I had a fair idea of what was going on. No, Bruce was a weed in more ways than one and I'm not surprised he drove Paul to distraction. But what's that got to do with your visit?'

'That's a bit rich. With the amount of press coverage it has received, I'm beginning to wonder what planet you're on. Don't you ever watch TV or listen to the radio?' Simon asked having decided that if Mr Glover was going to be uncooperative, he could afford to adopt a more belligerent attitude himself.

'No I don't and that ain't against the law. So, get on with it or bugger off.'

Touché, thought Simon. 'Okay, we're investigating what appears to be a case of murder committed on Bondi Beach yesterday. It just so happens that in the course of our investigation your name has come up. Seeing we have two Glovers put away for murder, we were laying bets you'd be involved somehow. You know, a pair isn't bad but three of a kind is better.'

Ralph scowled with annoyance. 'Jesus H Christ. Just because some bloody idiot gets themselves whacked on Bondi Beach, you have to come running over here to arrest me. No, no way, not this time, mate. I know nothing and I don't want to know.'

'You don't even want to know which bloody idiot got themselves whacked?' enquired Simon.

Ralph turned to Henry with an enquiring look on his face. 'Hey Henry, do you know anything about a murder on Bondi Beach?'

'Sorry Ralph. I did hear something about the police being on the beach early yesterday but apart from that, nothing. So, Inspector, who was it that got themselves put out of their misery?'

'For your information it's Chief Inspector Webster, and the bloody idiot to whom you refer was Robert Porter, MP.'

Ralph turned to Henry mortified. Before he had time to speak, Henry, in anticipation said, 'Ooh no, not me. Sure, I wanted to clobber the cretin but that's about all. I could never murder anyone, although I think I had good enough reason to murder Porter. But hell, there must be a stack of people with a better motive than I had. But no, I didn't do him in. Crikey, he was a politician so you can't be short of suspects. Anyway, how was he murdered; a psychopathic pistol packin' penguin?'

'No, not quite, he was stabbed. Although we are yet to receive the forensic report, from what we saw it certainly looked like he was stabbed a few times,' replied Simon. 'And just what was the motive you had for murdering him, Henry?'

Simon sat back and listened as Henry explained the

circumstances giving rise to Mr Porter, MP, providing Henry with a very good motive for doing him in. Without doubt, Simon thought, Henry seems a tad bitter towards Mr Porter, even a very dead Mr Porter. 'Well, it sounds like you had a perfectly reasonable motive, Mr Haynes. We will need to ask you some further questions but they can wait until after we get the forensic report. However, despite your denial of any involvement in the matter, even Satin can cite Scripture for his own purpose. And Mr Glover, did Mr Porter give you any reason why you should murder him, quite apart from the fact he was a politician?' Simon asked expectantly.

'No. Henry had told me all about his situation earlier and I can appreciate his feelings on the matter. And I can't believe there are too many people around, least of all a mob of politicians, who could give a rat's proverbial about the conservation of a few pink toed, snotty nosed tree frogs, unless there was something in it for themselves. Anyway, I have a sneaking suspicion these frogs don't exist. It's all just a beat-up by a bunch of disgruntled do-gooders eager to disrupt any suburban development that local councils are screaming out for. Bloody Porter probably jumped on their bandwagon 'cause he thought it might give him a few extra tree hugger votes in the next election. Then again, maybe these tree huggers don't exist at all and it's a set up by Porter with ulterior motives.'

'Any ideas what these motives might be?' Simon asked.

'You're the copper. You work it out.'

As Simon could see that there was little to be gained with further questioning of the two men at this juncture, he got to his feet and placed the notebook into his inside coat pocket. 'Well, thank you gentlemen. I'm sure I will need to talk to you again in the near future. Needless to say, the press regards the murder of Mr Porter, MP, as an outrage and they want results, quickly.' With that Simon nodded to the two men and left the office leaving the door open.

As soon as Simon had departed, Henry looked at Ralph, shrugged and said, 'So much for Mr Shakespeare; it wasn't Satin who can cite the Scriptures, it was the devil.'

Chapter 10

The two men wearing dark sun glasses were big, hairy and wore black leathers, the jacket emblazoned with two crossed devil's pitchforks with one bell above and one bell below the intersection of the forks. Fire and brimstone bordered the remaining area of the emblem making the jacket a most impressive looking garment. They pulled up in front of the house riding tandem on a big black Harley which looked more like a teeny motor scooter under the two giants. The helmets the men wore looked more like the old German military style helmet than those approved by the Australian Safety Council. But who was going to argue?

Having knocked, the door was soon opened by a tall, slim woman with dark short hair and brown eyes. She greeted the two men with her engaging smile and bid them enter the house where she led the two giants into a comfortable lounge room.

'My name's Georgie and this is my friend Susan,' she said and indicated to the blue eyed blond seated in one of the lounge chairs. 'Please, take a seat. I know one of you must be Jacko as Mr Lange told me you would be calling today.'

'Yes, I'm Jacko and this is my mate, Benny. We both met your husband a few years ago and I seem to bump into him every now and then. He's a real nice bloke, even if he is a copper. He did me and Benny a favour some time back so we figure we owe him one. Mr Lange told me you have a potential problem regardin' a gang of bikies who have moved in next door. He sorta suggested that maybe we can do somethin' about it.'

'Yeah, we're not real bikies, or anythin' like that,' Benny interjected. 'I know a few blokes who ride Harleys and I do some work on their bikes from time to time. I don't ask to be paid in cash, just to be able to ride their bikes now and then. Anyway, Mr Lange said we should dress the part as your problem involves a bikie gang.'

Georgie nodded. 'Yes, but let me explain. You may have noticed a "For Lease" sign outside the house next door which was for lease but isn't any longer. The house is owned by a lady, Judy Kemp, who is Ron Lange's girl friend. Judy had no say in who rented the place; that was left up to the real estate people. Unfortunately, the renters happen to be two people who ride big motor bikes and, from the clothing they wear, they certainly look like members of a bikie gang. Needless to say, the last thing we need in Collaroy is a horde of riff-raff rampaging around on noisy motor bikes. Cripes, it just wouldn't be Collaroy anymore.'

Jacko acknowledged the problem with a nod. 'Yes, I can see there might be cause for some concern. I take it you don't know which gang they come from, like Satin's Seraphs, The Heretics? But, by the same token, they've probably never heard of us either,' he said with a doubtful expression.

'According to their T-shirts they're called Krims Noir, whatever that means. And that prompts the question; what's the name you and Benny go by?' Georgie asked, intrigued.

'The only name we could think of, seein' there are only two of us,' Jacko replied, 'is The Bells of Hell. I'm Ding and Benny's Dong.'

Both Georgie and Sue looked at each other, and for the first time with a touch of apprehension. 'Yes,' Sue conceded, 'how very appropriate, but getting back to the problem. If I was in Georgie's position, I wouldn't be too concerned with who or what the two people renting the place next door are now, but what they might become.'

'Yeah,' said Benny, 'they might end up usin' the place to make drugs, or start a brothel or turn it into a tattoo parlor, or who knows what. Yeah, I bet that's why they wanted it. They want to grow Mary J in the back yard and sell it to all the blokes who come to hire the women.'

'Ah, for cryin' out loud, Benny, give it away. We're here to help the nice ladies, not be the grim bloody reaper. Sorry, Mrs Webster, Mrs Elliott,' Jacko said trying to restore some decorum. 'Now, what exactly do you have in mind to try and dissuade these yobbos from livin' there?'

Georgie shrugged having given very little thought to just how two hulking great "bikies" might intimidate two home renters to such an extent they may wish to cancel their lease on the premises located at 26 West Bank Lane, Collaroy. 'Well, we thought you might knock on their door and ask if you can buy some pot, just to confirm our suspicions. Failing that, we thought you might be able to come up with an idea of letting them know Collaroy is a dangerous place to live. Something like letting them know another gang is interested in the place.'

'Oh, I see. And Benny and I comprise the total membership of this other bikie gang,' replied Jacko with keen perception. 'Yes, that might work. However, there is one drawback to that idea that I can think of straight away. If it became general knowledge two unknown bikie gangs were, shall we say, vying for a particular piece of real estate, one of the heavy gangs, like The Heretics, could come and do away with the minor players. This could be good or this could be bad. While they might get rid of your two new neighbours, the chances are that they might also get rid of The Bells of Hell, and that would be most inconvenient. There's always some sort of turf war going on with the bikie gangs and the last thing the big boys would want is the introduction of a new bunch of brainless half-wits out to establish their own bit of turf.'

Georgie sat back in her chair, unconsciously bit her little fingernail and thought for a moment before she said, 'Simon, my husband, seems to think that we shouldn't do anything and just hope that they don't extend their lease on the place. Trouble is that if they do, then it's a bit late to do anything. I thought someone like you might be able to talk to them, find out what they're up to, then intimidate them to move out. Neither Sue nor I would be able to intimidate two flies climbing up the wall.'

'And this is all on the hush hush from hubby,' Jacko asked seeking confirmation.

'Yes, it is. Simon will think I'm a fruit cake if he finds out I'm trying to intimidate a bikie gang.'

'Okay,' Jacko said having obtained the basic gist of the requirement, 'I think the best we can do is leave it at the moment so we can all have a think about it.'

Georgie scowled. 'Yeah well, that's all very good but the place is creating some sort of a reputation already with these two riding around on their Harleys and bright lights shining from the house all night. We're not the only ones around here to think they're cultivating marijuana,' Georgie said, a trifle miffed that no definite plan had been decided upon. 'I'll get in touch with Judy and let her know we've spoken. She appreciates the situation we're in but until she has evidence of a breach of the lease there's not much she can do. In the meantime, we can just hope our two obnoxious miscreants don't turn a pleasant neighbourhood into a bikie battle ground.'

Chapter 11

It was the second day following the discovery of Robert Porter's body on Bondi Beach. The forensic report left no doubt that the high-flying politician had been murdered by person or persons unknown, a total of twenty two stab wounds found on the body. Of course, the report did state that only one of the stab wounds had been fatal, so it was within the bounds of possibility that Porter had stabbed himself twenty one times before inflicting the fatal blow.

Irrespective of the circumstances surrounding the death of Robert Porter, MP, the press was going to make sure the public was well informed and kept up to date with the progress of the police investigation, along with any other information it could provide irrespective of the relevancy to the case. Needless to say, journalists, in their own inimitable way and in what is euphemistically referred to as "investigative journalism", were in the process of searching for any scurrilous information they could dig up to keep the public's ghoulish appetite for the scandalous aroused.

Detective Chief Superintendent Paxton lounged back in his chair, his legs out straight his hands interlocked and resting on his stomach. He peered over his desk at the gathering in his office before his eyes settled on Simon. 'Okay Simon, I appreciate it's early days so far, but what have you got for us?'

'Not much, sir. I'm sure if Mr Porter had been of exemplary character, even of normal character, it would be difficult to find out who wanted him dead. As it is, Mr Porter was a politician, if you get my drift, sir.'

Paxton frowned. 'Yes, yes, I can understand that. There's always someone who thinks nailing a politician deserves a merit award, but that's beside the point. Other politicians have come to grief in similar circumstances, but not here in Australia. The closest we've come happened years ago over at Mosman when some idiot fired a gun at a politician; and missed.'

Detective Sergeant Noel Elliott, listening intently to the Chief Superintendent, decided to add his comment. 'Sir, everyone has a gripe with one politician or another and usually over broken promises. How about we cross-check promises Porter made during his election campaign and see which ones he's reneged on. Then there are those politicians who have been assassinated, but not actually killed, you know, character assassinations. A hell of a lot of politicians have been metaphorically assassinated by other politicians for various reasons, usually by those who think they can do a better job. All we need do is find out who wanted Porter's ministerial job or who did he upset enough to do away with him.'

With elbow now on the desk and chin held in hand, the other hand drumming a rhythm on the desk, Paxton said nothing but shifter his gaze from Noel back to Simon with a slow shake of the head and a despairing look on his face. Simon shrugged, shook his head and rolled his eyes, and then said, 'Come on, Noel, we already know of at least one person he's upset and you can bet your booties he's upset a lot more people than that. What we don't know is who he's upset enough to actually kill him.'

'I take it you have all read the forensic report?' Ron asked in an effort to touch on other aspects of the murder. 'It does have some similarities with Shakespeare.'

Superintendent Nigel Fisher looked at his boss and shrugged. 'Sorry, sir, I had no idea this meeting would turn out like this. And what's the forensic report got to do with Shakespeare?' he asked as he turned to Ron.

Ron pursed his lips, shrugged and spread his hands, palms upright, in the universal gesture of "I haven't got a clue". 'Nothing, probably. But look, I'm no Einstein when it comes to the English literature or Roman history. Everyone knows Julius Caesar was assassinated by being stabbed to death. Even Mr Shakespeare tells us that. But the history books tell us big Julie was stabbed twenty three times, with only one stab wound being fatal. This sounds very much like someone could be having a go at Simon here who wouldn't know his Hamlet from his Puck. As it is, our Mr Porter seems to be one stab wound short of a Caesar which, of course, may be significant, totally coincidental or totally irrelevant.'

Simon, a tad peeved by Ron's estimation of his literary acumen, turned to him, his face etched with a dark frown. 'And what's Einstein got to do with history or literature? As far as I know the only thing Einstein was good at was physics. And who the hell is Puck or have you developed a lisp?'

Chief Superintendent Paxton groaned before he picked

up a plastic ruler and smacked in on his desk with a resounding "crack". He achieved the required result; silence. 'Now I have your attention, gentlemen, I want you all to shut the bloody hell up. We're here to solve a murder case, not have a lesson on English literature.'

Noel cautiously raised a hand.

'Yes Noel, you have a question?' Paxton asked, still irritated by the progress of the meeting.

'Sir, I'm the junior rank here and acknowledge I have a lot to learn. But isn't "to shut the bloody hell up" splitting the infinitive?'

'Why yes, I suppose…Now listen here, Elliott, I don't give a damn if I'm splitting the bloody atom. Now, I'm telling you, keep your mouth shut and let's get on with it. Nigel, what have you told the press?'

Superintendent Fisher fumbled with his brief case and withdrew a document headed "Press Release" and handed it to Paxton. Paxton placed his reading glasses on the end of his nose and spent the next point five of a second scrutinizing the item. 'Well, we can never be accused of providing incorrect or misleading information. And you're sure we didn't have something better than "No comment at this point of time"?'

'Unfortunately, sir, that's about right. Simon did interview a couple of property developers over at Bondi, and one of them certainly seems to have a motive. Both Simon and Noel are pursuing Porter's professional and personal life with some interviews arranged for tomorrow morning with women Porter seems to have been involved with.'

Paxton appeared to have become very disconsolate. 'Strange, isn't it? Porter's body was found two days ago and today there's a full two page spread in the morning paper covering the incident. And all we can contribute is "no comment". Seems the press got to Graham Lee and Louisa and what they couldn't find out there they managed to weasel out of some political cretin up in Macquarie Street. Naturally, they've painted Graham Lee as the murdering bastard, what with his reputation as a gangster and his relationship with Louisa. Simon, you've spoken to both Graham and Louisa. Do you think they had an involvement?'

Simon shrugged. 'Well sir, they both had plenty of motive, but I can't see them murdering him, at least not like that. If Graham was going to bundle someone off the planet, I'm sure he wouldn't have done it on Bondi Beach. He's far more discerning. Don't forget that day out on Graham's boat when Louisa wanted a price on having Superintendent Fisher's wife done away with. He was very circumspect about it.'

'Yes, everyone here was there that day. It was quite amusing, except for poor Agnes,' said Fisher with a bit of a giggle. 'But I see what you mean. If Lee was going to do away with someone it would be done professionally. And what do you think of the Shakespeare angle, Simon?'

'I don't. I just believe there's something in the old adage that history repeats itself and when I see something from a Shakespearian play that's appropriate, I'll try to recite the line; force of habit from the old school days.'

'And did it help?' Ron queried. 'I mean, during your school days.'

'Nope, I failed English Lit dismally.'

'Okay you lot,' Paxton broke in, 'as I said from the beginning of this investigation, the press is out for blood and at the moment they appear to be doing a far better job than we are of catching the perpetrator. Simon and Noel, I'm not asking you for results, I'm telling you. And Nigel, I don't care what you give the press but next time please give them something, anything. Tell them Jack the Bloody Ripper is on the loose again. So, on your horses and if you can't find who stabbed Porter to death, find some obnoxious cretin who we can pin this murder on.'

Chapter 12

'Okay, Noel, just where are we off to?' Simon enquired as he slipped into the passenger's seat of the unmarked police car.

'I've set up a chat with a Mrs Cheryl Mason. She's one of the women on the list Buckmaster gave us. You know, one of the women reported to be a member of the Porter stable,' Noel replied as he started the car. She lives in the Hurstville area so must be a St.George fan, poor misguided girl.'

'Yeah, well don't mention football or horse racing. I think she may be a bit put out if you refer to her as a member of the Porter stud.'

Noel frowned as he negotiated the busy intersection of Broadway and George Street, near Central Station. 'Okay, but if the cap fits, wear it is what I say. Her husband is a minister in the lower house, so no wonder she's off for a bit on the side. There's only one thing more boring than being a member of the Lower House and that's being a member of the Upper House.'

'Cripes, and I thought I was the one who had this thing against politicians,' returned a surprised Simon.

'No, you've taught me a thing or two and I've become far more observant. That public servant bloke we spoke to at the council office, Boswell, yes, that's him, Boswell. If there was anyone to denigrate the credibility of a public servant, it was that bloke. So now I've caught your affliction; an aversion to public servants and politicians.'

'Yeah, well welcome to the real world,' replied Simon as he sat back to let Noel get on with the driving while he enjoyed a catnap.

Eventually Simon broke out of his slumber, rubbed his eyes with the balls of his hands and after a big sigh asked, 'Now this lady, Cheryl. What do we know about her?'

'According to all reports the marriage between Cheryl and Peter Mason is a happy one. They were married around seven years ago, just after he entered politics when he was twenty five. Done nothing apart from going to university where he finally graduated with an arts degree; whoopee duck. He did play rugby union for Uni so he can't be all bad. She's in her late twenties and said to be a very good looking woman. Hang on, we're nearly there,' Noel announced as he made a left hand turn off the Princes Highway and headed towards Kogarah Bay.

He eventually slowed the car and came to a stop outside a medium size brick home with a tidy front garden and neatly trimmed lawn. 'We're here,' said Noel. 'I was a bit surprised when Cheryl said she'd meet us at her home. I would have thought she would have preferred to keep a meeting with us confidential. You know, the nosy neighbours thing.'

'Yes, but the car is unmarked so we could be members of some religious sect trying to drum up business,' returned

Simon. 'Anyway, let's go and see what she has to say about the late Mr Porter, MP.'

The report of the physical attributes of Cheryl Mason was correct; she was an attractive lady. Cheryl had black short hair with a fringe cut straight across the eyebrow of her dark brown eyes. Wearing a pair of jeans which looked to be two sizes too small, high heeled sandals and a yellow La Coste polo, Cheryl ushered the two detectives into a lounge room devoid of the expected knick-knacks and dust catchers usually found in a lounge room. All the same, the room was comfortable and felt spacious without any undue clutter.

'I suppose you want to know about my relationship with Robert Porter?' Cheryl asked as she settled into a lounge chair. 'I do read the papers.'

'Yes,' Simon replied as he pushed an ottoman aside to sit on the lounge. 'Your name was mentioned during the course of our investigation. It seems you and Mr Porter had, shall we say, a liaison?'

Cheryl frowned. 'Look Chief Inspector, there's no need to be coy about it. We're all part of the modern generation and I'm married to a politician who expects me to stay at home and keep the house tidy. And I thought woman's equality was done and dusted. Of course, there are times when he is obliged to take the old cheese and kisses along to some function, just to make him look good.'

'Somehow I think I've heard this story before and, by sheer coincidence, that was from Louisa Porter,' commiserated Simon. 'And don't tell me, it was at one of these functions you met Robert Porter?'

'That's right. You could say I was suffering the seven-year itch and Peter didn't want to scratch, not that I don't love him, of course. Unfortunately, Peter is not adventurous and, to put it bluntly, he's exciting as a game of chess. I wanted a bit of excitement, he didn't. Simple as that. Peter introduced me to Robert at some function or other and he seemed a nice enough sort of person. He was living alone after the break-up of his marriage and was depressed and lonely. Well, that's the story he gave me and, apparently, I wasn't the only one to be fed that line. At the outset I wasn't aware of his reputation and by the time I was it was too late; the damage had been done. How women can fall for such garbage is beyond me, and I include myself as one of the stupid imbeciles. Talk about gullible.'

'And is your husband aware of what's going on, or went on?' Noel asked.

Cheryl shrugged and looked pensive for a few seconds. 'No, not at the time as he was too busy taking care of "business", if I can call it that although I suspect the business wore Chanel Number Five. Whether you know it or not, politicians have far more vices than just being able to sprout untruths when it suits them.'

'But he knows now?' Simon asked.

'Well, sure as hell he was going to find out sooner or later and it was sooner. He would have to have been as thick as a brick not to realise I'd been screwing around on him.'

'Yes, and how was that?' queried Simon, his interest piqued.

'Oh, you guys ask such awkward questions; just a moment while I fix a drink. You boys want one?'

'No thanks. We're on duty,' Noel blurted in a reflex response.

Having poured a gin and tonic from a sideboard, albeit ten thirty in the morning, Cheryl regained her seat. 'Okay, I don't know if Peter really knew about it at the time, but it was for sure he was going to find out one way or the other. Are you sure you need to know just how he found out?'

'Yes. We need to know the circumstances of your relationship with Porter so we can assess what influence that relationship may have had on both you and your husband,' replied Simon, pressing the point.

'Yes, I see.' Cheryl gulped her drink and sat with the empty glass held in her lap. After a moment's silence she took a deep breath and said, 'I could go into all the scientific and medical parlance, but to avoid any misconception as to the affliction from which I am currently suffering, gentlemen, it is, and to use the vernacular, a dose of the clap.'

'Holy hell,' was all Noel could muster as his jaw dropped.

Simon shook his head as he noted Cheryl blink a tear away from the corner of her eye. 'And I take it Peter is aware of your condition and the source of this, er, inconvenience?'

Cheryl sighed. 'Of course. He even drives me to the clinic each Monday and Thursday. Look. I can't undo what's already done. I'm embarrassed and ashamed and certainly something I'm not proud of.'

'Does, or did Porter know of your condition? Of course, that's assuming it was of Mr Porter's doing. And I do apologise if that question casts aspersions on your integrity or doubt as to the extent of your infidelity, Mrs Mason.'

'I know you gentlemen must think I'm some sort of sex maniac, which I'm not, but at the same time I wouldn't consider myself to be sexually anorexic either. But cripes, Chief Inspector, all I wanted was some excitement, not become the legislative assembly's lady of ill repute, perceived or otherwise. Honestly, I have never played up on Peter before and it was only on a couple of occasions that Robert and I got together, so to speak. And no, I didn't tell Robert although I possibly should have seeing I wasn't his only conquest. I know for certain he was having his way with several women in Macquarie Street, so I presume I'm not the only one to suffer.'

Simon sat forward, elbows resting on his knees and hands clasped together. 'Of course, you know that could provide you with one hell of a motive to murder Mr Porter?'

'Look, Chief Inspector Webster, if I had been on Bondi Beach at five o'clock in the morning, which I wasn't and never will be, and ran into Robert Porter, which I never did and never will because he's dead, but if I had I would've fed him to the crabs, which would have been quite appropriate, considering. If I had a motive for doing him in it was because of his stupidity and flagrant irresponsibility, quite apart from what he's done to me. That in itself would make you want to murder the creep, not that I did, murder him that is. Do I make myself clear?' Whatever despondency prompted the tear to Cheryl's eye had totally evaporated.

'Quite, and what about Peter?' Simon enquired. 'I can appreciate Peter may have had grounds for creating a by-election by eliminating Porter, even if you were a willing partner to Porter's escapades. Mr Porter's actions, apart from getting himself whacked, have placed your husband in a very awkward position. Peter could stand to lose some credibility, even his seat, maybe. And it certainly appears that, irrespective how much discretion you exercised, your little fling with Porter didn't go completely unnoticed around Macquarie Street. It seems at least some members were aware of what was going on. In fact, the situation reminds me of a speech I heard somewhere; the evil men do lives after them, the good is buried with their bones.'

Cheryl pressed her lips together and frowned. 'Gee thanks, Chief Inspector. So, my little indiscretion with Robert Porter will be inscribed in the annals of party politics for evermore?'

Simon shrugged his shoulders then shook his head. 'No, I don't think you have to worry. History will recall you as being nothing more than "the girl who did". People look upon men as being the predator and, in this case, you were just the unfortunate victim. As Shakespeare probably got it right, I'd say Robert Porter's fame, or infamy, is assured. So, if any name is inscribed in any annals, it will be Robert Porter's, not yours. Anyway, Mrs Mason, we thank you for your frankness and assure you of confidentiality. However, I think that in view of the circumstances you'd better let Mr Mason know we will need to talk to him, but we'll get that organised later.'

Chapter 13

It was about ten minutes into the drive back to Day Street before either detective spoke, and it was Noel who broke the silence. 'Well?'

Simon frowned as he absently gazed out of the window of the car. 'Well, what? I take it you want to know my thoughts of the lovely Cheryl Mason?'

'I thought that was the object of the exercise, wasn't it?' Noel replied as he abruptly braked to avoid a pedestrian who had mindlessly stepped off the footpath in front of the car.

Simon waited for Noel to terminate his abusive tirade directed at the pedestrian through the car's opened window, a tirade that took Simon a little by surprise having never seen Noel embark upon such a vitriolic castigation, albeit probably justified. 'Far be it for me to comment, Noel, but as your senior officer I feel obliged to point out that you appear to be suffering from a form of psychosis of which I have previously been totally unaware.'

Noel, his face still contorted in rage over his encounter

with the stupid pedestrian, was exasperated. 'Oh yes, do tell. Being eminently qualified in the science of psycho-analysis, just what Freudian psychological problem does your in-depth analysis lead you to believe the patient is suffering?'

'Road rage, you twit,' came Simon's simple answer. 'If things like that can get you hot under the collar now, just hang around for another twenty years and see what'll be going on then. People will be strolling around with tele-phones and music plugged into their ears, totally oblivious to what's going on around them. Anyway, back to your question; Cheryl. Who knows? The whole thing is very subjective and will remain so until we speak to Mr Cheryl Mason. The fact that Cheryl was having it off with Robert Porter may result in severe repercussions for Peter, depending on the moral standing of his colleagues. Seeing Buckmaster knows what's going on, it's fair to assume there are others around the hallowed halls of parliament who know as well. Whether they choose to do anything about it is another matter. At the moment we don't know Peter Mason's personal feelings towards his wife's behavior, and it's those feelings that should indicate whether he had the motive to kill Robert Porter.'

Noel gave an exasperated sigh. 'I can't believe either of the Masons would go so far as to murder Porter. Cripes, the injudicious exploits of politicians aren't seen as anything to get excited about. In fact, I think most people have come to expect a lot of them to carry on like footballers at their end of season, and not wishing to use the vernacular, knees-up.'

'Yes, I get your drift, but excited about what, the politi-cians or their actions?' Simon asked with a cynical smile.

'Yeah, both.'

. . .

NOEL SCREWED up a sheet of paper into a ball and had a three-point shot into the garbage bin located next to Simon's table and missed, which wasn't totally unexpected. 'Okay, boss, what now?' Noel asked with what appeared to be a total lack of enthusiasm. Noel was having a problem coming to terms with the obvious excitement senior officers and the press were getting themselves into over the death of a politician. Why should there be any more importance placed on a politician's murder than for anyone else's?

Simon pushed his chair back from the table, flexed his biceps in a muscle-bound pose and enjoyed a hefty yawn. On completion of the yawn, he clasped his hands behind his head and started to rock gently back and forward on his chair. 'Well, I think I'll go and have another chat with that bloke Buckmaster up in Macquarie Street. While I'm doing that, I want you to see what gossip you can pick up from another girl on the list he gave us. You know, another of Porter's conquests.'

Noel nodded as he flicked through his notebook. 'Yeah, okay. Hopefully next time Fisher comes around for something to tell the press, you'll have something to give him. I still think it's a bit iffy talking to these women as I doubt a woman could have done what someone did to Porter. I don't suppose anyone from Francis's mob has found the murder weapon?'

'No such luck, but I'm not surprised. A walk around the cliff from Bondi to Tamarama would give you ample opportunity to dispose of the weapon into the ocean. And as for a female perpetrator, remember that Lady MacB remarked that she didn't know the old bloke had so much blood in him. So much for fair maiden as a suspect.'

Noel got up from his desk and walked over to the white-board. In the middle of the board he wrote the name

"Robert Porter." Radiating out from the name he drew three lines and annotated the end of each respectively; "Political", "Personal" and "Others". Under the "Personal" heading he wrote the names of Louisa Porter, Graham Lee, Cheryl Mason and Peter Mason. Under the 'Political' heading he wrote the name Dayman Brothers.

Intrigued, Simon watched on. It was a rare occasion for the whiteboard, the only piece of advanced technology within the office, to be used. 'And what goes under "Other"'? he asked.

Noel ceased his writing, turned and with a pout, slowly shook his head. 'And what sort of an asinine question is that? You always have to have an "Others" for all the others that don't fall within the previous two categories. It's where I'll put the names of all the other people who we come across in our investigation.'

'Gee, sorry Noel. I'm not conversant with this modern high-tech investigating technique.'

Chapter 14

Gavin Buckmaster was a parliamentary backbencher and a member of the party currently in government. He had scraped into the political arena on the distribution of preferences having only received little over point two percent of the votes cast in his electorate. Needless to say, there were many members of both sides of the House who believed Gavin Buckmaster had as much right to his seat in parliament as the inimitable Guido Fawkes.

Simon was prepared for the standard bureaucratic pretence of security procedures he had to suffer before being escorted by a burly security guard to a very unpretentious looking office located deep within the bowels of the colonial style sandstone building, a building poles apart from the soaring sky-scraper that housed the premier and cabinet offices. With the door to Buckmaster's office already open, Simon politely tapped causing Buckmaster to cease his reading of a newspaper and look up.

'Ah yes, Chief Inspector Webster. Good to see you

again, and so soon too. I believe you would like to have another chat about Robert Porter? Please, take a seat,' Buckmaster offered indicating to a comfortable looking seat in front of his desk.

'Yes, thank you. To begin with, can you tell me the relationship between you and Mr Porter, just to establish whether I'm talking to the right person?'

'By all means. Robert Porter had two portfolios, Minister for Planning and Infrastructure and The Environmental portfolio. He tended to spend more time on the planning side of things while I tried to keep him up to date on environmental issues, notwithstanding the time spent looking after my own electorate. We had been working together for over twelve months so I got to know him pretty well, both professionally and personally.'

'So, what happens now, apart from a bi-election for his seat? And what will happen to the two portfolios?'

'Good question that I suppose only the Premier can answer. You see, Porter was a very ambitious man and he coveted the Premier's job. He'd risen in the ranks to hold two ministerial positions, albeit one a junior portfolio, that being the Minister for the Environment. That was a job he had absolutely no interest in, save for the fact he believed he could con the tree huggers in his electorate into voting for him again. You know, the cute and cuddly politician. That's why I was left to do most of the hack work on the environment, or green side of things, while he received all the plaudits.'

'So, you were aggrieved by the situation, you having to do all the work while he received all the brownie points?'

Buckmaster sat back in his chair, scratched the back of his neck and looked pensive for a moment before replying. 'No, Chief Inspector, I didn't kill Mr Porter if that's what you're driving at. Sure, he was annoying at times, but it was Porter who showed me how to organise the distribution of preferences to get me home in the last election – just.'

'And when is the next election due? Simon asked.

'Not for another eighteen months although Porter was already doing his homework on that issue. He was one of the few members who stood up at a Party meeting and supported Wally Ackerman in his bid for the position of Deputy Premier. Ackerman is also the Minister of Finance, although that's one position Porter never seemed to be overly excited about. See, Porter was looking at the bigger picture. Ackerman is a good deputy and would probably make a good premier so it naturally prompts the question; why did Porter support him to gain the deputy's position if both he and Ackerman himself have aspirations for the top job?'

'Well, if I was a cynic, I would say Porter may have been setting Ackerman up to do a job on him, metaphorically speaking. No good supporting someone you can't get rid of,' Simon said.

'If you're meaning to stab Ackerman in the back, that's just one of the hazards of being a politician, it comes with the job. Mind you, there are also some benefits that can be had. The only people who don't have to worry about receiving a knife in the back are the backbenchers. You see, the chances of being dirked are directly proportional to the position held. A minister might expect someone is itching to put the knife in and by the time you get to Deputy Premier, you know damn well there's a queue waiting to shaft you. But seeing you're speaking metaphorically, I'm unaware of anything dramatic or scandalous enough to bring Ackerman down. Well, not right now, that is.'

Simon pursed his lips and raised his eyebrows. 'When

you say "dramatic enough", does that mean there may be things going on which, taken collectively, could be prejudicial to Ackerman's career?'

'Come on, Chief Inspector, you possess a streak of healthy scepticism. You mightn't know exactly what goes on, but you suspect there is probably enough to blot the reputation of a few members. You'd be surprise at the number of politicians open to blackmail for one reason or another. Politicians are in a position to influence many weighty decisions on any number of issues. Because of this it is quite possible they may be susceptible to the occasional offer of recompense for supporting a specific agenda. Of course, the acceptance of any payment in any form, from cold hard cash to a bottle of wine can be construed as a bribe which can lead to blackmail. I may not know of any such payment, but no-one wants to be the first to blackmail a colleague, irrespective of how high up the parliamentary ladder they may be simply because everyone knows the blackmailer would stand to be blackmailed himself.'

'So, what you're saying is Porter may have had something dramatic enough on Ackerman?'

Buckmaster shrugged. 'Maybe. Who knows?'

'How does the rest of parliament regard Ackerman, discounting the obvious opposition's animosity?'

'He gets along with everyone, including the Premier, I think. At least that's the picture he tries to cultivate. Someone who goes out of their way to get along with everyone is something like being akin to a death adder; take your eyes off them and you're dead, metaphorically speaking, of course.'

'Of course,' Simon replied. God, big Julie really did start a trend, he thought.

'Another problem,' Buckmaster continued, 'is that while

those nearing the top echelons can sharpen their knives for any fortuitous opportunity that may come their way to further their position, ambitious backbenchers who think they're eminently qualified for a position that, in reality, far exceeds their intellectual capability, are out sharpening their knives so they can get a foot on the ladder. Mind you, if a backbencher had any brains at all, he, or she, wouldn't be a backbencher but be in private enterprise earning bucket loads of money. I think a lot of people enter parliament because of the very handsome superannuation scheme and the perks that go with it, like overseas "research" jaunts, or junkets. And honestly, have you ever come across a politician who's overworked?'

'No, can't say I have. And for all your denigration of backbenchers, don't forget you are one yourself. Do you consider you're intellectually superior to your colleagues on the backbenches and deserving of a foot on the ladder?'

'Yes to both your questions. Having delved into the prerequisites of becoming a politician, I decided I was eminently qualified for the job.'

'Oh yes, and just what are your qualifications for such an exalted position?' Simon asked, somewhat eager to learn just what scholastic credentials Mr Buckmaster considered crucial to a successful political career.

'Well, I'm sure you will agree that an impressive academic record is critical to all those aspiring to a position in which the citizens of the country can confidently place their trust. I happened to have graduated from university in several complex subjects pursued by few students. That in itself makes my academic record far more impressive than those who undertake the everyday mundane degrees. In fact, it is because of the complicated and onerous nature that so few undertake such esoteric subjects.

'These subjects included conceptual design and structural development techniques in Calameae material; the digital recording and appreciation of the aesthetic qualities pertaining to abstract impressionist art; and conceptual and representational reconstruction of anatomical features of the European female post 1962 using calcium salts, petroleum jelly and aliphatic acid which is, as you are undoubtedly aware, a terribly difficult medium to work.'

Simon heaved a sigh and slowly shook his head. This bloke's whacko, he thought. He's qualified in basket weaving, finger painting and making nude women out of plasticine. 'Yes, specializing in such difficult subjects would make you extremely qualified, probably more so than a lot of other members of parliament,' he said truthfully. 'Anyway, getting back to the problem at hand. As Porter may have been in the process of sharpening his knife to do away with the Deputy Premier, were there others sharpening their dirks to do away with Porter?'

Buckmaster gave a whimsical shrug. 'Not that I'm aware of, but I'd put money on it. You see, despite public perception, it's a dog eat dog environment in parliament. Everyone is just waiting for a colleague to stuff up, or snuff it, even those in the same party. Anyone who claims they're not interested in the top job, or a job further up the ladder, is lying on their back teeth. If a politician wants to serve more than one term, he soon learns that career progression in politics is a ruthless business. Do unto others before they do unto you sort of thing.

'I've no doubt Wally Ackerman is fully aware that the higher you go the bigger the target painted on your back. I'd say that as Mr Porter held two portfolios he would have been targeted by a number of backbenchers out to hijack the minor portfolio, the environmental one. Not much point in the Treasurer dirking the Minister for the Environment, is there?' Buckmaster asked as if everyone should be aware of the hierarchical standing of any particular politician.

'To be honest, Chief Inspector, the portfolio of Planning and Infrastructure is coveted by every person elected to parliament. No matter how squeaky clean a new planning minister is initially, it doesn't take long for him, or her, to be rolling in cash. The position is sort of like the Hyrda; get rid of one minister's head and a new one soon pops up. No matter how squeaky clean they are when they get the job, they'll soon be sullied by offers too good to knock back. That's one portfolio where one can come out bruised and battered from all the kickbacks and money thrown at you from sleazy people trying to work the system to their own advantage. They pay a politician for a favourable tender decision and the polly ends up pocketing zillions of dollars. Nine times out of ten the government could have had the same job done for a third of the cost. Sort of "here's a hundred grand if the government can see its way to give us the contract". And as Porter's aspirations were common knowledge, maybe some senior ministers would have been out to make sure he didn't get too far ahead of himself.'

'But, of course, we are speaking metaphorically, aren't we?' Simon asked.

Buckmaster looked astonished. 'Oh, but of course we are. But think of the fun we'd have if we weren't,' he said with a wry grin. 'In politics there's always bloodletting going on somewhere, so if it happened that we were talking literally, that would present a whole new ballgame. Porter may have been murdered for any number of reasons, not the least being involved with a number of women from the parliamentary staff, or his indiscreet liaisons with the wives of members.

'But if Porter thought he could bring down Ackerman, there must have been something going on that Porter knew about and, no doubt, Ackerman knew Porter knew. See, although Ackerman is led around like a puppy dog by his wife, he can be ruthless at times. I wouldn't want to pick a fight with him, unless I knew I could win, and even then, I don't think I'd take him on, especially if his wife was in his corner.'

'Well,' exclaimed Simon with an air of finality, 'I suppose there's only one way to find out. I s'pose I'd better organise a little chat with our wally Deputy Premier when he gets back from hacking his way through the Amazon jungle, if he gets back that is. While I would like to question Mr Porter, I don't think he would have too much to say on the matter. By the way, what do you know of Peter Mason?'

'Ahh, Peter. Nice bloke with a lovely wife Cheryl, a real pearl. He's the Minister of Sport and Recreation.'

'Now why aren't I surprised,' came Simon's rejoinder.

'Pardon?'

'Oh, nothing. Her name was on the list you gave us as having been one of Porter's women.'

'Yes, but everyone knows about that so it's not news now, and there are others. Come to think of it, there are probably a few little flings going on around the place now.'

'And the Premier knows of these little flings going on around him?'

'Probably, but who would be game enough to go up and ask him if he wouldn't mind requesting the Honourable Member for Woop Woop to refrain from shagging his wife? No, unless it gets totally out of hand, you know, a real

Roman orgy sort of thing, everyone will claim it's just par for the course.'

Simon sat for a moment, his mind in a fanciful world of lecherous debauchery. So, this is what goes on in parliament. How quaint.

Chapter 15

Although it was early April, the southerly breeze blowing along George Street was uncomfortably cool. Simon and Noel had finished their first cup of coffee in the coffee shop located on the corner of Bathurst and George, a venue the two detectives had used for several years now as it was within easy walking distance from the Day Street Police Station.

'One of these days Ron will get here on time,' remarked Noel as he turned his head towards the door in expectation.

Simon shrugged. 'Well, he's a busy boy, but he will be here soon enough, so just relax. See there you are, he's just arrived.'

Ron paused at the doorway and looked around the shop before spying his two colleagues. 'Hi Simon, Noel. Getting a bit brisk outside even if it is only April,' he said as he sidled into the bench seat next to Simon.

'Yes, Flitch, two flat blacks and a cappuccino,' Simon ordered as Flitch attended the table. Flitch was Felicity, a tall, slim, dark haired teenage girl who had taken over the waitress position previously held by Samantha. Sam had served the three men coffee for a number of years before she decided she needed warmer weather and moved to the Gold Coast.

'Two and one comin' up' she replied.

'Okay Ron, what have you got for us?' Simon asked.

'Well, for your information, I had to do more digging than an undertaker. And I don't know if there would be grounds for murder, although I'm being subjective there. Not much is being said by the blokes who usually know what's going on. I suppose that's to be expected as Porter's killing is a little out of their area of interest. Anyway, to start with, this bloke Ackerman. It seems he plays a very close hand and no-one appears to know much about him, apart from him being the Deputy Premier that is.'

'Yes, and I bet ninety percent of people wouldn't know the name of the Deputy Premier. I know now only because of recent events,' Noel remarked.

'Yeah, okay. The one thing I did find was that when Ackerman entered parliament, he was skint; didn't have two pennies to rub together. Six years later he's rolling in it and, being on a politician's pay, that's a real neat trick. Say he's on a hundred and fifty grand a year. In six years, and if he stacked every penny he got from his pay in the bank, that would make for nine hundred grand. His wife has her own business, something to do with development and investments, and she drives around in a bloody great Bentley. They live the high life and I hear he even owns one or two racehorses. Although politicians are supposed to declare their pecuniary interests, the Ackermans just bought a three million dollar house overlooking the harbour. Now for a polly to be able to throw that sort of money around might give the cynics cause for concern, especially as he entered parliament stony-broke.'

'So, Ackerman is on the take from somewhere and Porter found out. Ackerman found out that Porter knew of whatever the scam was and hit Porter, literally, before Porter could hit Ackerman, metaphorically. Simple,' Simon quipped, 'but what was the scam?'

Ron grimaced. 'Come on, Simon, I know I'm good but there are just some things I don't know. That's one that you'll have to find out for yourself, though I'll keep an ear to the ground.'

'And is there anything else of interest?' Simon asked, his doubtful expression reflecting his pessimism. 'Hang on a sec, here's Flitch.' After the coffees had been distributed, with an engaging smile, the conversation continued.

Ron rested an elbow on the table, held his chin in the palm of his hand and taped the side of his face with his fingers. After a few seconds of deep thought, he said, 'There are a few things that come to mind, one being Porter's earnest intention of getting his Bill for the legalisation on legalised casinos passed. He'd already tried on a couple of occasions and had the Bill defeated on party lines. From what I hear he had drafted another Bill with a few minor amendments and was confident of getting it passed. If it is passed, it will see the closure of the existing illegal casinos, and that might see a few people get their nose put right out of joint. And I have no doubt it's not "if" but "when".'

'Anyone in particular?' Simon asked as he spooned the froth from his cappuccino into his mouth.

'I hear Andrew Crawford is a tad upset, and despite what Graham Lee says, I think he, Lee, would prefer the status quo to remain. Apart from Graham's little business enterprise, Robert Porter had been a real ass by making things as difficult as he could for Graham and Louisa. He had really built up some overt hostility by not agreeing to a divorce.'

Simon pursed his lips before asking, 'Enough hostility to do him in?'

'Probably, but not the way Porter was done. Don't forget, Lee's all class and would never stoop so low as to dispatch someone in the way Porter was dispatched,' Ron replied with certainty.

Simon finished the last of his coffee and pushed the cup and saucer away into the middle of the table before raising three fingers and his eyebrows to Flitch; message received. 'Even so,' Simon continued, 'I'll leave the Lees, both Graham and Louisa, on my list of contenders for having done away with Mr Porter, together with Andrew Crawford and this developer bloke, Ralph Glover and his sidekick Henry Haynes. Then we have Cheryl and Peter Mason who had grounds for slitting Porter's throat. On top of that, we have a government full of politicians, from Deputy Premier down to backbencher, all eager to dirk each other to get higher than the next bloke. This Ackerman character is of interest but he was out of country when Porter was fixed up, or at least supposed to have been.'

'Humph,' was Noel's cynical response. 'Yeah, but that's according to Buckmaster. I don't think we should accept it as gospel until we check it out.'

Ron shook his head with a look of frustration. 'Okay, so Ackerman might or might not be a murderer, but stuffed if I know where he gets his money from. And this garbage about politicians having to provide a disclosure statement of their pecuniary interests is about as useless as a politician's electoral promise. No way in the world has Ackerman amassed what he's got on his parliamentary salary. Maybe you should go and have another chat with this bloke Buckmaster as he seems pretty responsive.'

Simon, looking rather pensive and with his chin resting on the palm of his hand, took a deep breath and finally said, 'You know, everyone on our list of suspects had motive, or at least we think they had motive. We certainly won't find any hard evidence against Cheryl or Peter Mason, and probably Graham Lee and Louisa Porter, not that that should eliminate them from our list. With everyone else there must be some real incriminating evidence available, somewhere. Andy Crawford was worried about legislation Porter was trying to introduce, and Ralph Glover and that Haynes bloke were both a bit hot under the collar with Porter for having intervened in development projects.'

Noel, at a complete loss as to what Simon was driving at asked, 'Okay, boss, so you think there's hard evidence buried somewhere. So what? It's not as though we know what the nature of that evidence could be, or where it's located if it does exist at all. That makes looking for something we don't know what we're looking for a tad difficult.

'So, we have a hunt around and see what we come up with,' came Simon's logical response.

'Yeah, like where?' Noel asked.

'I reckon it would be interesting to take a peek through Porter's home,' Ron chimed in.

'Gee, now why didn't I think of that?' remarked Noel, sarcastically. 'Ohh, that's right. Porter's solicitor has taken over control of the premises, which are locked up tighter than Fort Knox. And I think the chances of obtaining a search warrant are as likely as a snowball's chance in hell.'

'We can easily apply for one, but you're probably right.

We can't really go up to a magistrate and tell him we want to search the place, but we don't know what we're looking for; it's just because someone doesn't, didn't, like the man and we want to find out why,' Simon said grudgingly.

'So, as we won't have a search warrant, you plan to break in and have a look around for anything of interest? How stupid of me,' came Noel's snide comment.

'Yep,' Simon replied as he folded his arms and lent back on his chair, 'and you only got one thing wrong. It won't be me; it'll be us as it'll give us good practice for when we have a look through the next residence on the list.'

'Oh yes. And whose might that be?'

'Our illustrious Deputy Premier, Walter, call me Wally, Ackerman.'

Chapter 16

It was a cold and windy night, the clouds scurrying across the sky occasionally blotting out the waning moon and bringing an intermittent shower of rain. The houses in Ocean Road, Double Bay were opulent but as they came with a price tag in the millions, so they should be. The particular house of current interest was shrouded in darkness which was not unexpected as it was night-time, about one o'clock in the morning. The couple previously holding residence in the now unoccupied two storey mansion had split up over a year ago; the lady of the household off to shack up with a gangster, while the latest occupant and husband of the wayward wife, the late Robert Porter, MP, recently stabbed to death on Bondi Beach.

'Hey, how'd you do that,' Detective Sergeant Noel Elliott asked his accomplice, Detective Chief Inspector Simon Webster.

'Tricks of the trade,' Simon replied as he replaced the two metal lock picks in his jacket pocket. 'Despite what the

Hollywood actor can do with a hairpin, I've always had to use at least two picks. This lock is a single cylinder deadbolt where you need a key from outside and you just turn a knob on the inside of the door to lock it. All comes with experience, Noel.'

'Well, I'll be,' exclaimed Noel as Simon pushed the front door of the house open.

'No, no lights. The place is supposed to be empty and prying neighbours may be inclined to get a bit too nosy. Use your flashlight.'

'What flashlight? You didn't say I'd need one,' came Noel's indignant reply.

'Oh, for God's sake. Use the utility belt flashlight,' Simon suggested.

'What utility belt flashlight? Who the bloody hell do you think I am – Batman? The best I've got is a penlight.'

'Okay, so use it, you idiot.'

'Well, with that halogen lamp you're carrying, we may as well turn the lights on.'

Simon muttered something under his breath before admonishing Noel. 'Look, just shut up and get on with it. Now, as we haven't a clue as to what we're looking for, go have a look around for anything that may suggest we should be looking for it, or anything that's odd. You start upstairs and I'll do down here.'

IT WAS about an hour later that the two detectives met on the staircase, the search of their respective areas completed under somewhat difficult conditions, their meagre lighting affording little assistance to their ferreting. 'Well,' Simon asked as he sat down of the stairs, 'anything useful?'

Noel sat on the step above Simon with a bundle of papers and extraneous items. 'Yeah, I came across a few papers in his bedroom, along with some adult toys which doesn't surprise me, not with his reputation. The papers include a couple of letters between Dayman Brothers and Porter, and also a copy of a letter from Ackerman to a company, Eastern Development and Investment. I think we should take them back to the station and go over them as I think we'll find them quite interesting.'

Before Simon could reply, he froze and held his finger to his lips before dousing his lamp. 'Shush. Someone's at the front door.' The two detectives heard the front door quietly open and close, the intruder making every effort to be as quiet as possible. Simon held up his hand in the universal stop sign for Noel to maintain his position and to remain silent. The sudden quietness within the building only intensified the sound of the wind raging outside. Still, someone else was in the house. The seconds turned to minutes before there was the crash of something smashing onto the lounge room parquetry floor.

'Shit!!' The lights blazed on, seemingly in every room of the house which, from a house of darkness, was now transformed into one of brilliant radiant luminosity.

Simon and Noel maintained their seat on the stairs as a man appeared from the lounge room in front of them. 'Well, I'll be buggered,' exclaimed Noel, 'if it's not Andy Crawford. And what brings you out at this hour of the day?'

After the initial surprise of confronting the two detectives sitting in a very relaxed manner on the stairs of the mansion owned by the deceased Mr Porter, MP, Andy said, 'Well, I think I may ask the same question, but I thought the inclement weather provided a good opportunity to do a little snooping. But before we go any further, I take it you don't have a search warrant or you wouldn't be searching the place at this hour of the night?'

Simon declined to respond to the question. 'My, my. For a gangster you are a very astute man. But we are the police and you're not, so we will ask the questions. Before we go any further, let's get all these lights out as everyone in the neighbourhood will want to join the party.'

Andy, after turning off all the lights that had managed to turn themselves on, selected a stair just below the two detectives and sat. It wasn't until then that Simon asked the inevitable question, 'Now Andy, what are you up to?'

'Look, everyone who's ever bet on a roulette wheel knew Porter was up to no good with his attempt to legalize casinos,' Andy replied as he rested his back against the banister. 'Obviously that would mean the end of business for me and a lot of people like me, Paul Stack and Graham Lee to name a couple. I came out here just to see if I could find anything relating to his draft legislation. Hell, he tried to get it through Parliament a couple of times and eventually he would have received the support needed to get the Bill through both Houses.'

Simon didn't appear to be listening to Andy Crawford. Again, he held his finger to his lips and turned his lamp off. Again, there was the unmistakable sound of the front door opening. This time, however, as soon as the sound of the door closing was heard, Simon switched on his lamp illuminating the three men sitting on the stairs. Although the entrance to the house was still shrouded in darkness, there was the image of a man standing next to the door, apparently unsure as to what he should do next.

'Ah, for Christ sake, you wouldn't read about it. Just

how many more are going to show up? Turn on the lights, shut the bloody door and lock it, whoever you are before we get anyone else wanting to have a look around the place,' commanded Simon. Once the second intruder, or was it the fourth, had switched on the lights, his identity was immediately established. 'Aha, if it's not the inimitable Mr Henry Haynes, I do believe. Don't tell me; you're here to find anything on Mr Porter, MP, and his involvement in redevelopment gazumping. Am I right?'

'Crikey, I know what I'm here for, but what about the rest of you lot?' Henry finally managed to ask after his initial shock of finding the suspected deserted house full of people had dissipated.

Simon reclined on the steps, his elbows placed on the step above the one he was sitting on. 'Well, it seems you and Mr Crawford have specific, although totally different, reasons to be here. Why Sergeant Elliott and I are here is none of your business, however you will appreciate we are conducting a murder investigation. Now, Henry, how about you answer my question.'

'And just what was your question? I seem to have lost the plot for a moment.'

'How about Mr Porter's involvement in Dayman Brothers?'

Henry's face contorted with anger. 'Geez, and wouldn't I like to know? I just know it was Porter's fault our company went broke and he had something to do with it. And wouldn't I have liked to have got my hands on the bugger; I'd have slit his bloody throat.'

Simon sat up and looked at Noel with a "there, I told you so," look. 'Okay, Henry, just because you've denied killing Porter, going around saying you could have slit his throat doesn't really help your situation at all. You know, mens rea and all that legal stuff.'

'Yeah, I know and I'm sorry about that. But just because some bloody mongrel beat me to it doesn't mean to say I wouldn't have if I had bumped into him.'

'And you're sure you didn't go down to the beach and hack him to death?' Simon suggested.

'Hell, no. Who in their right mind would get up at that time of the day, even if it was to eliminate a parasitic political twerp?'

'Good grief, pardon my ignorance. Look, I'm sorry but we're going to have to terminate our little meeting,' Simon said as he hauled himself to his feet with the aid of the banister. 'With the place lit up like a Christmas tree, a police patrol will eventually call around, and Noel and I would prefer not to be here when they do. And I suspect neither of you gentlemen wish to be apprehended while trespassing on the household of a Minister of the Crown, even if he is dead?'

Henry looked at Andy and raised his eyebrows. 'Don't know about you, mate, but I'm out of here,' Henry declared.

'I'm with you,' rejoined Andy. 'Just one thing, Chief Inspector. If, on the off chance, you uncover anything to do with Porter's casino Bill, I'd really appreciate any information you might dig up. I suppose Henry would also like any info relating to his problem that you uncover. Of course, your assistance in both these matters would be greatly appreciated, recognizing, of course, that you do not possess a search warrant to be legally here in the first place, have broken into the premises illegally and are in the process of removing documents and other items of interest from the premises without lawful excuse. I'm sure the solicitor handling Mr Porter's estate would recognize the significance of such action, should he be made aware of tonight's activities. And while I would never tell you how to suck eggs, any revelation the papers you remove from the place may contain, you could never use that info in a court case.'

Chapter 17

'Well, this is a real fine mess you've got us into, Ollie,' Noel remarked with more than a hint of vexation. 'Fisher wants an update in half an hour and what have we got for him? All we have is a growing list of suspects without any real evidence for us to even pretend we're making headway. On top of that, we're being blackmailed by a bloody gangster.'

'Okay, you've made your point, so stop grumbling and go through these papers,' Simon said as he dropped a pile of documents onto Noel's desk. 'We want anything that supports what we don't know about possible motives. One thing I did find was Louisa's personal docs which I'll pass on to her. It's not as though anybody can refute that they weren't always in her possession.' After fifteen minutes Simon sat back, his fingers interlocked behind his head. 'Anything?'

Noel sifted through his papers until he came up with a photocopied document. 'Strange, but Porter had a photo-copy of Ackerman's travel arrangements, along with claims for travel expenses, incidental allowances, outfit allowance, meal allowance and a host of other allowances I've never heard of before. Hell, there's a pile of claims here that will cost the tax payer a fortune, quite apart from the cost of getting his first class air tickets for himself and his wife. And I bet they shack up in five star hotels, just so their trip isn't too arduous.'

Simon pursed his lips and started rock gently back and forward on his battered chair. 'Now, what in the world would Porter want with those? It's got nothing to do with him, apart from the fact that he pays his taxes along with the rest of us, I think. The letter from Eastern Development and Investment to Porter is also very interesting. In a very round about sort of way, they're offering Porter a very big bundle of money to review the Dayman's Rose Bay property development contract. I think Ron should have a closer look at what went on, you know, the subtle approach technique.'

'So, what's the next move, apart from visiting Fisher and telling him absolutely nothing? He will be a very unhappy chappy if he can't include the name of the murderer in his next press release. And what are we going to do with these papers? We can't hold them for evidence as they were illegally obtained.'

Simon stopped his rocking and folded his arms. 'We'll just have to put them back and that will legalise them. No-one saw us actually take the papers, Crawford just assumed we were going to take them. Replacing them should be easy enough, provided we don't get another crowded house. But that's the least of our worries. You know, Noel, I would love to have a peek around the Ackerman's place, and right now would be the perfect time with him and his wife jaunting around overseas.'

'And what do you hope to have a peek at, specifically, that is?'

'Oh, I don't know. Anything that might be of interest.'

'Yeah well, you'd probably find the Kama Sutra would be of interest, but not necessarily of interest in the matter currently under investigation.'

Simon shook his head. 'Look Sergeant, seeing we don't know what we are looking for, we are faced with another situation where we won't have the latitude of doing a search under the facade of a search warrant, which it can't be as we don't know what we're looking for. A poke around may prove far more beneficial. Once we find out what's in the place, we can then seek a specific warrant listing the things we've already found but didn't take. Until then, who knows what may be of interest?'

'WELL, I'LL BE STUFFED,' exclaimed Noel as the two detectives entered the Bathurst and George Streets coffee shop. His exclamation was prompted by the fact that Ron, not only having arrived before the detectives, had already ordered and had the coffees delivered. 'Gee, thanks Ron, you must be anxious to tell us something,' Noel said as he slid onto the table's window seat.

'No, but Simon said he wanted a chat, and from what I hear the hierarchy aren't too pleased with your progress.'

Simon sat down and pinched the bridge of his nose with thumb and forefinger, his eyes screwed shut. 'Yeah, we know, and Fisher has just conveyed his feelings in no uncertain terms. When I told him an arrest was imminent he went into a state of near apoplexy, poor sod. I don't think he believed me. Anyway, Ron, we have a small job for you. Can you dig up all the information you can on the company Eastern Development and Investment; who's on the board, the CEO, anything you can drum up? You better check out its progress on the stock market for the last couple of years, too. That might prove interesting.'

Ron pursed his lips and tilted his head to the side in a gesture of curiosity. 'Hang on, I thought you were doing a murder investigation. This sounds more like fraud to me.'

'There's no doubt a murder has been committed, but I have an idea this will blow out into something bigger than Ben Hur. At the moment we're looking at anything and everything that could give us a lead as to a clear motive. I think we can downgrade the Masons as suspects for the moment although I've no doubt the lovely Cheryl would have been itching to kill Porter. One bloke I'd like to have another chat with is this Gavin Buckmaster. Despite him being a politician, he seems a very straight sort of person which doesn't ring quite true.'

'Getting right off the subject, how are the new neighbours settling in,' Ron asked with an air of indifference.

Simon gave a "couldn't care less" shrug. 'Apart from Harleys announcing arrivals and departures, which accounts for more than half the visitors to the place, I haven't any problems. Georgie seems to think they're neighbours from hell but I honestly don't know what she's on about.'

Ron just nodded and chose to discontinue this particular line of conversation. He was all too well aware that Georgie had it firmly entrenched in her mind that her two neighbours were nothing short of reprehensible villains out to make inroads into the drug scene. 'Yeah okay. When do you want the info on this company Eastern Development and whatever?'

'The sooner the better,' Simon replied. 'I haven't a clue

what the connection is with Porter's death but somewhere along the line all these little pieces are going to come together to give us the real picture.'

'Yeah, something like a Jackson Pollock masterpiece,' Noel remarked sarcastically.

Chapter 18

Despite the fact it was now well into April and already having incurred the first wisps of cooler weather, it was still warm enough for the get together to be held on the back lawn of Simon's Collaroy bungalow. It was virtually back to the good old days with Graham Lee and Louisa Porter, Ron Lange and Judy Kemp, Noel and Sue and, of course, Simon and Georgie, all casually seated around the small garden table loaded with the obligatory potato chips and nuts.

Simon had considered the problem but had decided Graham and Louisa did not pose a conflict of interest, albeit both remaining on his list of suspects for the brutal murder of Louisa's devoted and ever-loving husband Robert Porter, MP. The police hierarchy had been aware of the friendship that existed between Simon and Graham and Louisa before appointing Simon as the investigating officer. As a consequence, Simon believed any criticism of this association with the two suspects was Chief Superintendent Paxton's problem.

While the girls indulged in the occasional wine, or two, the men were content to chew the fat and maintain a steady flow of empty beer cans into the strategically placed metal garbage bin. Unfortunately, the current topic of conversation held by the girls was of interest to the men, while the men's topic of conversation was of interest to the girls. As a consequence, neither group was capable of meaningful discourse, both more intent to eavesdrop on what was being said in the other group. Becoming increasingly irritated by missing snippets of vital information, Georgie's exasperation finally got the better of her. Picking up an empty beer can, Georgie hurled it into the garbage bin with a resounding "clunk". As this was far more clamorous than the usual dainty "clink" of a gently lobbed can, it had the desired effect by drawing everyone's attention to an irate Georgie.

'Look,' Georgie said as she ran her hand through her short, dark hair, 'I don't know about the rest of you, but I feel I'm being terribly rude to the other girls here by not paying as much attention to their conversation as I should. From where I sit there appears to be two topics under discussion and I would like to listen to both. So, Simon, we girls are talking about our neighbours and your conversation is about the murder. Let's get on with one at a time so we all know what's going on.'

'Fine, if everyone else is happy with that?' replied Simon as he sought a response from the others. As no objection was forthcoming, Simon said, 'Okay, but girls before boys.'

Georgie looked troubled as she poured herself another Chardonnay. 'I'm quite happy with that but before we start, Simon, I want your assurance that you won't start a domestic in front of all our friends.'

'Of course, my sweet. Why should I start a domestic?'

'Just promise.'

'Okay. I promise. No domestic. Now, get on with it.'

'Right. From the very beginning I had my doubts about our neighbours, especially as they didn't try to hide the fact that they were members of a bikie gang. They dress like bikies, they look like bikies and they ride Harleys. Now if you look like a duck, waddle like a duck and quack like a duck, you're a duck. On top of that, every night they leave one of the spare bedroom lights blazing with a zillion watt light globe. Now, ever since the swinging sixties, people have known you need that sort of setup to grow marijuana, so these people are into cultivating their own pot supply.'

Simon shrugged, looked at Graham who was well versed in the drug trade and the cultivation of Indian hemp, and slowly shook his head. 'Yeah well, just because they leave a light on in some bedroom doesn't convict them of being into marijuana cultivation,' he said, leaving no doubt as to his scepticism.

'So you're basing your hypothesis on this bright light idea?' Graham asked as he tried to conceal the hint of a smirk.

'It's not just the lights but all the other stuff as well. Bikies are always into selling drugs,' replied Georgie quite indignant that she should be doubted.

'Maybe. And they're into tattoos and prostitution, gang wars and killing people too,' suggested Noel who was also trying to conceal a smile.

'Well, seeing everyone has their own idea on the subject, and if Georgie has no objection, I might be able to throw a bit of light on the subject,' Ron said.

'And why should Georgie have any objections. I think she needs all the help she can get?' Simon asked, a tad concerned that there might be something going on to which he may not be privy.

'Oh Simon, don't be so obtuse,' Georgie replied. 'As you're in denial and don't seem the least perturbed about our neighbours, I asked Ron if he could somehow confirm my suspicions.'

'And just how can I be in denial? I've never been to Egypt.'

'And what's Egypt got to do with the price of eggs?' Sue hastened to ask.

'Just a joke. I'll explain it one day,' Simon said with a smile. 'Now, come on Ron. Have you confirmed that our neighbours are cultivating the herb superb?'

Ron cast a glance at Georgie before answering. 'I only got word yesterday. My informant went to your neighbours under the guise that he had heard on the grapevine they were into growing a quality product and he wanted to try some. The bloke wasn't there but the girl said yes, they were into hydroponics, but they were having trouble with the HBS lighting, whatever that is, and the crop had been delayed. So it seems they are growing weed but it isn't ready for reaping, just at the moment.'

'It's not HBS, it's HPS and stands for high pressure sodium,' Graham explained. 'It's a type of light used for many purposes, outdoor entertainment areas but more for hydroponic cultivation where you need a very bright light for about twelve hours a day. As they probably use about a six hundred watt lamp, you can bet they'll need to sell a lot of whoopee-weed to pay the electricity bill.'

'See, told you,' cried an elated Georgie. 'I knew it. They're members of a bikie gang and into selling drugs. So Simon, you're the policeman. What are you going to do about it?'

Simon rolled his eyes and shook his head. 'Well, the first thing I'm going to do is have another beer,' he announced and plunged his hand into the icy depths of the Esky to fetch another can. 'The second thing is to ask Ron if he can provide the name of his informant, appreciating the fact that such info is usually confidential.'

'It is, usually,' replied Ron with a shrug and a deep breath, 'but as the information is out, and as Georgie knows who the informant is, I s'pose I can tell you that it was Jacko.'

'Oh, for God's sake,' came Simon's indignant response. 'You don't mean Jacko from The Spinning Wheel casino, the bloke who works for Paul Stack?'

'Yep, that's the bloke,' Ron replied, taken aback somewhat by Simon's lack of confidence shown in Jacko's ability as an informer.

'Good grief, there are seven of 'em and you had to choose Dopey,' Simon exclaimed. 'Look, Noel and I are into a nice juicy homicide at the moment, the neighbours don't keep me awake at night and I couldn't give a rat's proverbial what they're up to. As long as they keep their gang wars, drugs and all their other goings on on their side of the fence, and they keep it down to a quiet roar, c'est la vie.'

'Okay,' remarked Louisa, 'now we have next door sorted, how about we get onto something important, like who do I have to thank for carving up that hideous husband of mine and how much did the weasel leave me.'

'Crikey, you think Robert made provision for you in his will?' Noel asked, a little surprised that Louisa might even consider such a possibility.

'No, not really, and I couldn't give a damn. I'm just glad he's gone to that big political party in the sky. But it would be nice to know who knocked him off,' replied Louisa with a smile.

'We have a few enquiries open at the moment and it's not as though we're short of suspects,' Simon said as he gently lobbed his empty beer can in to the garbage bin. 'It seems that, irrespective of how righteous a politician may appear, sometimes the "under the table" inducements just can't be ignored. Which reminds me, Ron. How are we going with Eastern Development?'

'Don't wish to muddy the waters, Simon, but that's one I'll come over to Day Street and have a chat with you about. I haven't quite finished but I think you'll find it's pretty interesting,' Ron replied.

Simon nodded his acquiescence and said, 'I await all aquiver in anticipation.'

THE PARTY CONDUCTED on the back lawn of 24 West Bank Avenue broke up rather late, but not before coffee had been consumed in copious quantities over the last hour and a half. With the departure of the guests, Simon and Georgie cleared the director's chairs and garden table into the garage and had commenced the kitchen washing up. Georgie paused in her dish washing and said, 'I think it must be the warm day and the couple of glasses of wine because I'm ready for bed.'

'Yeah,' Simon replied, a tea towel slung over his shoulder as he placed the crockery into the sideboard. 'I don't think I'll have to do any reading tonight to send me off.' Simon was one of those lucky, or unlucky, people depending on the book, who needed to read only one page of a novel before falling fast asleep.

Having completed the tedious task of post party housework, Simon and Georgie prepared for bed. It was Georgie, standing at the wash basin in the bathroom, a tooth brush in hand who turned her head to listen. 'Hey Simon, sounds like next door are having visitors tonight. A couple of Harley motor bikes just drove up the street.'

'Hell, I hope someone was riding them and anyway, how do you know they were Harleys?'

'Come on Simon. No other bike sounds like a Harley.'

'Yeah okay, I heard them. Nothing illegal about that,' replied Simon as he pulled the bed cover back. 'Sounds like they're not staying though as I can hear them coming back down the road.' It was as the noise of the two bikes reached their loudest, directly outside 24 West Bank Avenue that the explosion occurred. It took Simon all of two seconds after the crashing sound of the lounge room window disintegrating that he realised what had happened. Christ, a bloody ride-by shooting. 'Georgie,' he yelled, 'you okay?'

'I think so, but what's happening?'

'Just get down and stay in the bathroom. They might want to have another go. Now where's my bloody mobile?'

'And what's a bloody mobile?' yelled Georgie.

Chapter 19

'Well, all I can say is you've gone and upset someone in the extreme,' Noel said as he shook his head in disbelief. The two detectives sat in their Day Street office engrossed in discussion after Simon had spent some considerable time describing the previous night's event in lurid detail. Although he had been in the bedroom at the time of the incident, Simon was at pains to describe the scene as the lounge room window shattered into myriad shards of glass almost giving him a pane in the neck, as he frivolously described it. 'And you say you have no idea who sent you the message?'

'Not that I can think of, apart from that Glover character who's all bitter and twisted at me for putting his brother and uncle in the slammer.'

'And have you told Paxton about it?'

'Yeah, that was the first thing I did after I rang Manly CIB as we live in their area. Paxton's sure it's connected to the Porter killing; maybe it is.'

'And is that bloke Brown, Spring-Brown doing the investigation?'

'Yep, not that he's got much to go on. Two motor bikes drive past, return a minute or two later and while passing blast the lounge room window with a twelve gauge double barrel shotgun.'

'If it was someone riding a bike it must have been a sawn off blaster they used, unless someone was riding pillion. That would suggest there were three people involved unless there were two people on the other bike as well. That would make four people involved. But then again...'

'Oh, shut up, you pillock,' Simon interrupted in exasperation. 'I don't really care if it was someone riding shotgun on a Wells Fargo stagecoach, it's Spring-Brown's problem, not ours. And anyway, we have enough on our plate. Now, just where were we before this impolite ride-by interruption?'

'Ron said he'd call in this morning to give us what he's got on that Eastern Development thing.'

'Oh yes, that's right. I'm beginning to think Pandora's box is just about to be opened and there'll be one hell of a mess around the place. I used to think a good politician was one you would never hear rabbiting on about some stupid bloody idea and who just got on with the job. It's like this Deputy Premier bloke, Walter Ackerman; quiet as a church mouse until you start to have a look around and see how much he spends on overseas travel.'

The ringing of Noel's phone interrupted the conversation and after a second or two Noel replaced the receiver. 'That was the front desk. Ron's here so I'll go down and escort him up.' It was only a couple of minutes before Noel returned to the office with Ron in tow, his friendly dark brown eyes matching the smile etched across his face.

'Hi Ron,' Simon said. 'Pull up a pew and tell us what you know.'

Ron dragged up the only remaining chair in the office, a new office chair meant to replace Simon's battered relic that Simon had preferred to retain over the "new you beaut modern racing chair", as Noel described it. 'Before we start, let's hear your side of the story seeing everyone is talking about the shooting at your place last night. Any comment?'

Simon pursed his lips and gave a shrug. 'Know nothing about it but I will be having a chat to one of the Glover family. Apart from that, the only thing I can think of is that it's a case of mistaken identity.'

Ron's blood ran cold, the smile on his face quickly disappeared. Bloody hell. Jacko and Benny. 'Well, glad no-one was hurt. But moving right along,' Ron said, anxious for the current topic be dispensed with, 'this Eastern Development and Investment mob. It's a private company so it's not listed on the stock exchange which isn't unusual as they probably like to dole out the company profits to share-holders as quickly as possible. Odd thing is that the managing director goes by the name of Monica Sainsbury Ackerman. She owns fifty one per cent of the shares, the rest distributed throughout the family. And before you ask, the answer is yes, she just happens to be the wife of Walter, and no, he has no interests in the company, or so the records indicate.'

Simon harrumphed. 'Yeah, I bet. Someone's working a fiddle here and I bet it was Porter, with a little help from Walter. Having no interest in the company means Walter probably thinks he has no pecuniary interests to declare to parliament. Monica just sits back and waits for the contracts to come in then farms them out to the subcontractors in which she'll also have an interest. I bet that in the case of the Rose Bay development, Dayman Brothers had the contract but got the whole thing squashed by Porter so Monica's mob, and by default Wally, would finally get the contract.'

Noel finished rolling a sheet of paper into a ball and had his shot into the garbage can next to Simon's desk – and missed, as per usual. 'So,' he said as he decided against another shot, 'the Ackermans can be choosy and select any development they want. Porter just found some excuse to overturn a local council decision, like the greenies tangerine spotted tree frog or whatever at Rose Bay, and bingo, another fortune to the Ackermans and a kickback for Porter.'

'Looks like it but we would need proof; just another good reason for having a peek inside the Ackerman's house,' Simon said, his eyebrows raised questioningly.

'Do you mean a discrete peek or a fully-fledged warranted search?' Ron asked.

'Let's try for a warrant ASP and get over there before Wally and Monica get back from their overseas jaunt,' Simon suggested.

RON, together with Judy, met Georgie and Sue at a coffee shop in the Queen Victoria Building on George Street. The meeting had been hastily organised by Ron who couldn't help thinking that possibly, in some small way, the ride-by shooting at 24 West Bank Lane was of his making. That he acted as the conduit between Jacko and Georgie was never in doubt, albeit with some trepidation as Ron believed the problem was a domestic affair between the Websters and the gangland idiots next door. His lack of enthusiasm to involve himself had now been vindicated by subsequent events. Irrespective of what Simon may think, Ron firmly believed the shotgun shooting of the Webster's front window was far too coincidental to be a matter of "mistaken identity".

'I'm sorry, Georgie, but what the bloody hell did you ask Jacko to do? Whatever it was, he certainly stuffed things up unless, of course, you asked him to run rampant with a shotgun.' Ron said, his mood displaying a hint of annoyance.

Georgie gave Ron a look of staunch rebuttal. 'Hey, now just hold onto your horses. To begin with, and Sue can back me up on this, we didn't ask Jacko to do anything, not specifically anyway. Yes, we asked him if there was any way he thought the neighbours might be intimidated into thinking a move away from Collaroy might be in their best interest. But why on earth would we ask Jacko to shoot up our house? If there was any shooting up to be done, it should have been on the house next door. And Simon has already decided the people most likely to have done it are involved with that Glover tribe of unscrupulous miscreants.'

'So, have you spoken to Jacko about the shooting?' Sue asked.

'No,' Ron replied, 'but I will. I can't believe Jacko, or even Benny, would have pulled the trigger. The problem is, we don't know if they spoke to anyone about your neighbours and what they're up to. If they spoke to The Mafia they wouldn't have driven around on Harleys and used a pea shooter. They'd be more inclined to have turned up in a black limo and used a machine gun. And I think Simon's idea about a member of the Glover family is a bit astray. I very much doubt this Glover bloke would be out to intimidate Simon. He's more likely to seek his revenge on Simon in a more drastic and permanent way rather than by just blowing in your lounge room window. Simon mentioned he will be having a chat to Ralph Glover anyway.'

'Well whoever did what, I'm sorry, Judy, for trying to get rid of your tenants but I'm sure if we can move them on we'll end up with some little old lady who'll fit in nicely,' said Georgie. 'So, Ron, are you going to speak to Jacko or would you like Sue and me to go up to The Turning Wheel and speak to him?'

'No, you can leave that to me. And the place is The Spinning Wheel; the owner, Paul Stack, believes one good turn deserves another,' replied Ron. The girls ignored a very poor attempt of some humour.

Chapter 20

Simon and Noel sat waiting in the coffee shop located in the Mitchell Library, a stone's throw from the colonial sandstone buildings of Parliament House. The venue for the meeting, suggested by Peter Mason, MP, had been agreed to as it was considered that, at this point of the investigation into the death of Robert Porter, MP, a more relaxed atmosphere was appropriate. Quite apart from the pleasant ambience of the coffee shop, it took Peter Mason, MP, just a few minutes leisurely stroll down Macquarie Street to meet the detectives.

It was not difficult for the detectives to recognize Peter Mason, as was it a simple case for Peter Mason to identify Simon and Noel. The thought crossed Noel's mind that it was pointless wearing mufti as there was something about being a copper that was easily recognizable, uniform or no uniform. 'Glad you could make it, Mr Mason. I appreciate you must be a very busy man,' Simon said after the initial introductions had been made and refreshments ordered.

'Not at all. Cheryl mentioned you had been out to see her, about Robert Porter, I believe?'

'Yes, that's right. We're conducting the investigation into his death and, unfortunately, your name has come up. This chat is solely to clarify the situation and in no way should you feel that we are on a witch hunt,' Simon said in an endeavour to calm any anxiety Mr Mason may have.

'No, that's fine. I've nothing to hide so let's get on with it,' Peter said as he poured himself a cup of tea.

'First of all, we would like to know a bit about your background. I believe you are the member for South Sydney and currently the Minister for Sport and Recreation.'

'Yep, that's right. The Premier hoisted me to the position in the belief I knew something about sport. Buggered if I know where he got that idea from, apart from the fact I used to play the odd game of rugby.'

'And you don't? Know anything about sport, I mean.'

'Look, mate, the only thing I know about sport is the LA Lakers play baseball, the horses run the wrong way round in Melbourne and The Ashes are played at Wimbledon.'

Simon looked at Noel, a blank look on his face. Holy hell, Simon thought. And I suppose the Treasurer qualifies for his position because he had a piggy bank when he was a kid. Simon began to feel depressed. 'I believe that, in view of the circumstances, the Premier has cut short his visit to the USA?' he asked seeking clarification of the situation.

Peter Mason gave a shrug. 'Yes, that was the news the Chief Whip gave us but it seems the Premier has had second thoughts. He now believes there's nothing to be gained by rushing home and getting himself involved. I suppose Walter Ackerman would have been the logical person to provide the eulogy in the absence of the Premier, but he's absent overseas as well.'

Noel shook his head and frowned. 'Pardon my ignorance, Mr Mason, but who's the head honcho in parliament at the moment seeing everyone seems to be either overseas or dead.'

Peter Mason rested his elbow on the table and held his chin, tapping his cheek as he thought about the question. After some deep thinking he said, 'I hadn't thought about it, but now you've raised the subject, I suppose it's me. Most of the other ministers are out of the country on fact finding missions which only leaves me and a couple of others, apart from the backbenchers and they don't count.'

'Oh, and what about Mr Buckmaster?' Simon asked the de facto Premier.

'Yes, well, he's still in town but he's a backbencher and has to be very selective of where he gets to go. I heard somewhere his next trip is to Singapore.'

'I thought he was virtually an aide to Robert Porter handling all the environmental stuff? And what's Singapore got that's so interesting?' Noel asked, fully aware that the question would be met with a totally unsuspected and stunning response. He wasn't wrong.

'Yes, he is but he has a far greater interest in formula one motor racing and Singapore has a grand prix. If you were a cynical person you could check the major sporting events held worldwide and see that most of the politician's overseas trips coincide with some sporting or social event.'

'For your information, Mr Mason, I am a cynic and getting cynicaler,' responded Simon. 'But we're not here to discuss the pros and cons of political perks. Now, if we can focus on the problem at hand which is the murder of

Robert Porter, MP. You mentioned that your wife had informed you of our visit to see her?'

'Yes, she said you would be talking to me sometime or other.'

'And did you know your wife was quite frank with us. In fact she was so frank she even gave us the idea you may have been a bit upset with Mr Porter; upset to the extent you may have wanted him dead?' Simon said with an interrogative inflection.

Peter Mason heaved a sigh and gave a shrug. 'Good grief, gentlemen, I can't hold Cheryl accountable for her current predicament. Obviously, I didn't pay her the attention she both sought and needed, or maybe even demanded, as I was too busy with my own personal life, if you get my drift. You know, something about the pot calling the kettle black. Anyway, the only thing that really annoyed me was that Porter should have been more discreet, or at least more careful, as most of us are.'

'So, being "annoyed" with Porter doesn't amount to having a raging desire to kill the man?' Simon asked.

'Look, if there was anyone who should have been annoyed it's Cheryl. I'm sort of surprised that when she became aware of her problem she didn't go round and blow Porter's brains out. You see, Cheryl is sweet as apple pie, up to a point. Push her past that point and all hell can break loose. No, Chief Inspector, the word "annoyed" has very different connotations to different people.'

'Then I take it you weren't annoyed enough to kill Porter?' Noel asked, his eyebrows raised in a questioning manner.

'Hell no. I mightn't have liked the man as he always seemed to be involved in some dodgy scheme, not that I ever knew for certain what the scheme was. He gave a lot of people the impression he was up to something dubious but no-one knew anything about the details. Everyone around Parliament House, and probably the general public, know the Minister for Planning and Infrastructure can, if so inclined, make a bundle by facilitating the requirements of big property developers. I would be very surprised if Robert Porter hadn't indulged in the pastime,' Peter Mason added as if it were just a matter of routine.

'Did anyone else know, or think, Porter was pandering to these developers?' Noel asked.

'I have no idea what other people know or what they are thinking, although it would be a very handy attribute to possess. No, I can only hazard a guess,' Mason replied as he contemplated the advantages of being able to read the minds of other people.

'Then guess,' Noel said, his manner becoming brusque.

'Well, with our illustrious Deputy Premier Walter Ackerman married to a successful developer, I'll leave that to your own judgment.'

After the meeting had broken up and Mason had made his way back to Parliament House, the two detectives ambled down Macquarie Street towards Circular Quay. 'Well, it almost sounds like there is collusion between ministers and backbenchers. Mason and Buckmaster are virtually saying the same thing,' Noel commented.

Simon pressed the pedestrian button at the traffic lights and stood hands in his pockets, waiting. 'Yes, and both stories seem to suggest something was going on between Ackerman and Porter. And we still have this Glover and Henry Haynes to have a little chat with. The light turned green.

Chapter 21

Simon had decided he could justify the confrontational approach should the forthcoming discussions degenerate into a verbal stoush, as he anticipated. With that decision and his resolve firmly set, Simon, with Noel in tow, chose to ignore the niceties of protocol and paid scant regard to the attention of a petulant secretary who stated categorically that the two visitors had to be announced to Mr Glover prior to entering the office. Having walked straight through the open door into his office, the detectives found Ralph Glover ensconced behind his desk and Henry Haynes, looking grumpy as usual, occupying the office's only lounge chair.

'God luv us, Henry, Holmes and Watson again. You'd think they'd leave us in peace since we've already told them we had nothin' to do with killing that politician bloke. Now, what is it this time, Mr Webster?' Ralph asked.

'Just like to ask a couple of questions. Now, you can either be polite and answer the questions in a civil manner or we can haul you off to the station and do it the hard way,' Simon said with a touch of impatience.

'Okay, okay, keep your shirt on,' replied Ralph, his mood taking on a more conciliatory note. 'Best you take a seat and let's get on with it. Do you want Henry to stay?'

'May as well,' Simon replied as he and Noel sat themselves on a couple of collapsible metal chairs. 'It'll save you the time of telling him everything after we've left. The first question I have is pretty straight forward. I appreciate there is no love lost between us over your family's incarceration, which you hold me personally responsible. However, I find your antipathy towards me goes a little too far when you hire thugs to do a ride-by shooting of my home. I want the names of these gun totin' morons you hired.'

'You're joking,' Ralph exclaimed with a look of genuine surprise. 'You mean someone had your home shot up? Henry, do you know anything about this?'

'Not me boss,' Henry replied. 'I don't like coppers but hell, I'd never go that far. Sure, I mightn't buy tickets for the policemens' ball, but crikey, that's a bit over the top.'

'So, you both say you know nothing about it?' Noel asked before he realized it was a stupid question.

'God help me. Your sergeant is pretty hard of hearing,' Ralph quipped. 'I think we've both told you that we know nothing about a shooting. But I'll tell you once more, so watch my lips; neither Henry nor I know anything about a shooting, or a stabbing. Now I think that's clear enough, Chief Whatever Webster. And is there anything else a little less repetitious you want to talk about?'

Simon folded his arms and thought for a moment. 'Yes, there is one other thing. Henry, are you aware of a company called Eastern Development and Investment?'

'Of course. They're going gangbusters at the moment,'

Henry replied. 'I don't know how they did it, but they're the mob that ended up doing the Rose Bay development. They must have convinced someone that there were no endangered tree frogs living in the area. Apart from the Rose Bay shemozzle, they seem to be picking up big well-paid contracts at a rather surprising rate.'

Noel look at Simon and raised his eyebrows. Well, well, well. That is interesting.

CHIEF SUPERINTENDENT PAXTON'S office failed to exude the usual aura of peace and tranquility. In fact, right at the moment the atmosphere was a little tense, the pre meeting social chitchat having collapsed into a strained and awkward silence. Those summoned to the office were now waiting in dreaded expectation for the Chief Superintendent to complete his reading of a folder whereupon he deftly tossed it into his "out" tray. Of the visitors to the office, it was only Detective Superintendent Fisher who was at ease; he wasn't responsible for the progress, or lack thereof, of the investigation into the death of Robert Porter, MP. In fact, the attendances at Fisher's press meetings had dwindled significantly as more topical and up-to-the-minute news items replaced the news of the brutal murder of a politician. Newspaper reporters and radio commentators, having bled the story to death, had consigned Robert Porter to the history pages and were now focused on more important news; the football season had kicked off.

'Okay, Simon, let's have it. Seeing you've discounted the suicide angle, just who did kill Porter?' CS Paxton asked knowing full well that Simon didn't have a clue as to the identity of the culprit.

Simon crossed his legs, sat back and unconsciously

started to flick the top of the biro pen he was holding. 'Sir, we're beginning to think the murder is not just a simple murder case based on the usual reasons one gets themselves done away with. You're aware of the usual motives, jealousy, revenge, hate, money and all those other stupid excuses people get themselves murdered. Well, in this murder it seems like there's a multitude of different motives that could have been used by any one of at least half a dozen people.'

'Look, Simon, I'm beginning to feel like a mushroom, so will you please stop with the crap, and the clicking, and tell me something a bit more enlightening than "it could have been anybody for any number of reasons."'

'Okay sir, but I will précis it down,' Simon said. 'We don't know why Porter was killed but we think he was using his position as Minister for Planning and Infrastructure to receive kickbacks from companies for favourable treatment in the allocation of development contracts.'

CS Paxton's head drooped as he massaged his eyeballs with the balls of his hands. On completion of this little exercise he sat back, elbows on the leather arm rests, his hands clenched on his stomach. He looked at Simon for a moment before he passed his gaze to Noel, Fisher and finally Ron who couldn't help feeling a trifle uncomfortable. 'Jesus H. Christ, Simon. What planet have you been living on? Everyone knows a politician with altruistic motives is as rare as a taxi on a Friday night. And since when haven't most politicians had their snout in the trough with their own little schemes aimed at subsidising their own not insignificant fortnightly pay packet?'

Simon refrained from answering what he considered a rhetorical question. However, he couldn't help thinking, with much surprise, that maybe he wasn't Robinson Crusoe and that there were others who shared his opinion of a politician's moral behaviour and ethical inclination.

'Ron, you've been very quiet on the subject. What have you discovered that these incompetents haven't?' Paxton enquired.

'We think one of those companies that paid Porter was a company called Eastern Development and Investment which happens to be owned by the Deputy Premier's wife, Monica Sainsbury.'

Both Superintendent Fisher and Chief Superintendent Paxton looked somewhat nonplussed by Ron's revelation. 'You're kidding. Simon, is this ridgy-didge?' Paxton asked, with a look of grave concern. Paxton was fully aware of the ramifications should the revelation prove correct.

Simon shrugged. 'Sorry sir, but that's what it looks like. Although married to Walter Ackerman, Monica chooses to use her maiden name of Sainsbury. We appreciate the sensitivity of the situation and are treading cautiously. As you can see, if we are correct about the payment of kick-backs, the murder of Porter may be just the tip of the iceberg, not forgetting that there's a failure to submit a disclosure of assets by Walter Ackerman irrespective of what name Monica chooses to use in the running of her business.'

'Well I'll be buggered,' muttered Paxton. 'Alright. I want you to pursue this line of enquiry, but please, and I'm not telling you, I'm begging you, just show a bit of be discretion. If you're right it could bring down the government. No, on second thoughts it would bring the government down. Fisher, not a word of this to the press. In fact, as far as they are concerned, play out the murder of Porter for as long as possible with as little as possible, if you get my drift.'

As the four visitors left the office, it was Noel who remarked, 'holy hell, talk about a bugger's muddle.' As indeed it was.

Chapter 22

It was eleven thirty at night as the car made its way along New South Head Road towards the very exclusive harbourside suburb of Vaucluse. The occupants of the car were in no hurry to reach their destination; the later the better, quite apart from the fact that the last thing they wanted was the undue attention of a police patrol car and a speeding ticket.

'Pardon my ignorance, boss, but aren't we going in the wrong direction? I thought Ackerman lived out Parramatta way,' Noel, the passenger and navigator, queried.

'Good God no,' Simon replied. 'I thought everyone was aware the Deputy Premier was the member for the west Sydney electorate of Parramatta while he resided in his eastern suburbs mansion at Vaucluse. I think he overcame whatever problem there may have been by buying a bed-sitter flat somewhere in the Parramatta district, not that he ever lives in it.'

'Well, pardon my ignorance,' Noel countered. 'Anyway,

just what are we s'posed to be looking for when we get there?'

'Haven't a clue. We'll know whatever we're looking for is what we're looking for once we find it.' Having been unable to provide a magistrate with anything more than "because we want to look around", and unable to say with any certainty that an offence had been committed, apart from Porter's murder, the magistrate had very little difficulty in denying the application for a search warrant.

'Gee, I'm glad you explained that to me otherwise I would've been totally in the dark,' Noel said, unenlightened. 'You are sure Wally and his wife are out of country at the moment?'

'No, I don't think anyone can be certain where they are. Buckmaster seems to think they're in Paris before going down the Amazon so I'll go along with whatever he tells me. Ahh, this looks like the place,' Simon said as he pulled into the curb in front of a palatial brick wall fence behind which stood a palatial two storey, white brick mansion. As the occupants of the house were on an extended overseas trip, Simon was not surprised to find the large wrought iron gate providing access to the stone driveway shut. After a moment of inaction with the two detectives seated in the car, Noel suddenly realised the problem; the gate.

'Sorry boss. I was miles away,' Noel said as he re-entered the car for the long drive to the house.

'And no way in the world could a mere polly afford a shack like this on just his pay packet,' Simon said as the lights of the car illuminated the mansion. 'I've stayed in smaller hotels than this, and the distance from the gate to the house is further than I'd go for a holiday. Bloody Ackerman has to be guilty of doing something shonky.'

'Aahh, now I'm with you, boss. This bloke Ackerman is guilty of doing something illegal but we don't know what that something is. We have a hunt around tonight for something to indicate whatever the illegal thing he's doing is so we can have a further hunt around for specific evidence to prove he's guilty of that something he's done that's illegal. But I think the hard part will be finding whatever that something is to indicate he's done something illegal in the first place. And you think that whatever he's done will prove significant to Porter's murder?'

Simon clicked his tongue and nodded. 'Got it in one, Noel, I think. That's if he's done anything illegal. We can only assume he has because of his wife's business arrangement with Porter. So, let's get going and see what our Deputy Premier has been up to, if anything.'

Being such a plush neighbourhood, the next door neighbour's house was quite some distance from the Ackerman's home. This, along with the brick fence that enclosed the property and its prodigious garden surrounds, seemed to mock the "Neighbourhood Watch" sign attached to a verandah column adjacent to the front door. The thought crossed Noel's mind that you could drive a removilist van up to the door, empty out the place and be gone without anybody paying any attention at all.

Simon, after recent practice, had become quite adept at manipulating the lock on the front door of a house, and tonight was no exception. It wasn't long before the two detectives had illegally entered the mansion of Walter Ackerman, MP, and his wife, Monica. Equipped this time with decent torches, and Simon with a small camera for photos of the something that might be illegal, the two detectives found themselves in a marble floored reception area. From this site access could be gained to a number of rooms on the ground floor and, by way of an ornate curved staircase, access to the rooms above.

Noel let out a quiet whistle. 'Wow. Someone has a bucket of money; but who is it, Monica or Wally? And I see what you mean. You don't end up in a place like this without getting a little dirt on your hands.'

'Bugger,' Simon said in annoyance. 'You've just raised a very good point that I've overlooked. I've no doubt we'll be able to find out their banking details somewhere around here. Tomorrow I want you to see just who does hold the purse strings. In the meantime, you check around down here and I'll have a peek upstairs.'

Noel, having searched the formal lounge and dining rooms, an informal living room cum lounge room with an adjacent dining area and kitchen, finished his peeking well before Simon. The only thing he considered peculiar and out of the ordinary was a rather large polished wood presentation plaque located above an ornate open fireplace in the formal lounge room. Apart from the attached small brass plate with the words "Presented to Walter Ackerman in appreciation, Langkawi, Malaysia June 1981" inscribed, that was all the presentation consisted of. There were brackets to support whatever it was that had been presented, however there was now nothing to even suggest what had been presented in the first place, unless, of course, the brass inscription plate represented the sum total of the presentation. Noel made a note of this rather unique plaque, together with details of a small window found open at the rear of the building, before heading for the stairway to see how Simon was getting on with his peeking.

Noel caught up with Simon in a small room, probably a bedroom but used as a study. It was the brand spanking new IBM electric typewriter, a bookcase loaded with binders and files, a paper shredder and an office table, with the obligatory phone and office chair that provided both detectives with sufficient evidence to hazard a guess as to the function of the room. 'Anything useful, boss?'

'Yeah, but I'm getting a little confused. This appears to be Monica's study whereas I expected it to be Walter's. On second thoughts, what would he need a study for as she has her own company to run. Much as I would like to know what's in all these binders and files, we are pressed for time and I'm reluctant to take anything as we are in here illegally.'

'Any banking details?' Noel asked as he flicked through a binder.

'Yes, I did find the banking details for Eastern Development, and for both Wally and Monica. According to one of her ledgers she's made some big transfers to an account and I'm putting my money on it that it belongs to Robert Porter. That's another one you can check out tomorrow.'

Noel nodded in acknowledgement. 'And anything else?'

'There are a few other things that I've taken photos of but nothing in particular. Look, let's get out of here and you can tell me what you've found on the way home,' Simon replied, a little anxious of being found guilty to trespassing on the property of a Minister of the Crown.

Chapter 23

Ron walked along Palmer Street to The Spinning Wheel where he met Jacko standing outside the front door, as previously arranged. Jacko, at first appearance, was pleased to see Ron as he held the expectation of some sort of tribute for having fulfilled Ron's request for assistance. 'Well, we passed on the details just like you asked me to, Mr Lange,' Jacko said, a smile on his face and full of confidence. 'My mate Benny spoke to one of the boys who had dropped off his Harley at Benny's place for repairs. Seems Benny told him what was going on with your neighbours and how they were members of a bikie gang and into hard core drug stuff.'

Ron looked pained. 'So, you don't know exactly what Benny told this bloke?'

'No, not exactly. Why, is there a problem?'

'Yeah well, sort of. They shot up the wrong house.'

Jacko's smile broadened. 'Aah, come on Mr Lange. You're havin' me on.'

'Nope. They shot up the Webster's house,' Ron replied

simply. 'They're getting an emergency glazier in today to put in a new window.'

Jacko groaned, covered his eyes with his hand and slowly shook his head. 'Geez, I told Benny a dozen times to remember the number of West Bank Lane. Benny told me the job was done, but he didn't tell me it was the wrong bloody house.'

'He probably doesn't know.'

'Crikey, I'm sorry Mr Lange. Look, I'll whip round and see Benny and tell him we got it wrong. Maybe he's still working on the bloke's bike so we can get this thing sorted.'

Ron looked rather dejected and wondered whether he should quit while ahead. Still, the problem remained and he had given his friends some sort of assurance he would attend to the matter. 'Okay, Jacko. But please, whoever you get this time, make sure the number is 26 West Bank Lane, not number 24.'

Ron strolled back down Palmer Street to William Street, found a phone box and, with great reluctance, rang Georgie.

The following morning Ron met Georgie and Sue at Manly Wharf, Ron having decided a quiet forty minute trip on the ferry might be a relaxing tonic for his frayed nerves following his talk with Jacko. He accepted the fact that his selection of Jacko as the person to persuade Georgie's next door neighbour to reconsider their lease options had not been such a great idea. It was now time to reveal to Georgie the true facts of the matter.

'CRIPES, A BIT NIPPY THIS MORNING,' Noel remarked as he removed his coat and hung it on the coat rack behind the door. 'Still, it is May. And what time did you get in? Looks like you've slept here.'

Simon sat back on his chair, shrugged and clasped his hands behind his head. 'Yep, came in about five to drop off the film down at the lab. They have a bloke ferreted away in the dungeon twenty four seven, just in case something important comes along and you need the prints in a hurry. Here's a magnifying glass I picked up to help. Let's have a look over whatever we've found at the Ackerman's place before you get onto that banking stuff.'

'Good thinkin' boss. I would like to know if we've found the "something" we were looking for,' Noel said as he dragged his chair up to sit on the opposite side of Simon's desk.

'Yeah well, don't forget most of the stuff I've taken photos of comes from Monica's study, not Walter's. But before we get started, didn't Buckmaster tell us the Ackermans had gone to the UK and Europe before heading off down the Amazon?'

'That's right. So?'

'Well, I don't care if it is springtime in the UK, it can still get bloody cold over there. It appears the Ackermans left all their winter woolies at home in their cupboard, which is a bit surprising. I doubt that it's significant but file it away, just in case. Now let's have a look at whatever we've got.'

The quality of Simon's photography left much to be desired but was adequate to meet the detectives' requirements. Simon took his time over a photograph of a ledger headed "Eastern Development and Investment Operating Account". 'Noel, you'd better take this along when you check the bank records. It shows Robert Porter having been paid substantial amounts of money at irregular intervals

while large sums have been deposited into the same operating account. When you check the bank accounts, get a
copy of the statements that coincide with the debits and
credits of the ledger payments; let's see if there are any
shonkies going on.'

'Okey-doke, boss. Just getting away from banking for a
second, this looks a bit suss.'

'What's that?' Simon asked as he ceased his gazing
through his magnifying glass.'

'According to a diary entry, in June '81, the Ackermans
went to a new holiday resort at Langkawi somewhere in
Malaysia. This gels with a presentation made in June '81 to
Wally Ackerman although all the presentation consisted of
was a brass inscription plate, nothing else. I wonder if that
"holiday" was a fact finding tour.'

'That'll be easy to find out,' replied Simon. 'Old Buckmaster will be able to access the records of all the jaunts
taken by everyone. And that window you found open. Any
sign of forced entry?'

'None, but it wasn't the most secure of windows.' Noel
replied. 'Anyone could've gained entry and it may have
been left open accidently. But nothing seems to have been
disturbed, apart from the presentation plaque, so who
knows? There are a few entries in a diary where Monica
has written "Bob" and a time. You don't think "Bob" could
be Robert Porter do you?'

'I suppose it could be. It looks like they did have some
sort of business arrangement going on, so it's quite possible.
Again, it's something we should keep in mind. Maybe I'll
do a bit of work on the whiteboard while you're out so we
can see what's what.'

Starting with the work already carried out by Noel, it
took Simon another hour to write in the names of others

who had raised their head in the course of the investigation, among them being Walter and Monica Ackerman, or Monica Sainsbury, their link to Eastern Development and all tied back to Robert Porter.

Simon's work was interrupted by a phone call which, after placing the felt tipped marker on the board and returning to his chair, he answered with undue haste. On completion of the call Simon rested one arm on his hip, the other elbow on the desk, held his chain and tapped his nose with his forefinger as he contemplated the significance of the call. The chances of finding the murder weapon were about one in a million. However, apparently some scuba diver, diving off the rocks between Bondi Beach and Mackenzie Point to the south, had found an item he considered might be of some importance to the police. Aware of the recent murder, the diver handed the item to the Eastern Suburbs LAC where Detective Inspector Francis had sent it to forensics for analysis. Until the significance of the find could be determined, whether the murder weapon had been found was a moot point.

Chapter 24

The door to Gavin Buckmaster's office was open as usual, Buckmaster ensconced behind his desk and in the process of doing The Daily's crossword puzzle. He declined to stand and, after nodding to the escorting security guard, ushered Simon into the office. 'Detective Chief Inspector Webster, please take a seat,' he said indicating to the same comfortable looking lounge chair Simon had sat during his earlier visit. 'Now, what can I do for you DCI Webster?'

'Nothing really desperately important and probably doesn't have anything to do with our murder. It's just that during our investigation some matters have come to light with which we would prefer to have a better understanding. I'm not sure you're the person I should be speaking to. Maybe I should be speaking with the Chief Whip.'

'That might prove a little difficult as he's overseas at the moment. If you let me know what the problem is maybe I can fix it, or at least point you in the right direction,' replied Buckmaster.

'Yes, of course,' Simon said as he withdrew his note-book from his coat pocket and flicked through the pages. He paused for a moment then asked, 'These study trips politicians are forced to take. How are the plebs, like me, to know it's not just another junket at the taxpayers' expense and that they really are expected to do some work?'

'Ah yes. I've heard this question a dozen times before. You see, DCI Webster, on completion of a study tour, the person undertaking the tour must submit a report covering the aim of the study jaunt, I mean trip, the lessons learnt, and the names and positions held by the people with whom discussions had taken place. No, there is a whole plethora of statutory requirements to be addressed. So, you see, these study tours are very trying and physical demanding ventures, even after you get home.'

'Oh yes, I can appreciate the problems. They must be a real nuisance. And these statutory reports are submitted on completion of the tour?'

'That's right. The report has to be submitted within a specific timeframe, as laid down in…'

'Yes, I know; the statutory requirements. And just how many of these reports have you seen?'

'Buckmaster shrugged. 'You know, you're the first person to have asked me that question and to be honest, I've only seen two or three.'

'That many? And which members took the time to write these reports?'

'I can only remember the first one I read. Forgotten who wrote it but I think he was

on a study trip taken to Namibia in the late sixties. Whoever it was wrote a very comprehensive three page report.'

'And you don't recall any other report?'

'Well, yes and no. Those that I have seen are virtually the same as the Namibia report. One bloke went to Iceland and his report stated he landed in the capital of Windhoek.'

'And no-one questioned it?'

'Hell no. In reality, politicians are too busy to write their own report. Everyone has a copy of this Namibia report and they just amend a few dates and names. No-one sits around to examine and correct it. As long as a report is submitted in accordance with the statutory requirements, everything is kosher.'

Simon sat back, elbows on the chair's armrests, his note-book in his left hand tapping it with a pen held in his right. 'Okay Mr Buckmaster, I need to know the exact itinerary for Walter Ackerman during his study tour conducted in June 1981.'

'No problem. Just a moment, I have that register right here. I was bringing it up to date with the Premier's and DP's tours. Now, when was it you said, June '81?'

'That's right.'

After a few page-turning moments he stopped. 'Ah yes. I don't know how you knew he was away, but from 20 May to 2 July he was in Amsterdam, Copenhagen, Stockholm, Oslo and Helsinki. And before you ask, yes, his wife Monica went along as well.'

'Holy hell. That must have cost the taxpayer a packet?'

'Yes, that would have been a terribly expensive tour, quite apart from the fares. There's accommodation allowances, cold weather allowances, meal allowances, inci-dental allowances, inconvenience allowance and a dozen or so other allowances that I can't recall off the top of my head.'

'And naturally they have to acquit these allowances with receipts on their return?'

'Good God, no. If that were the case politicians would have to take an accountant along with them just to make sure the allowances were used for what they were intended. And to suggest a politician would use the money for any other purpose other than that for which it was intended is positively outrageous, scurrilous and slanderous.'

'Yes, quite so. And all these allowances would have been paid before they left Sydney?' Simon asked, totally ignoring Buckmaster's pretentious diatribe of feigned indignation.'

'Of course, although I would never dream of carrying that much money around with me. It must have been around twenty thousand. But why this sudden interest in study tours?'

Simon sighed and shook his head in wonder. 'Mr Buckmaster, what would you say if I told you that during the month of June 1981, the Ackermans were lavishing it up at a new holiday resort in Malaysia?'

'I'd say you were nuts.'

'Does anyone go out to the airport to make sure the politicians climb onto the aircraft to take them to the specific destination of the scheduled study tour?'

'Come on, Webster, get off the grass. They're big boys and don't need anyone to hold their hand.'

'Okay, I only said "if I told you". Let's leave it at that for the moment, but if I'm correct, and someone else was aware of the scam being perpetrated, that person could well find himself very dead. If I were you, I'd be very discrete as to who you mention this little discussion with as that person just might make sure you don't blow the whistle.'

. . .

'RIGHT, Noel. Let's have a look at the ledger accounts against the bank accounts. After having a quick squiz through the business operating ledger there seems to be some payments needing some explanation. There are quite a few made to Robert Porter, which wouldn't be surprising if he were touting for Monica's company. There's also a very large payment of fifty thousand made to Wally Ackerman about eighteen months ago.'

'Hang on, boss. Wouldn't that just about coincide with the last election?'

'Pure coincidence, Noel. Now, let me have a look,' Simon said as he checked the bank statement. 'Yep, the payment was made alright. Now, I wonder if that was to support Wally's electioneering. A political party is required to divulge all contributions but I'm not so sure about payments to an individual, especially if that individual is your spouse. Sort of means a very rich man could buy as many votes needed to get into parliament, or could be that Walter is pocketing some re-election contributions.'

'Yes, but aren't all politicians supposed to reveal their pecuniary interests?'

Simon pulled a face and said, 'And the operative word is "supposed". I always thought pollies were one step above a used car salesman as far as principles, integrity and morality go, but I'm beginning to think a used car salesman is a pillar of virtue in comparison. Right at the moment I'm beginning to feel sorry for Ralph Glover and his mate Henry. How can people like that compete with the Minister for Planning and Infrastructure, and a woman hell bent on making money?

'By the way, while I was clicking away with the camera I must have taken a photo of a very strange letter. It's from Peter Mason to Eastern Development and Investment.

Apparently, a lot of people knew of Robert Porter's plan to introduce his Bill for legalizing casinos. Mason had advised Monica Ackerman in the letter that he had been approached by an Andrew Crawford, you know, the Red Ruby man, with a business proposition alluding to the debate and vote on the Bill. There wasn't anything specifically mentioned apart from the fact that Crawford had hinted to Mason that a substantial fiscal advantage may be available should he, Mason, lobby and vote against Porter's Bill.

'Mason blatantly pointed out that he, as Minister for Sport and Gaming, would be desirous to know if Monica would be amenable to enter into a discussion relating to future arrangements, should the Bill be passed. Obviously Mason was, or is, in the process of hedging his bets to see which is the more profitable option; lobby against the Bill and be paid off by Crawford, or support the Bill and be paid off by Eastern Development. According to the bank statements there's a comparatively recent payment made from Eastern Development to Mason which amounts to about a year's salary. With Porter's death it means sod all to Mason as to who introduces the Bill now as the situation will remain the same; go with Crawford or go with Ackerman. The Bill will be passed sometime in the future and a very large property development scheme will be on the drawing boards. And along with that comes every weasel out of the woodwork to make as much money as they can, legally or otherwise.'

Noel let out an airy whistle. 'Well, that certainly puts the cat among the pigeons and Crawford right up there with potential murderers. I suppose with everything as it is, we turn a blind eye to Mason's little scam?'

'The only thing Mason appears to be doing is sitting on

the fence trying to work out the most lucrative way to jump. Maybe he'll jump both ways. Hell, who needs a stack of gun powder? With all the shenanigans we've uncovered we could create far greater havoc to parliament than any little scheme dreamt up by Guy Fawkes.'

Chapter 25

It was late, very late when most honest citizens have been tucked up in bed for hours. Anyone found roaming the streets at such an hour of the morning had to be either a thug on the prowl for some poor inebriated old sod with the intent to belt the tripe out of him and rob him of his last dime, or a drunken sod too drunk to find his way home.

Georgie obviously heard the sounds of the motor bikes long before Simon as it was Georgie who gave Simon a not too gentle shaking. 'Simon, wake up, something's happening.'

'Crikey, not again. It's your turn, so you go fix it,' came the uninterested response.

'No. Something's going on outside. There's motor bikes in the street.'

'Come on, Georgie, give us a break. It's the middle of the bloody night and the street's where the bikes should be. Be damn strange if they were anywhere else.'

'Simon, something's happening next door. Can't you hear the bikes?'

'Cause I can hear the bloody bikes. They wouldn't be Harleys if they didn't make a loud noise. But so what? The people are having a few bikie visitors around. As long as we're not invited, who cares?'

'But there's no-one home. They drove off around six thirty last night and I'm sure they haven't returned.'

'Look, my little angel, there's a couple of Harleys stopped out the front which isn't a Federal offence. Just let me get back to sleep and wake me when something dramatic happens, like when someone drops a bomb on the place, okay?'

'Oohh, men!' Georgie grouchily pulled the doona up and turned her back to Simon as he settled down to an interrupted night's sleep. And that's when it happened.

The initial sound was a window breaking followed by the Harleys roaring off down the street at a great rate of knots. 'See, told you,' Georgie proclaimed as she jumped out of bed and ran to the lounge room window. 'Goodness gracious, Simon, I think they've gone and torched the place. You can see the flames through the window.'

'Bugger, and what's with this "goodness gracious" bit,' Simon responded having never heard Georgie use such an expletive before. 'Okay, well ring the bloody brigade, you idiot. And don't just stand there contemplating if you should open the marshmallows. I'll try and check out if there's anyone inside before it all goes up.'

'Well, don't you dare be a hero, Simon. Do what you can then get out of there,' Georgie screamed as she headed for the phone.

It was all of seven minutes before two fire brigades, their sirens wailing to clear the deserted streets of traffic, pulled up outside Number 26 as that was the house currently in a state of conflagration and well on the way to being burnt to the ground. Simon, his inspection of the house completed, located the brigade officer in charge and advised him that he had conducted a search of the premises and was able to report the house was unoccupied. While the brigade officer appreciated this vital piece of information, he was not at all pleased that Simon had entered the building that was now well on the way to total destruction, despite the valiant efforts of the firemen.

There was little the brigade could do to save the weatherboard cottage and within the hour it had been razed to the ground. After the mopping up operation had been completed the brigade officer approached Simon who, along with Georgie and other curious spectators, despite the hour, had watched the unexpected and unusual event. 'Sorry I got a bit tetchy about you entering the place earlier, but this house went up like a bomb,' commented the fire chief. 'I'll be calling in the arson squad as even I can detect the use of an accelerant.'

Simon's heart missed a beat. 'You mean someone actually burnt the place down?'

The fire officer nodded confidently. 'I'll put a week's pay on it. The speed of the fire was devastating which is why I wasn't pleased to hear you had been in there.'

Simon looked at Georgie and opened his mouth to ask a question but thought better of it. The history of previous residents of Number 26 West Bank Lane, including Dorothy who had dropped dead on seeing a spider, along with two other suspicious deaths, had taught Simon not to ask questions as eventually the true story would be revealed.

On turning to the fire officer Simon asked, 'And did you find anything out of the ordinary, apart from the fact someone burnt the place down?'

'Funny you should ask,' the officer replied. 'I've seen a

couple of fires as a result of faulty wiring, but nothing like this. I can't say with any certainty at this stage, but one of the bedrooms seems to have had a hydroponic setup with a mass of unapproved wiring installed for more lighting. I've seen marijuana plots with such a setup but this was a little different; maybe a new strain of weed.'

JUDY AND RON, having received a very early morning phone call from Georgie, arrived at 24 West Bank Lane just after Simon had left the house and headed for the footpath on his way to catch the 190 bus for the city. 'Hi Simon,' Ron called as he closed the passenger's side door of the car after Judy had got out. 'Bit of a mess, isn't it?' Detectives from Manly had placed a "crime scene" tape around the block of land the house once occupied while the arson squad conducted their investigation by sifting through the ashes of the building.

'Doesn't look pretty,' Simon agreed. 'Both the arson squad and Manly CIB are working on it, hence the no go tape. The arson squad should be finished soon as they've been here for a couple of hours. Terribly sorry, Judy, but I have to run or I'll miss my bus. Georgie's up and about so just go straight in.' With that Simon headed off towards Pittwater Road while Ron and Judy proceeded along the path to the front door.

Georgie did not look well. Dressed in a pale blue dressing gown, no makeup, no engaging smile, no twinkle in her dark brown eyes, her dark short hair a mess. No. Georgie Webster did not look like the usual gregarious Georgie Webster. 'I'm just about to have a coffee, Ron, Judy?'

'No thanks, we've just had breakfast,' Judy replied for

both of them.

'I'm so sorry, Judy. I had no idea it would turn out like this,' Georgie said as she poured the hot water into the three mugs, oblivious to Judy having declined the offer for coffee. 'Simon doesn't know what we had in mind, but I think he suspects something.'

Ron's face reddened with embarrassment. 'Well, how do you think I feel right now. Judy's the most important person in my life and I'm responsible for having her house burnt down.'

Georgie held her mug of coffee with both hands unconsciously warming them against the chill autumn morning. 'I can't believe Jacko or Benny would have asked someone to go quite so far. They both seemed such placid fellows despite their looks.'

'Jacko and Benny wouldn't hurt a fly, but they've obviously spoken to somebody who has a totally different perception of what constitutes a bit of intimidation and what's downright terrorism,' Ron replied. 'No way would they have asked anyone to burn the place down.'

'Come on, Ron, I'm not looking for anyone to put the blame on, especially you. I had a hand in this myself as I agreed with Georgie that something had to be done to get them to break the lease. Poor old Benny and Jacko won't feel too good when they find out what's happened,' Judy said with a smile. 'Come to think of it, we might be able to use this bit of a setback to our advantage, so let's look on the bright side of things.'

Ron looked at Judy and raised a questioning eye. 'I know it's early days but what do you have in mind?'

'Simple. Clear the mess away and build a nice new brick bungalow,' replied Judy. 'Correct me if I'm wrong, but can I hear a couple of motor bikes coming up the street?'

Judy wasn't wrong. Peering out through the new lounge room window Georgie confirmed the arrival of Jason and his female companion riding their Harleys. They stopped outside the ruins of the place they had called home, just behind the two cars from the arson squad. After dehelmeting they advanced, hand in hand, to the cordon tape boundary where an arson squad detective met them and engaged them in conversation.

'Wish I knew what they were talking about,' remarked Judy as she tried to snatch a peek through the curtains.

'Probably something to do with their hydroponic setup and marijuana cultivation. Although the victims of an arson attack, they could get themselves arrested for growing pot,' Ron suggested.

'Well, I don't know about you, but I'm going out to have a chat with my tenants, or ex tenants, bikie gang or no bikie gang,' Judy said as she headed for the front door. 'I've got to know what's going on as I'm sure the insurance company will want to know. I've already told them the assessor could find me at number 24 if I'm needed.'

'Hang on Judy, let me get a pair of jeans on and I'll come with you. If Ron has a touch of the guilts, where does that put me? I should have taken Simon's advice and minded my own business instead of creating this debacle,' Georgie said despondently as she headed for the bedroom.

Jason and his female companion were sitting on the gutter beside their bikes, the girl resting her head on Jason's shoulder. 'Sorry to interrupt, but my name is Judy Kemp. This is, was, you neighbour Georgie Webster and Ron Lange, my partner.'

The two young thugs sitting in the gutter and wearing their Krims Noir T-shirts looked up, the girl brushing away a tear, obviously upset at having their home, along with all their possessions, burned to the ground. 'Oh, hi. I'm Jason Redding and this is my lovely lady, Rhonda. This has to be the worst day of my life and right at the moment I haven't a clue what we're going to do.'

It was now Judy's turn for a twinge of the guilts. Crikey, maybe they aren't such nasty people. 'Yes, it is a bit of a mess. I was the owner of the house, now the owner of this pile of ashes. I've been in touch with the insurance company and they're sending a loss assessor out to have a look around. Irrespective of whether it's arson or not, my insurance company should meet temporary accommodation costs. I'll hang around to speak to him anyway.'

'Thanks, Ms Kemp, any assistance would be greatly appreciated. And yes, the arson people seem to think the place was fire bombed,' Jason said as he scrambled to his feet. 'I just can't understand why anyone would want to fire bomb our place.'

'Look, let's not stand around out here wondering,' Georgie said, her conscience suddenly pricked into the appeasement mode, 'how about we go inside and have a drink.'

'That's very kind of you, Mrs Webster. It's a bit early for Rhonda or me to have a drink at this hour of the day, if we drank that is, but we're teetotalers. However, a cup of tea for both of us would be greatly appreciated, thank you.'

On returning to Number 24, Georgie and Judy retired to the kitchen to make the brews as Ron and the guests made themselves comfortable in the lounge room. Once the girls had returned and the tea and coffee distributed, Ron, being forthright and blunt, had to seek the truth. 'Alright Jason, I take it you and Rhonda are members of an outlaw motorcycle gang, what with your leather jackets and Harleys?'

'Well, yes. We are members of a motorcycle club, but we're just a bunch of normal people who like to ride Harleys, and it's a club, not a gang. Individually, there might be one or two people in the club who wouldn't baulk at bending the rules of society but, overall, it's just a group of people with a common interest. Just because a person rides a Harley shouldn't be any reason to immediately label that person as a member of some bikie gang.'

'No, I realise that,' replied Ron who was beginning to feel a trifle insecure. 'Okay, what about the T-shirts you wear with "Krim Noir" written on the back. Doesn't that mean "Dark Criminal" or something? And what about the very bright bedroom lighting that's on all hours of the night? The last time I saw lighting like that was in a hydroponic setup for growing marijuana.'

Georgie and Judy listened on in rapt attention. Ron had, in a very brusque and provocative manner, arrived at the nitty gritty of the subject by virtually accusing Jason and Rhonda of being evil bikie gang members involved in the cultivation of whacko-tobacco. 'Oh, now I see what you're getting at, Mr Lange,' said Jason, with a clearer picture of the situation. 'Look, how about I just shut up and let Rhonda answer all your questions. Seeing you have directed all your questions to me, I take it you think I'm the brains behind the organization. Maybe you'll accept Rhonda's replies with the honesty they'll be given without any intervention from me. Okay?'

'Okay Rhonda, the black T-shirts with "Krim Noir" written on the back?' Ron asked. 'Are they part of a distinguishing feature within your bikie group?'

Rhonda looked at Jason and shrugged. 'Before we start, I'd like to ask Jason one question.'

'Okay,' replied Ron. 'But one question only.'

'Gee, thanks, Mr Lange. Jason, do you want me to be polite or should I treat this moron as the last of the seven dwarfs?'

'No, be polite. I think Mr Lange is probably the spokesperson for Judy and Georgie, so he's not the only one to think we're related to Al Capone.' Both Judy and Georgie couldn't conceal their embarrassment, both going a bright shade of rosy pink.

Rhonda looked at Ron. 'Okay Mr Lange, the T-shirts. First of all, I have a question for you. Do you know what a Krim Noir is?'

'No, I haven't a clue in the world as to what a Krim Noir is. We just thought you couldn't spell and you meant it to mean something to do with criminals,' Ron replied, suddenly conscious that he was going to be enlightened by some stupidly profound response.

'Well, there you go, see. For your edification the krim noir is a tomato, originally from Russia, or from the Crimea to be more precise. Now, your next question, Mr Lange. Oh yes. The bright bedroom lights. You were correct on this point in that we did have a hydroponic system. Our aim was to grow the krim noir hydroponically as there seemed to be very little work done in this area. Most of the tomatoes are either garden or hot-house raised so we thought we'd have a go at hydroponic cultivation.'

'So how come you moved to Collaroy to pursue your horticultural endeavours?' Ron asked at the risk of another perfectly logical answer.

'Jason is a green-keeper and he just scored a job as head green-keeper to the Long Reef Golf Club. And as Long Reef is just over the road, the house here at Collaroy was perfect for us.' Yep, Ron had blundered again. Perfectly logical.

'Well, what about all the bikies riding up at unearthly hours of the night,' Georgie asked, striving to make up some ground in the ever deepening debacle of her own making.

Rhonda looked at Georgie with something akin to a look of pity. 'The motorcycle club to which we belong was founded by a group while we were at university, the common denominator being we all liked riding Harleys. We were all doing a horticultural or agricultural course, although we were in different years. As we all had an interest in what comes out of the ground, other members of the club became interested in what we were doing and were usually anxious to see for themselves how we were progressing. Although we have all finished uni and moved on, the bike club keeps most of us together. We have many friends, including some who don't ride a Harley Davidson, and we aim to keep their friendship. As a consequence, we won't dictate what hour our visitors may turn up as we are always happy to see them. Simple enough?'

Ron looked at Georgie whose usual unflappable composure was now in a state of significant turmoil. Bugger. Why in the world didn't I take Simon's advice and had taken the time to find out what the situation was before going to extremes, Georgie thought.

On the other hand, Ron was looking at the broader picture without too much certitude. Here I am sitting in the same room as a possible homicidal maniac; well, Georgie had been indirectly responsible for the death of poor Dorothy, quite apart from her involvement in the daylight robbery of a bank in the middle of Sydney, and a close encounter with the death of two squabbling neighbours. And now arson, not forgetting my involvement, he thought.

Chapter 26

Noel studied the whiteboard with an intense interest, the number of names having increased dramatically; and all leading back to Robert Porter, deceased. 'Are all these suspects?' he asked with a touch of sarcasm.

Simon tossed his pen onto the table, pushed his chair back from the desk and clasped his hands behind his head. 'Yes, getting a bit crowded, isn't it? And we still haven't had a chat with this bloke Wally Whatsaname and his wife.'

'Ah, you mean the inimitable Deputy Premier, Walter Ackerman and Monica, call me Sainsbury Ackerman. Maybe they've been headhunted by a tribe of headhunters somewhere deep in the Amazon jungle, that is if they went to Brazil at all.'

Simon relaxed and folded his arms. 'And that's something we have to keep tabs on. Let's see if Buckmaster would like a cup of coffee as he just might be able to tell us where the Ackermans really are. Failing that, all we can do is wait for their homecoming. I have this thing at the back of my mind that having rorted the overseas junket scheme at least once, he'll do it again. To go on a study tour to such vastly different locations as Europe and Brazil would mean the Ackermans would have been entitled to a heap of allowances, if for no other reason than to reimburse them for the inconvenience of having to take the trip in the first place. No, for them to fiddle the system, they probably get their zillion dollars of allowances then troop off to a reclusive caravan park somewhere out the back of beyond and lie low for a while. But let's see if Buckmaster's in,' Simon said and reached for the phone.

'NOW, what can I do for you gentlemen?' Mr Buckmaster asked as he pulled a chair out from a table of the sidewalk café on Macquarie Street. Before sitting, he raised his eyebrows to the waitress and placed his order for one black coffee. Simon and Noel didn't get up on Buckmaster's arrival but continued to sip their brews. 'I suppose you're still working on the Porter case?'

Cripes, for a politician this bloke is quite brainy, Simon thought before answering. 'Yes, that's right. We still have a couple of loose ends to tie up. You've already given us some information on the Deputy Premier, but we need to know a bit more. Obviously, we can't go on waiting for his return from his study trip so we thought you might be able to fill in a few gaps for us.'

'I can understand that so I hope I can be of assistance,' replied Buckmaster as he tweeted his nose; the coffee was a bit strong. 'What is it you would like to know, specifically?'

'Okay. For starters, when do you expect the Honourable Ackerman to return home?'

'Quite soon, really. We expected him to get in touch with us but he hasn't said a word since flying out to

London. I suppose I shouldn't be too surprised as he would have been very busy, what with all the work he had planned to do.'

'So, you're sure he and his wife actually did get on the plane?' Noel asked. 'At least, the plane to London, that is.'

'Of course they got on the plane to London. Haven't I told you that already?' Buckmaster replied testily.

'Okay, moving right along. What do you know about Walter's wife, Monica?' Simon continued, unfazed by Buckmaster's touchy demeanour.

'Not much,' Buckmaster replied. 'I know she has her own business running a construction company or something or other. As long as Walter Ackerman remains out of the picture and not involved in any way, it's all pretty kosher as far as pecuniary disclosure goes. And that's what you were after, I take it?'

'Well, I always thought a politician was required to disclose his financial situation, including where all the money comes from,' Simon said.

'Now, Detective Chief Inspector Webster, if you took the time to read the articles relating to such matters you would find that most of it is subjective. There are words like "substantial", "likelihood" and "reasonably expect". What you might consider a substantial sum of money, I might consider a mere drop in the ocean.'

'Yeah, okay,' said Simon, his patience getting the better of him. 'But we're here to conduct a murder investigation, not check on the probity of politicians, which would be a rather useless exercise anyhow. So, let's get back to Monica for a moment. Just who has she been pally with? I mean, is she pally with other politicians?'

Buckmaster's head dropped as he slowly shook his head. 'Look, on that score I haven't a clue but I'd expect so, being the wife of the Deputy Premier. I know she was pally with Porter and he was pillow pally with a lot of women. I honestly don't know if Porter's and Monica's pallyness extended that far, but they got on well together.' Buckmaster contemplated for a moment then added, 'Now I come to think of it, it probably did.'

'And what about Walter and Monica. How do they get on?'

'The relationship between Monica and Wally is strange. I know Wally wouldn't mind having Porter's ministry under his own belt but he'll get that only if Monica thinks it a good idea, which she doesn't. Wally is a wimp and wouldn't get anywhere unless Monica told him how to get there.'

'So, in your opinion, what is the relationship like between Monica and Walter?'

'She's lovely but tough as guts. She's a hard-nosed business woman and someone I'd hate to meet in either the boardroom or a dark alley.'

'Yeah, well that's all very nice, but I didn't ask for your opinion of Monica.'

'Look, their relationship is far from lovey-dovey and if you didn't know Wally you might get the idea he's gay, which he's not. There's so much opportunity to play around and he's in the perfect position to exploit those opportunities, but doesn't. Hell, I know I would if I was in his position. Wally's time spent checking up on what the Minister for Planning and Minister for Local Government are up to leaves him no time to carry on with women, including Monica from what I hear. He's paranoid about what might be planned for future rezoning and development opportunities. As a consequence, any spare time Monica has is her own and what she does with it is her business.'

'This bit on Walter keeping tabs on ministers. You

mean to tell me that that sort of information on rezoning and development isn't held in the strictest confidence?'

'Of course it is. It's just that "the strictest confidence" is probably held by a hell of a lot of people,' Buckmaster replied as if such information was common knowledge.

'Look, Buckmaster, I'm trying to find a motive for the death of Robert Porter. Every time I talk to you the list of motives, together with the list of suspects, gets bigger and bigger. If it's not rorting the system for every penny you can get your sticky little fingers on, especially with these shonky overseas study trips, it's trying to get rid of the minister who holds the portfolio that provides the most potential source of extra income. On top of all that, we have our parliamentarians doing their utmost to create their own version of Sodom and Gomorrah. Bloody Porter, it's all his fault.' Detective Chief Inspector Simon Webster was becoming cranky.

Noel, aware of Simon's disposition, looked for the waitress. 'Two Irish coffees, and hold the coffee, please.'

Chapter 27

Chief Superintendent Paxton leaned forward, his chin resting on the palm of his hand, elbow on the table while tapping a constant tap on the table with his other hand. He had his eyes closed as his five visitors filed into his office and seated themselves in an arc in front of him. Needless to say, Paxton was not a happy chief superintendent. In fact, he couldn't quite remember the last time he had been happy. With the Commissioner of Police now on his back seeking an explanation as why no-one had been arrested for the murder of the Honourable Robert Porter, MP, it was plainly evident that the Minister for Police was on the Commissioner's back.

The visitors sat in a strained silence waiting expectantly for some well-chosen disparaging comments from Detective Chief Superintendent Paxton. It was rather surprising that when the words did come, they were delivered in a cool, calm and collected manner, quite the opposite to the antici-pated old fashioned bollocking those in attendance expected. 'Right, gentlemen,' Paxton said as he picked up a pencil and sat back in his chair. 'I'm not going to open this little chat with an admonishment as to the success, or lack thereof, of your investigation. I realise you are doing the best you can under extreme difficulties, those difficulties being asinine politicians who have the remarkable propensity of being able to undergo total memory collapse whenever it suits them, but don't quote me on that score. However, despite whatever anomalies, fraudulent activity, swindling, cheating or rorting you may have uncovered in regards to the alleged political gravy train in the course of your investigation, Simon, we are not on a bureaucratic witch hunt. That is not our job. Murder is.'

'Yes, we're well aware of that, sir, but there is a lot going on that may impinge on the investigation,' Simon replied as he clasped his hands together on his lap and arched his thumbs. 'Unfortunately, I will concede the course of the investigation has led us to believe there may be some irregularities and abuses of office or, as you so succinctly refer to it, exploitation of the gravy train.

'Now, while we appreciate this is a murder case, the abuse of the system may have significant implications in the murder of Robert Porter. We have already established that one minister is alleged to have received kickbacks and I've no doubt this is only the tip of the iceberg. It's not so much the nature of the gravy train, but the extent and scope the gravy train has been, and continues to be, exploited, by whom and how much those involved are profiteering. One would think any person with half a brain between their ears, and who is abusing the system, would try to go about it with some discretion. However, as everyone is aware of the illicit activity going on, quite apart from their own shenanigans, knowledge of such activity that has the potential to lead to blackmail, and a motive for murder, is negated by the law of reciprocity; you squeal on me, I'll squeal on you, except louder.'

'You mean you've uncovered more than just the payment from developers to a minister?' questioned Paxton with an anxious look.

'As I have pointed out, sir, we believe there may be certain activities being perpetrated by politicians that members of the public are unaware, and if they were there would probably be hell to pay.'

'Well, nearly everyone already believes politicians can manipulate property development schemes to fit their own agenda, and they're probably right, so there's no reason why they shouldn't believe politicians manipulate every-thing else they can get their hands on. The general public has been so accustomed to politician's errant ways and stupid antics, I doubt there's anything that would surprise them now.' replied Paxton. 'Okay Simon, go where the flow takes you but remember, above me there's a commissioner and above him is a minister. If I lose my job because you've trodden on someone's toes, they'll be investigating another murder.'

Paxton turned to face Graham Gallymore before he continued. 'Right, Gally, your turn. I'm told an item that may be of interest was handed in to you. Can you tell us what that's all about?'

Gally pressed his lips together and scratched his right ear before answering. 'Yes, we had what is commonly called a kris handed in by some alert scuba diver. A kris is a sort of heavy knife generally found in Malaysia. Buggered if I know how the diver found it, but he did, thank heavens. Having been in the ocean for a couple of days didn't help with the examination, but finally we were able to identify it as the murder weapon. We detected enough microscopic samples of blood to be able to match them with Porter's, and the stab wounds to Porter's body fit the kris exactly. As an expert witness I would say yes, we have the murder weapon.'

Paxton heaved a sigh of relief on receipt of the first bit of positive news since the commencement of the investigation. 'Holy hell, at least someone has some good news.' He then swiveled his chair to face Superintendent Fisher sitting on the end of the arc. Now Nigel, how are you and the press getting on? I take it they're losing interest by now?'

'Depends what paper you read, and your political persuasion. Some tabloids have moved on while a broadsheet is continuing to vamp up the whole thing and calling for resignations. Seems another story is starting to bubble away in the cauldron, and that happens to relate to politicians' entitlements. Everything relating to politics and politicians has been relegated to page ten of the papers and replaced on page one with the weekend footy results. All I can say is keep going, Simon, as future developments might rekindle both public and press interest.'

Paxton nodded his acknowledgement and turned to Ron. 'Mr Lange, you're very quiet.'

'Yes, sir. As Simon said earlier, there's a heap of things going on at the moment. One of the things that keeps cropping up is Porter's Gaming Bill and the impact it will have on illegal casinos. With Porter's demise it seems no-one wants to run with it, at the moment anyway. On top of that, there's a rumour going around that Peter Mason just received a bundle of money. And guess where it came from?'

'No, don't tell me. I bet it was either our old mate Andy Crawford, who doesn't want the Bill passed, or Eastern Development, ergo Monica Ackerman nee Sainsbury, who wants the Bill passed,' replied Paxton with a shake of the head in wonderment. 'Any idea when the payment was made, like before or after Porter's death?'

'I see what you're driving at, sir, but it doesn't make any difference,' Simon interrupted. 'If it had been Crawford who paid Mason to lobby against Porter's Bill, just because Porter is dead doesn't mean that Mason won't have any lobbying to do. Some do-gooder will eventually present the Bill and Mason, being the Minister for Sport and Gaming, is now in a position to influence its outcome.

'On the other side of the coin, we know that it was either Monica Ackerman or her company, which I suppose is the same thing, who paid Mason this particular bucket of money. We believe the payment was made to secure Mason's support for the Bill and the lucrative development contract that will come with its passing.'

'So, Mason gets an incentive from the Deputy Premier's wife to support a bill to legalise casinos. Now, isn't that just dandy,' Paxton murmured.

Simon nodded his head. 'Seems so, but I think our Mr Mason still hasn't made up his mind which way to go. I'd say he's out to make as much money as possible before the preverbal hits the fan. We don't know for sure just how much money Mason has received for his support, one way or the other, as there's bound to be lobby groups operating for and against the Bill. Irrespective, I wouldn't mind betting there's another cheque in the mail for the greedy little bugger.'

Paxton frowned and, with both hands resting on his table, twiddled with the pencil. 'Okay, but wouldn't that put Mason's life in a pretty precarious position. Sounds to me like he's out to double cross everyone and if someone is capable of doing Porter in, they wouldn't have any qualms of nudging Mason off the planet.'

'Well, we won't know that until everyone finds out that they're being double-crossed. And that's what makes this case so interesting. There's sufficient motives and suspects that we could run a sweepstake. I just don't think we have hit on the real motive,' Simon said with a troubled look.

THE RAIN WAS BUCKETING DOWN, the wind blowing a gale from the south and Simon was an angry chief inspector or, to use the vernacular, Simon was one pissed off chief inspector. Anxious for a change from the Day Street scenery, he and Noel made their way in silence up the hill to the coffee shop on the corner of Bathurst and George Streets. After ridding their umbrellas of the excess water by rapidly opening and shutting them, much to the chagrin of passers-by, they entered the coffee shop and headed towards their usual table where Ron Lange was seated, gazing out of the window, his mind in a state of reverie.

Shunted from his day-dreaming, Ron voiced, 'Lovely weather, if you're a duck, and what's so damn important that we have to troop around the city in weather like this?' he enquired just as Fitch arrived to take their order.

'G'day, Fitch,' said Noel, eager to engage someone in cordial conversation, well aware that Simon wasn't predisposed to carry on with anything nearing civility just at that particular moment. 'Just the usual, two flat blacks and one cappuccino, thanks Buttercup.'

'Buttercup? What's with the Buttercup?' Fitch asked seeking some sort of explanation as to what Noel may have in mind. After all, the only thing given the name

"Buttercup", as far as Fitch was aware, was a cute jersey cow.

'Just a term of endearment,' Noel replied with a smile. 'If I called you "sweetie" I could be had up for sexual harassment.'

Fitch rolled her eyes. 'Two flat blacks and a cappuccino.'

'Okay, Romeo, now you've got that all sorted out, can we get on with it?' Simon scowled.

'Gee, what's got into him?' Ron asked Noel. 'Grumpy, isn't he?'

Before Noel could reply, Simon butted in. 'Yes, I'm certainly not Happy and Paxton thinks we're all Dopey.'

'Well, that leaves us with four others, so I think we're doin' pretty well,' Noel said with a display of literary sophistication.

'Okay, just listen for a change,' Simon urged. 'For starters, we have a murdered politician and we haven't a clue as to who creamed him. What we have got is a bag full of possible suspects, none of whom even qualify as being a definite suspect. Next, we find that half the politicians on the planet have an additional income that makes their legitimate pay look like petty cash. If our murdered politician ever considered becoming a whistle-blower there would be any number of pollies wanting to make sure he kept his mouth shut.'

'And don't forget Ralph Glover and his mate Henry, especially Henry as Robert Porter didn't do him any favours,' added Noel as Fitch arrived with the coffees and a wry smile for Noel.

'See what I mean?' quipped Simon. 'I'm fed up with just stumbling around in the dark and getting nowhere. As a consequence, Ron, I want you to check the background of

Porter's women, or at least those that we know of. I'm looking for something of a character trait that might suggest the female of the species really is more deadly than the male. And you, Noel, get yourself over to Immigration and try to find out just where on the planet our illustrious Deputy Premier and his wife are right now. It's for bloody sure those wankers up in Macquarie Street haven't a clue as to where they are. And while you're doing that, I want to go and have a chat with Glover and Haynes again.'

'Just a chat?' Noel asked, skeptically.

'Okay, so it might end up as a confrontation. It's time we started to rattle a few branches and see what falls out. Maybe we'll find the murderer, or maybe we can delete some suspected suspects.'

Noel drained the last of his coffee, replaced the cup on the saucer, and relaxed back on the seat. 'I take it you are going to let Paxton in on this little quest for knowledge? And what about Fisher and the press?'

'I can't blame Paxton thinking we're a bunch of inept imbeciles. Unfortunately, whatever I say to him only compounds the problem and makes me think I'm wasting both my time, and his. No, this time we're on our own and bugger the consequences, and the press. The only way we can re-establish our credibility is to produce the murderer, and that's what we'll do.' At least Simon gave the impression he was over his state of annoyance and anxious to get on with finding the Bondi Beach Butcher.

Chapter 28

'I don't know if there is a law against being disrespectful to a police officer, but that would have to be the biggest load of crap since they did away with the dunny cart. And you sit there and try to tell me that Henry and I colluded to whack that bloody shyster of a politician. I'm sorry, Detective Chief Constable Webster, or whatever, but you'll just have to go and pick on some other poor bastard to hang that one on, but it ain't gunna be me, or Henry.' Ralph Glover was peeved, certain in the knowledge that the chief whatever was out to make an arrest, any arrest. And if that meant some poor innocent bugger being stitched up for the murder of Robert Porter, MP, so be it. Ralph Glover couldn't give a damn who the police hung the murder on, but one thing was certain; it was not going to be Ralph Glover, or Henry Haynes.

What Simon had originally envisaged was a quiet discussion with Messrs Glover and Haynes in the uncomfortable Bondi Junction office of Glover Property Development. His expectations had been fulfilled, almost, save for the fact that the "quiet discussion" had degenerated into the "confrontation", as previously predicted by Noel.

Simon quickly tried to arrange his thoughts into some semblance of order. While both Glover and Haynes had motive, individually and collectively, to kill Robert Porter, Simon acknowledged that that motive was pretty flimsy. Any property developer with an ounce of intelligence, including Ralph Glover, was well aware that to tender for any sizeable project was much the same as playing a game of Russian roulette, with the odds stacked firmly against you. In reality, the bigger the contract, the more chance you would have of being gazumped by a more economically cashed-up developer willing to pay mega bucks to those within the decision making administrative bureaucracy; whoever pays the polly the most wins.

Simon was only too aware that such payments are never admitted. He simply accepted that ever since the first bureaucrats landed in Sydney Town two hundred years ago, those at the top of the tree received remuneration of some kind in return for preferential treatment. It was just a fact of life. The man in the street is generally unaware of a politician's vulnerability to shonky dealings with resolute cashed-up businessmen eager for favourable political decisions to further their own agenda. As a consequence, everyone is happy except for the poor unfortunate skint developer who will forever remain skint at the expense of the rich developer who's willing to remunerate the appropriate compliant politician. And to add grist to the mill, Simon, being a devout skeptic, couldn't believe that the majority of those at the top of the pecking order had got where they had by being squeaky clean.

'And you, Mr Haynes? Are you of similarly mind?'

'Bloody oath,' affirmed a just as peeved Henry Haynes.

'If it hadn't been for that, that bloody brainless bureau-cratic upstart politician, I'd still be working for Dayman Brothers. No, he sold us out to that female from Eastern Development. Pound to a penny that Jezebel will weasel her way into any future development worth tendering for. With her hubby being the Deputy Premier, it's a complete waste of time for the likes of Glover Property Development to tender for anything more than an outside crapper for a boy scout jamboree, even with Porter dead and buried. No, Chief Inspector, I haven't a clue who the killer is but whoever it is did me a favour.'

'Any particular reason for the use of the word Jezebel?' Simon asked without anticipating any great revelation.

Henry scowled. 'Okay, so I might just as likely have called her Cinderella, but if the cap fits you have to wear it. She's as rough as a cross-cut saw, or at least she was, prob-ably still is but rough in other ways. Madam Ackerman, or Sainsbury, was just that; a madam although I, along with a lot of other people, would say she was a prostitute. She worked her way up from street walker, to massage parlor, to escort agency and finally a high-priced call girl. Maybe she has to act with a bit more decorum nowadays, but I'd still hate to meet her in a dark alley.'

'Crikey,' exclaimed Simon. 'And just where did Wally find her, or shouldn't I ask?'

'Good God, Chief, you're supposed to know these things. Even I know a bit about Monica Sainsbury Acker-man,' Ralph chided. 'I think it started one night when he needed a companion for some political function and someone recommended Monica. After all, a lot of people knew Monica intimately well. As long as she looked good and knew what knife to use, at the dinner table I mean,

Wally was happy. It's for sure he had no idea she was a call-girl. Well, not then anyway.'

'So, is Monica a Macquarie Street partner pilfering player?' Simon asked.

'Probably,' both Henry and Ralph chorused.

Simon heaved a sigh, looked at the floor and shook his head. 'Well, bugger me. So, I suppose we can at least thank Wally and Monica for raising the standard of propriety within Parliament House to that of a knock-shop.' Ralph and Henry smiled.

Chapter 29

The introduction extended by Peter Mason to his Kogarah Bay home was cordial and without a trace of rancor. Considering the reason for the visit, Simon wondered just how long the friendly disposition would last. It was just after eight in the evening and, in view of Peter's considerable "work" commitments, one of the rare times both he and Cheryl were available to be interviewed together. Simon and Noel were ushered into the lounge room where Cheryl, dressed in a black Adidas track suit and a pair of brown fluffy slippers, reclined on a sofa, her legs drawn up and tucked underneath herself.

'Ah, Chief Inspector Webster and Sergeant Noel. You bring tidings of the Porter massacre I take it?' Cheryl asked with a smile.

'Well, yes, but I have a few questions I would like to ask first. Mind if we take a seat?' Simon asked as no offer appeared to be forthcoming in the foreseeable future.

'No, sorry. Please pardon my rudeness,' replied Peter as

he removed his tie. 'It's been a long day, especially with so many members out of town at the moment.'

'And that prompts my first question as no-one seems to have any idea as to when the Deputy Premier and his wife will be coming home. Do you have any idea?' asked Simon.

'The last thing I heard was that Walter is coming back by himself. Seems pretty strange to leave your wife stuck half way up the Amazon, but I might not have the story straight,' Peter confessed.

Simon shrugged. 'Well, I s'pose that's something we can chase up later. Right now I'm more interested in your dealings with Robert Porter – you know, the bloke who's dead.'

'And what dealings did you have in mind, Chief Inspector?' came Peter's abrupt response.

'Well, as you're the Minister for Sport and Recreation, doesn't that include gaming, or gambling?'

'Yes, it does, but what's that got to do with Robert Porter?'

'His Bill to legalise casinos.'

'So, just because Porter's dead won't stop the Bill. Someone will introduce it into parliament and there'll be a vote on it.'

'And which way will you be voting, Mr Mason?' Simon asked as Noel jotted notes in his notebook.

Peter Mason blanched. 'I'm sorry, Chief Inspector, but I fail to see what that has to do with Robert Porter's murder.'

'And I'm sorry too,' Simon said with a touch of annoyance. 'You're on the merry-go-round and burning the candle at both ends. Depending on who pays you the most, and we are aware some such payments have already been made, you'll either support the Bill, or support the illegal gaming lobby group against the Bill.'

'So what? There's nothing illegal about fence sitting, unless someone finds out,' interrupted Peter.

'Yeah, well I take it that it's purely coincidental this all came about just after Porter's death,' Simon continued. 'You didn't like Porter because he virtually held the purse strings for any future development proposal. The only way you could get in on the gravy train was to get rid of him as you knew there was a bundle to be made should his Bill be passed. Quite apart from that, you did harbour some animosity towards Porter for the deed he dumped on Cheryl here.'

'Look, Porter was a sleaze and got what he deserved. Sure, he and Monica Sainsbury were in cahoots. She was prepared to pay him zillions of dollars for the contract to develop a casino site once his Bill was passed. With him dead, I'll probably have a greater influence on who may be awarded the contract, should the Bill be passed. Obviously, I could, and I emphasise the "could", lobby in favour of the Bill as, at this moment in time, I haven't made up my mind. As far as Cheryl goes, c'est la vie. But for the Grace of God go I.'

'What do you mean, "but for the Grace of God go I,"' demanded Cheryl. You know I played up on you, but what's your story?'

'Okay, so Monica and I discussed a business arrange-ment, which included fringe benefits,' returned Peter indig-nantly. 'She had to be nice to me to win my support and I couldn't reject her proposition as it meant a lot of money to us.'

'Holy hell. And all this because that dim-witted Porter wanted to legalise gambling,' Cheryl said as she shook her head in bewilderment.

With the debauchery debacle being played out between the Masons, Simon was eager to get on with the job. 'Okay, I couldn't give a stuff as to who's up who because right now I'm more interested in who killed Robert Porter. I have this strange idea one of you decided to become the homicidal maniac, but I don't know which one. I'd therefore prefer to have someone confess to Porter's killing than have to go through all this investigating twaddle.'

The debacle suddenly ceased and a silence prevailed over the room. It was Peter who, after a searching look at Cheryl, seemed to understand the question first. 'Now, you just hang on a second, Chief Inspector. Sure, there might possibly be some slight misdemeanours and irregularities going on in Macquarie Street, but nothing unusual. As soon as you enter parliament you receive an official briefing on what you can and can't expect to get away with, along with a list of those positions offering the most profitable non-parliamentary pecuniary returns. By some strange coincidence, it was Robert Porter who held the position regarded as number one on the list of those offering the most favourable returns. The only unusual thing at the moment is Porter's dead and everyone will want his job. And before you ask, no, I don't want it because whoever gets it will always be looking over their shoulder. Neither Cheryl nor I had anything to do with Porter's death and to even think such a thing is totally preposterous.'

'And I second that,' voiced Cheryl in a very forcible manner. 'Sure, I could have killed the bugger, but I will recover from my affliction. Porter's affliction is far more serious; he's dead. And if Peter ever plays up on me again, you'll probably find another body on Bondi Beach.'

'Well, what's good for the gander is good for the goose,' replied Peter.

'Yes, but you chose to play up with a woman of ill repute, you moron.' It was obvious Peter had no knowledge of Monica's history.

Chapter 30

Flitch delivered the three cups of coffee. Being nine thirty in the morning, the coffee shop was nearly deserted; too late for the workforce on their way to work, and too early for the public service morning smoko. You could generally tell the public servant entering the coffee shop as he, or she, was never in any hurry and always wore the little identification card either hung around their neck, or attached to their clothing, just to remind themselves who they were. Ron Lange sat with his two detective friends although today it was Ron Lange's turn to be an unhappy man.

'I really don't know what's going to happen, but I should have guessed anything involving Jacko would be fraught with danger. No-one told those bikies to burn down the bloody place, and I haven't a clue as to who gave them that idea,' Ron said as he absently stirred his unsugared coffee. 'I could hazard a guess, but that's all it would be, a guess,' he lied.

'Well, if we can believe we know nothing about it, that's the way it will turn out,' Simon said hopefully. 'Neither

Georgie nor Sue know anything about the fire and that's the story they're sticking to. I don't think Jacko or Benny would reveal to police who they actually spoke to as they both know that might entail an increase to their life insurance premiums. No-one actually saw anyone do anything and all we heard were two motor bikes. So, all in all, I don't think there's too much to worry about, so cheer up, Ron. It's not as though you're responsible for anything. Anyway, we're not here to discuss an insignificant case of arson that nobody knows anything about. So, Ron, what have you got?'

'Well, whatever that bloke Bushmaster told you about what goes on behind closed doors appears to be pretty accurate.'

'Buckmaster,' corrected Simon. 'You mean…?'

'Well, they're both snakes, but yep, seems being a polly provides you with the excuse to be wherever you want to be with whoever you want to be with and whenever you want. Obviously, the story told to the poor housebound spouse varies but the polly knows they can rely on their associates to confirm the cover story as they're all playing the same game. One backbencher told his wife he couldn't say where he was going as it was confidential. All he did say was that Pierre Trudeau was in town.'

Noel frowned. 'You mean Robert Porter's love, or lust, for other women was not an isolated case?'

'Hell no, it's a real shabby little mess. I don't think Wally Ackerman helped matters very much when he married Monica Sainsbury. Everyone, except Wally that is, knew Monica's reputation and her previous occupation. That's when the flood gates opened and everyone started jumping into bed, anyone's bed.'

'And as far as her business interests go?' Simon queried.

'In a word, ruthless. She really exploits her position as the wife of the Deputy Premier and I don't think Wally really knows what's going on. She had a thing going with Porter. What we don't know is whether that "thing" was an emotional or financial attachment. I would be very surprised if it had been emotional, not with her past, anyway. Physical, possibly but no emotions involved.'

Simon pursed his lips and furrowed his brow. 'So, apart from throwing bags of money at Mason, has Monica approached any other politician with a bag of money?'

'Don't know,' Ron replied. 'She thinks Porter's Bill will be passed this time and she wants the contract for the development of a casino site, along with the six star hotel that'll go with it. Any politician in a position to influence both the vote and the awarding of the contract would be high on Monica's list for some sort of payment in appreciation for services rendered, should she get her way.'

'And Porter was in the process of receiving some gratuitous form of appreciation in expectation of support when someone did him in,' Noel said as if the whole situation was perfectly logical.

Ron shook his head. 'Maybe, but we don't know that. We know of their relationship but, as I said, we don't know the basis of that relationship.'

Simon raised his eyes to catch Flitch's attention whereupon he held up three fingers for another round of caffeine fixes. 'Well, seeing Robert Porter is unavailable for comment, I s'pose the only other person able to shed a bit of light on the subject is Monica Sainsbury Ackerman. Which reminds me, Noel, what did Immigration have to say?'

Noel harrumphed. 'Looks like Buckmaster got this one

wrong; somebody should have made sure the Ackermans got on the flight to London because they didn't.'

'Didn't what?'

'Get on the flight for London.'

'Don't tell me. They decided to fly off on some jaunt to some exotic, or erotic, place,' Simon quipped.

'That's about it. They flew to South America, Buenos Aires I think,' Noel said as he referred to his notebook. 'Yes, that's right, Buenos Aires. Once there, who knows where they went although they were planning to take a trip down the Amazon, from Manaus to somewhere else. I suppose if Monica wanted to get ahead, the Amazon is the place to get it, albeit a very small one,' chaffed Noel with a smile.

'That might be right as Buckmaster said they were on a study tour starting from Manaus after their supposed trip to the UK and Europe,' corrected Simon. 'And have you got a date as to when they left for Argentina?'

'Yes. According to their Immigration Department departure card, they left Sydney on the fifteenth of March, which happens to be just a matter of hours after Porter was stabbed. Of course, that might be purely coincidental. I checked with Qantas, the usual government carrier, and found that two business class tickets to London in the names of Monica and Walter Ackerman had been cancelled. They had been booked on a flight to Heathrow on fourteenth of March. In reality I s'pose the tickets weren't actually cancelled as they were replaced with two first class tickets to Buenos Aires,' Noel added with a look of appalled resignation. 'There's a zillion frequent flyer points credited to Walter's account.'

'Can't say that this Wally is endearing himself to anyone,' Simon said, his antipathy towards politicians plunging even deeper into the abyss of repugnant loathing.

'I wonder if Buckmaster, or anyone else, knows just what Wally was up to from the time he was s'posed to fly to London to the time he flew to Argentina?'

Ron pulled a face and replied, not that Simon had expected a response. 'Come on Simon, it was only a matter of hours anyway, and he was supposed to be sipping champagne on his flight to London. You don't think anyone really cares what he was up to, or even the shonky he's perpetrated? Quite apart from the official briefing on how to diddle the system given to new parliamentarians, they also receive a booklet "Lurks, Perks, Shonkies and Scams," written by some bloke who now lives in Monte Carlo.'

'No, you're absolutely right as no-one could give a fig. It's for bloody sure no politician is going to derail the gravy train, and while the general public continues to think politicians are the paragons of virtuous incorruptibility, the train will continue to choof along its merry way. And now I have that off my chest, I take it there's nothing to confirm Peter Mason's story that Wally's coming home by himself?' Simon asked.

'No, not a whisper. Maybe Buckmaster has heard something,' Noel suggested.

Ron frowned and folded his arms. 'You know, the more I listen to you two buggers waffle on, the more I get the idea this Wally bloke has some questions to answer.'

'I'd agree with that,' Simon replied, 'especially after having had a chat to our property developers over at Bondi and the Masons. Somewhere along the line I thought maybe Ralph Glover or Henry Haynes could have been considered a suspect for Porter's murder. Unfortunately, they didn't progress past the potential stage, as neither did Cheryl and Peter Mason, not that they both didn't have very personal motives for getting rid of Porter. No, it's as you say, Ron, we need to have a chat to Wally, once we find him. But in the meantime, Noel and I will have a chat with Buckmaster, again.'

'Oh yes, I almost forgot,' Noel said as he came across a particular page in his notebook. 'Monica Ackerman is a pommy. She came out here in the 60's and still possesses a current UK passport although she does have Australian citizenship.'

Simon pursed his lips and thought for a moment. 'Well, well, well. Dual nationality and two passports. How very convenient.'

Chapter 31

Although well aware of the impending visit, Gavin Buckmaster didn't try to conceal the newspaper opened at the cryptic crossword page when the security guard wrapped on the already open door. 'A couple of guests to see you, sir,' he announced before ushering the two detectives into the office.

'Aah yes. Thanks Bennedict,' Buckmaster said to the guard as Simon and Noel entered the office. 'Detective Chief Inspector Webster and Sergeant Elliott, good to see you again. Please,' he said and indicated to two chairs in front of his desk. 'And what can I do for you gentlemen today?'

'Bennedict?' Simon asked with a look of bemusement.

Buckmaster smiled and nodded. 'That's right. His genealogical foundations are in the USA, and his father's name was Joshua Arnold. All very logical, really. But you didn't come here to talk about a security guard's name?'

'No, not quite, but I'm not surprised Bennedict lives here and not in the USA. Anyway, we came here to talk about your boss, Wally, and his wife,' Simon replied. At that moment Simon was wishing he had done more homework; he hated asking questions when he didn't already know the answers. 'Most importantly, have you heard when Walter and Monica might be returning from their overseas jaunt?'

Buckmaster looked troubled by the question. After a moment's hesitation, and apparently having reached a decision, he replied. 'Yes and no.'

Well, ask a stupid "yes no" question and that's the answer it deserves, Simon thought. 'Right, now you've given me the short answer, could you please be a tad more explicit and explain?' Simon asked.

Buckmaster settled himself back in his chair, rested his elbows on the arm rests and clasped his hands together, all with an air of confidence and superiority; quite pretentious for a backbencher, Noel thought. 'I received a phone call from Walter, I mean the Deputy Premier, last night around two in the morning. He rang from Buenos Aires saying he was on the way home and that Monica would be returning a few days later. If that is correct, he should be here tomorrow sometime. God knows when Monica will decide to come home despite what Walter says.'

Noel looked puzzled. 'Correct me if I'm wrong, Mr Buckmaster, but I believe state ministers and their spouse travel on diplomatic passports if the trip has been paid by the government?'

'Yes, that is correct, and the Ackermans' trip has been paid by the government which means they're travelling on diplomatic passports,' Buckmaster replied.

Noel, as a taxpayer, was getting hot under the collar. 'Yes, but the original itinerary was for them to go to England, Europe and then Brazil with the costing calculated on that itinerary. But they didn't go to either

England or Europe. Instead, they decided to cancel the ticketing for both those places and fly off to Buenos Aires, first class and holding diplomatic passports. I thought the wife of the Deputy Premier, who just happens to be the Minister for Finance, had to travel with her husband and couldn't go swanning off by herself waiving a red passport around?'

Mr Buckmaster pursed his lips and scratched an ear. 'Yes, that is correct, but we were unaware of what plans the Ackermans had made. Good God, there has to be a certain amount of trust in these things and if you can't trust your politicians, who can you trust. And let's face it, nobody's averse to a bit of the good life when it's available, and politicians do avail themselves if and when the opportunity presents itself. Wouldn't you?'

'That, Mr Buckmaster, is a totally irrelevant, immaterial and stupid bloody question as I'm sure the situation will never be presented. But quite apart from this latest scam, and getting back to Mr Porter's untimely death, it seems we are running out of likely suspects and we really do need to talk to Wally and Monica. So, Wally's on his way home and Monica is still somewhere in Argentina, supposedly in Buenos Aires?'

'As far as I know, not that Walter mentioned specifically where Monica is, or was. He said they had been up at Manaus for a while before catching a ferryboat down to Santarem from where they flew back to Buenos Aires. To get to BA from Santarem they would probably have to go back to Manaus, then to Rio and catch a plane from there. Despite all the flight connections, he did say it was a wonderful trip, one that he's always wanted to do.'

'Yes, and I've always wanted to travel on the Orient Express but unless I become a politician or win the lottery it

219

ain't going to happen, not in this lifetime anyway,' remarked Noel with a touch of insolence.

Simon frowned at Noel for his sour comment then said, 'Look, I think it something of a waste of time doing anything until Wally and Monica get home. Mr Buckmaster, we would appreciate any news of their arrival details as soon as they become available as we would like to provide transport from the airport.'

'No problem. I was going to arrange a government limo but I'll leave the transport up to you then. I'll give you a ring at Day Street as soon as I hear anything.'

'NOW LET ME GET THIS CLEAR,' CS Paxton said with a deep frown etched across his face, 'as you've exhausted all other avenues of enquiry, you now intend to pin the rap on our Deputy Premier, Walter Ackerman?'

'Well, we've interviewed everyone else who may have had an interest in plunging the knife into Robert Porter. Wally and his misses, Monica Sainsbury, are the only two we haven't,' explained Simon. 'We would've if we could've but they've been overseas. Wally's on his way home and I believe Monica is still in South America, somewhere.'

Chief Superintendent Paxton was not at all happy with the situation. His Detective Chief Inspector had arrived at the solution to the heinous crime by naming Walter Ackerman as the perpetrator of the foul deed. It wasn't so much the solution to the crime that worried Paxton but the process taken in arriving at that solution; in this case the process of elimination.

'To start with, Chief Inspector Webster, would you kindly refrain from calling our Deputy Premier "Wally". Everyone knows "Wally" in the Australian idiom refers to a stupid or idiotic person. Such denigration of our trusted politicians cannot be tolerated, and Nigel,' Paxton said turning to Superintendent Fisher, 'you dare refer to Walter Ackerman as Wally Ackerman in any of your press releases and I'll have your guts for garters.'

'Understood loud and clear, sir,' came Fisher's response, aware that he may have already unwittingly passed on a disparaging comment relating to the Deputy Premier's mental condition to the press.

'And what evidence have you for your conclusion that Wally, I mean Walter, Ackerman is the guilty bugger?' Paxton demanded. 'From what I've heard there's sufficient motive for nearly every member of parliament to have done him in. And then there's all this garbage about kick-backs for favourable decisions within the tender process.'

Simon frowned. 'Well, first of all, Porter's womanizing within the hallowed halls of Macquarie Street was not confined to Mr Porter alone; others were indulging in the past-time. As a consequence, everyone knew what was going on but no-one was prepared to do anything about it; a case of the pot calling the kettle black, sort of thing. And as far as the kick-backs go, it was Monica Sainsbury Ackerman who was exploiting her husband's position to gain lucrative contracts for her company, Eastern Development. There is one other point, and that leads us back to the time before the last election. From bank statements it would appear Walter Ackerman may have been defrauding the Party of political donations, and Porter probably was aware of such fraud. If he did know, it would've certainly provided Porter with blackmail material.'

'And because all these perverse reasons involving philandering, blackmail, kickbacks, fraud, and Porter's Bill to legalise gambling came to a head at the same time, everything went pear shaped?' Paxton queried.

'That's right. Our investigation does suggest a number of people had a bit more of a motive for killing Porter than others. I'll admit, with some of the suspects the motive is pretty flimsy. People like Andy Crawford, who is a very wealthy man, would have been prepared to pay Porter oodles for his Bill on casinos to be dropped. Obviously, someone negated the need for such a payment because Porter's now dead. But did Crawford kill him to avoid paying? The stupid thing is that there are others who will run with the Bill, not that I suspect Crawford ever thought that far ahead.'

'So, Crawford could still be a contender?' Paxton asked, leaning forward, elbows on the table while his hands fidgeted with a pencil.

'Yes, I s'pose so but I don't think he would kill Porter,' Simon replied.

Paxton, hoping everything would go away, shook his head, his eyes closed. With unconscious effort the pencil snapped. 'Bugger. God, I wish this would all go away. Okay Webster, until you interview the Ackerman family we're guessing, at least, you're guessing. Nigel, not a word of this to the press. Understand?'

'Yes, boss.'

Chapter 32

Noel took aim at the waste paper basket next to Simon's desk then lobed the screwed up ball of paper, and missed which, according to Simon's estimation, disproved the adage "practice makes perfect". 'So, Whacky Packy is not a happy chappy?' Noel said as he lolled back in his chair, legs outstretched, his hands clasped behind his head.

'You could say that, but seeing I've been rebuked for referring to Walter Ackerman as "Wally", I'll rebuke you for calling the Chief Superintendent "Whacky Packy". I don't want to play all my cards yet so I'll presume Paxton is unaware of the scams being perpetrated by our trusty pollies, at least not all of them.'

Noel nodded. 'Okay, but we seem to be placing a hell of a lot on the outcome of the interview with Walter, if and when it takes place.'

'Yes, I know. I'm hopeful Buckmaster will give us a ring sometime today with some details of Wally's return. In the meantime, there are a couple of things I want you to do as a matter of some urgency. I can't believe Wally would leave

Monica stranded by herself somewhere in the Amazon jungle, so I want you to get in touch with the police in Manaus. Let's try to confirm if they did travel from Manaus to Santarem and details of any subsequent travels the police may be able to dig up.'

'Okay, boss. I'll get right onto it as it all sounds a bit suss to me. By the way, have we deleted Andy Crawford from the list of possible suspects?'

'Geez, Noel, how the bloody hell would I know. Crawford's name has been bandied about like a pop star with a personal problem. Seems like all our other suspects knew Crawford was trying to pay people off to defeat the Bill. Obviously, Porter wasn't going to be interested in any of Crawford's financial incentives as he was happily tucked up in bed with Monica Sainsbury Ackerman, figuratively speaking.'

Noel harrumphed. 'I think you mean literally speaking if what I hear is true. So, the only people we have eliminated, well, sort of eliminated, are Henry and Ralph over at GPD at Bondi, and the Masons. What about Graham Lee and Louisa Porter, or should I say the soon to be Louisa Lee?'

'No. They're out of it for the reasons we've already discussed. Graham is too tidy to do away with anyone in the manner Porter was. The killing was a frenzied attack by some homicidal maniac who was obviously a touch angry at the time. A normal person would only stab once or twice, not dice him up for hamburger mince.'

'What about Louisa then?' Noel suggested. 'After all, she did seek a price on the elimination of Superintendent Fisher's wife. What was her name? Agnes, that's it, Agnes Fisher.'

'And that answers your question. If Louisa wanted to

kill her hubby, she would have paid some hit man to do it, just as she thought she would do with Agnes,' Simon replied.

Noel pursed his lips and contemplated. 'What about Buckmaster then? He seems to know everyone else's business. He has his foot on the first rung of the political ladder and, no doubt, has aspirations of greater things. The higher you go the bigger the gravy train opportunities.'

Simon shrugged his shoulders before clasping his hands behind his head. 'Didn't think of him. He seems a nice enough bloke but, apparently, so was Jack when he wasn't Ripping. Anyway, enough of this speculation. Get the hell out of here and go ring the police at Manaus. Just because they're half way up the bloody Amazon shouldn't mean they don't have a telephone.'

'GORBLIMEY, haven't you got anything better to do than annoy people. I told you I had nothin' to do with that body fished out of the harbour and you're still pestering me.' Paul Stack was sitting behind his expansive desk, almost hidden from Simon's view. Simon, expecting to renew his acquaintance with Jacko, had been ushered into Stack's office after having been confronted at the front door of The Spinning Wheel by an unknown doorman.

'I see you have a new doorman. Jacko not around?' Simon asked with a genuine concern for Jacko's whereabouts.

'Yeah. He said he needed to have a few days off so he and his mate left town for a while. Strange, it was kind of out of the blue. He didn't say where they were going or how long they'll be away. Doesn't really matter as he'll still have a job here when he does decide to come home.'

'Which brings me to my next question, Mr Stack. Robert Porter's Bill to legalise casinos will be introduced into parliament soon and is expected to be passed. How do you see that impinging on the operation of The Spinning Wheel?'

'It won't.'

Simon baulked as it was not the response he had expected. 'Ah, could you enlighten me as I thought legalising casinos would be the end of places like this?'

'Look, there are some people like Andy Crawford getting all hot under the collar about it and he's trying his damndest to do something about it. It's all a load of crap. A legal casino will open up casino gambling to the population at large, something they've never had. Sure, they'll cater for high rollers in very selective and exclusive rooms where a minimum bet will be at least a grand. But the main clientele will be the riff raff who will think a casino is the social Shangri-la and the place to be seen, even if you don't gamble. You know, James Bond and all the beautiful women sort of stuff. We'll still have our regular clientele, maybe even more as this place, and others like it, are for gambling, not for wankers to get rotten drunk, chase women and end up being the biggest pain in the bum in town.'

'And Andrew Crawford doesn't see it that way?'

'Hell no. He sees it as a disaster with these places being shut down by the police. He even suggested, in a roundabout sort of way, that I might like to do a job on Porter. Can you believe that, me of all people? See, old Andy just goes like a bull at a gate and doesn't think too far ahead.'

'So, he was seriously considering bumping Porter off?'

'Oh, I'm sure he was.'

'Think he did?'

'Nope.'

'Why?'

'Someone beat him to it. He doesn't realise someone else will introduce the Bill so he's happy forking out bundles of money to anyone who'll listen to his waffle about the problems legalisation will supposedly cause. Nice bloke but....' Stack shrugged and gestured with his hands, palms up.

'And this is the general consensus of opinion throughout the industry?'

Stack didn't answer, just pursed his lips and nodded.

'So, unless there was some disgruntled operator, who you would no doubt know about, we can take it no-one in the industry knocked off Robert Porter?'

'That's about the size of it, Chief Inspector.'

'And you don't think the police will close down your business once the Bill is passed, as it will eventually?' Simon asked.

'No, they won't for the same reason they haven't already. They know that as soon as they close a place down it will open up somewhere else. The police would be running around like a chook with its head chopped off trying to keep track of places.'

'So, for you, Porter's Bill means business as usual?'

'As far as I'm concerned, they can do what they like with it. Who cares? I suppose the only people interested will be some developer who'll build the place at some outrageous price and the politician who receives the kickback for giving the developer the contract. And to hell with any tender procedure.'

Chapter 33

The dramatic conclusion to the investigation into the murder of Robert Porter, MP, had been meticulously planned with every possible detail and anticipated contingency thoroughly examined. Noel, not being as meticulous as Simon, had on rare occasions, come to the conclusion that a Cecil B. DeMille's production would be far easier to stage. Nonetheless, after a lot of coercing, cajoling, and in one case nothing short of a downright threat, Simon had assembled a coterie of guests in the formal lounge room of Walter Ackerman's palatial harbourside home. Chairs from the dining room had been commandeered to facilitate the large number of guests while outside the premises the paparazzi had gathered in strength waiting for the perpetrator of the political assassination to be marched off to the nearest police lockup.

The venue for the gathering had been decided on following the eventual arrival back in country of Walter Ackerman who had agreed to the suggestion put to him by

Simon. Ralph Glover and Henry Haynes sat together on a two-seat settee chatting quietly as if they didn't have a care in the world. Cheryl and Peter Mason, obviously in some sort of domestic dispute, were seated on lounge chairs some distance apart, Cheryl fidgeting with an empty glass in her hand and looking as though she was itching to be elsewhere. Gavin Buckmaster poured a scotch and soda from the cocktail cabinet before returning to one of the dining room chairs strategically placed for a view of the harbour.

Sitting at one end of a three-seater lounge was Andrew Crawford while at the other sat a very glum Paul Stack. Taking into account the serious nature of the evening's get-together, Paul was out to make a statement. In his crusade against the recognized standards of fashionable dress, Paul was wearing a pair of black slacks, an orange shirt and a sickly fluorescent green tie. At first glance Paul Stack probably presented a very reasonable impression of the general expectation of what a Kings Cross pimp might look like. Sitting close together and sipping cherry were Graham Lee and Louisa Porter. Graham appeared to be taking considerable interest in those around him with the occasional nod when eye contact was made with an acquaintance. The remaining red corner invitee, Walter Ackerman, eager for the local gossip since his absence, moved a dining room chair next to Gavin Buckmaster with whom he was now engaged in ardent conversation.

The thought had crossed Noel's mind that those invitees considered to be possible suspects had, by mutual or tacit arrangement, congregated in one general area of the lounge room while those invitees representing the law, another area. As a consequence, Noel viewed the segregation as the corners of a prize fight ring with the suspects in the red corner and the law occupying the blue.

Those arbitrarily assigned to the red corner were either chatting amiably or trying to ignore the situation while the team in the blue corner, all dressed in mufti of varying degrees of formality, were in hushed conversation. Simon, as host for the evening's entertainment and at a total loss as to the path the events would lead, had decided to adopt a position in front of the ornate open unlit fireplace where he now stood, hands clasped behind his back. With Noel standing beside him, arms akimbo, the two men looked over the guests in the red corner before turning their attention to those in the blue corner. Chief Superintendent Paxton, whose patients had finally run out, had issued Simon with an ultimatum; find the culprit or turn in your badge. He was standing next to a sideboard chatting to Superintendent Nigel Fisher, probably about the possible outcome of Simon's investigation and the ramifications it might have on the government.

One person allocated to the blue corner and sitting on one of the dining room chairs enjoying a can of Four X beer was Ron Lange. Ron was not pretentious and, as a dyed in the wool banana-bender now living in Sydney, steadfastly refused to change his allegiance from the Queensland brewed amber fluid, if provided with a choice. It was fair to say Ron was neutral in regards to the matter at hand, notwithstanding his work conducted for Simon on the case. Irrespective of the significance his input may have had on the investigation, Ron had as much of an idea as to who killed Robert Porter as did Simon; none.

'Ladies and gentlemen, may I have your attention please?' Simon requested. 'It's now six o'clock and, as I have no wish to be here at midnight, let's get this show on the road.' After a certain amount of shuffling of chairs and all the guests had taken their seats, Simon began. 'Right, but before we start we'll have a basic ground rule. There will be no interruptions without my consent. I am in control and there will be no interjection while I am addressing a particular person. Just one other thing. Although you have all been invited here this evening, any departure before the conclusion of this little soiree may be seen as being somewhat incriminating. As a consequence, I would suggest to anyone contemplating such action to forget it.

'Now, having got that out of the way and being totally presumptuous, I take it you are all aware of the object of tonight's gathering. If you don't, let me fill you in. Robert Porter, MP, was brutally murdered, not in his home by some deranged homicidal intruder, or in some sleazy alleyway by an underwhelmed irate voter, but in the middle of one of the most acclaimed beaches on the planet; Bondi Beach. As to who killed Mr Porter, I can assure you that by the end of tonight's meeting the perpetrator of the crime will have been identified.'

As this announcement was news to everyone in the blue corner, a few questionable glances were exchanged, notably between CS Paxton and Superintendent Fisher who returned Paxton's gaze with a pout of the lips, raised eyebrows and a shrug of the shoulders. Noel, totally mystified, gave Ron a searching glance and received a similar response with a shoulder shrug. Noel quickly came to the obvious conclusion; he had missed something along the way. It was either that, or Simon had flipped his lid and was about to embark on a career ending oration. The countenance of those guests alluded to being in the red corner, without exception, noticeably darkened with the thought that he, or she, was about to be identified as the killer, or was sitting next to a homicidal maniac.

. . .

GRAHAM LEE, having been given a "heads up" on the format of the night's proceedings by Simon, was not surprised when he became the target of Simon's first accusation. 'Mr Lee, we are all aware that you and Mrs Porter have been shacked up now for a couple of years and are contemplating marriage. And just when do you propose to wed the bereaved Mrs Porter?' Simon asked as he commenced pacing back and forward in front of the fireplace, his hands still clasped behind his back.

'There wasn't anything we could do until scumbag decided to agree to a divorce. He was well aware of our intention to marry but he had the idea a divorce was too trite and common for a politician. Quite okay for royalty but not for our politically correct derelict. Apart from that, he was of the idea a divorce wouldn't do his political career any good,' Graham replied as he took Louisa's hand.

'So, you decided to hurry things along by stabbing him to death? I can't say I blame you as he certainly provided you with sufficient motive,' Simon quickly responded.

'Good God, no. When I have someone removed it's done with class, not like an apprentice butcher trying to carve up a carcass. No, neither Louisa nor I had anything to do with his murder, but when you identify the bugger who did, I'll buy whoever it is a beer or two.'

As Simon and Georgie were close friends of Graham Lee and Louisa Porter, Graham's latest revelation caused Simon some perturbation. He stopped his pacing and said, 'Mr Lee, you just said "When I have someone removed." Could you please clarify that remark, like, just how many people have you had "removed"?'

'Freudian slip. Should have been "if I had to have someone removed", which I don't, and never have. Robert Porter was an annoyance but we could live with that.'

Simon, his hands now in his trouser pockets, recommenced his pacing back and forward, head down in an effort to give the impression he was deep in thought. In fact, that was the impression Simon was going to great lengths to convey to both Chief Superintendent Paxton and Superintendent Fisher. In reality, Simon couldn't suppress the feeling that the hole he was digging for himself was now a gaping chasm, the return from which seemed very remote and getting remoter.

'Alright, Detective Chief Inspector Webster, I take it you're going to use the SWAG method to identify the murderer while we sit here and have to listen to each person deny that they are the killer?' The irate question came from CS Paxton who, with arms folded, had adopted an aggressive attitude towards Simon's apparent glib method of finalizing the investigation.

Simon stopped his pacing and stood at ease, hands behind his back. 'Sir, everyone here with the exception of you, Superintendent Fisher, Sergeant Elliott and Ron Lange and me, of course, had motive for killing Robert Porter. I feel that by extracting the details of each person's motive you will be able to have a better understanding of the type of person Porter was, and of the person who did him in.'

CS Paxton didn't say anything but slowly shook his head. I s'pose it will be interesting to see whether Webster turns into a pumpkin at midnight, he thought. Noel, now sitting back listening to proceedings, finally surrendered to his curiosity and, on rising from his chair, addressed CS Paxton. 'Excuse me sir, you just mentioned the "SWAG" method of identification. As I have not heard of this method before, could you please explain its basic fundamentals as I'm sure it must be a highly developed method of identifying those guilty of serious crimes?'

CS Paxton didn't rise from his chair but sat back and looked at Noel with what could be described as a look of surprise at Noel's lack of knowledge of the vernacular. 'Yes, I'm only too happy to broaden your education, Sergeant, if the ladies will excuse the language,' he said and nodded to Louisa and Cheryl. 'Sometimes all the technical and scientific gadgets at our disposal fail to point us in the right direction during an investigation. To overcome this problem we can, but not too often I'm happy to say, adopt the SWAG method which, in plain language is the Scientific Wild Arse Guess method. Quite simple really, but a method we do not encourage.'

'Aah, thank you sir.' Noel nodded his appreciation although a little embarrassed at his lack of discretion for asking a question that prompted such an undignified answer.

'Moving right along,' Simon said as he resumed his pacing, a little annoyed at having been derelict in Noel's education. 'Mr Ralph Glover of Glover Property Development, I believe you are familiar with the bureaucratic twaddle that goes on when trying to develop a site?'

'Yeah, but what's that got to do with Porter's death?'

'Mr Glover, it might come as a surprise, but we have known for some time the practice of kickback payments made by developers to politicians seeking their favourable consideration. Our interest in that matter is solely to establish if there were grounds for murder, and of course it does; by both you and Mr Haynes for starters.'

'Well it's not so much the "twaddle" as you put it, but the people who are in control of the twaddle,' replied Ralph Glover with a touch of resentment in his voice.

'Care to be a bit more specific? Like, do you mean at local council level or further up the line?' Simon asked.

'Hell, you could start with the janitor at the local council chambers and work your way up to the Premier of the State. They all feel they have God's gift to make things as difficult as possible for you and, if they have a chance of making a quid out of it at the same time, they'll make it even more difficult.' Yep, Ralph Glover is one irritated property developer, Simon thought. Simon was well aware that Glover Property Development was being squeezed out of the development industry as it was unable to compete with the more affluent companies. These cashed up developers, willing to pay politicians bundles of money to get what they wanted, had no conscience; business was business. In fact, Simon felt a touch of sympathy for Ralph Glover, despite the fact that his hair was in a ponytail.

'So, as Robert Porter was one of these people in control of the twaddle, you vented your anger on him by sticking a knife into him a few times, twenty-two times, to be exact?' Simon asked hoping for a positive reply which he didn't get.

'Naah, I've already told you I didn't kill him. But strange you should ask again as Henry and I were talking just the other day about how you'd go about bumping off a politician. Oops, sorry Henry, but I know you didn't murder the bugger. At least, I don't think you did.'

'Aha, so you admit to having given the idea of killing Porter some consideration?' Simon persisted before Henry could get a word in.

Ralph Glover shook his head and frowned. 'Come on, Chief Inspector. Who hasn't considered blowing away a politician at some time in their life? Porter was a menace to anyone in the development and construction industry. If politicians refused the kickbacks offered, we'd all be on a level playing field. This time Porter took the kickbacks so it's no bloody wonder someone killed the pea-brain. Pity it wasn't sooner, but then I s'pose it's better late than never.'

Chapter 34

For Simon the evening was not going well. He had hoped his direct approach by challenging the possible suspects would lead to useful information becoming available. It hadn't, and members of both corners knew it. The thing that worried Simon was just that; the cross-examination of "possible" suspects. Everyone on the planet was a possible suspect, it was just how possible the suspect was that mattered. No-one in the red corner had actually progressed passed the potential possible suspect stage to qualify as a real, ridgy-didge suspect, while those people in the blue corner were possible suspects, albeit highly unlikely. At least Simon did have the satisfaction of believing that somewhere within the possible suspect's red corner, the probability factor favoured the presence of Porter's murderer. But where? Simon was a confused detective chief inspector.

With frustration setting in, Simon was getting annoyed. He now stood in front of the fireplace, arms akimbo, his eyes firmly set on Henry Haynes. 'Since we have heard from Ralph Glover that he and Henry Haynes had spoken of murdering Robert Porter, both men are one small step away from being arrested for conspiracy. Unfortunately, I very much doubt we will ever know if an agreement had been entered into to do away with Porter. Irrespective of the outcome of their conversation, Henry Haynes had motive, and opportunity to murder the man. I'll admit the means are somewhat contentious at the moment but I'm sure we'll be able to come up with something to satisfy that minor issue.'

'Aah, don't talk such utter crap,' Henry sneered. 'As Ralph has already told you, half the bloody electorate and nearly every property developer in town would like to have blown Porter away. So much for your motive. As for your means, I wouldn't bother to try and stitch me up with that one. Every household in the country has at least two carving knives in the kitchen drawer readily available as a murder weapon, so there goes your means. As for opportunity, well, I won't even go there as everyone and anyone has open access to Bondi Beach.'

'Yes, Mr Haynes, a lot of people wanted Porter dead, but you had a particular reason for wanting him to peg out. You worked for Dayman Brothers. Its financial crisis and subsequent forced sale to Glover Property Development can be directly attributed to Robert Porter's intervention, ostensibly on behalf of a group of tree huggers. Of course, in reality his intervention was on behalf of himself and Monica Sainsbury. You knew the shonky Porter had pulled so you drove to Bondi Beach and killed him, with or without Ralph Glover's assistance.' Simon felt elated. He had found the murderer.

Henry Haynes looked at Ralph and shook his head. 'This bloke is definitely whacko,' he said before turning to Simon. 'Just a couple of points, Chief Inspector. First of all,

I live in Lamrock Avenue so it's a lot quicker to get to Bondi Beach by walking than driving. Second, I don't have a car so I couldn't drive to Bondi Beach even if I had wanted to. Third, how in the bloody hell did I know Porter would be running along the beach at that particular time? Fourth, yes I was peeved with Porter, as were everybody else on the staff of Dayman Brothers, because he was directly responsible for the fall of the Company. Fifth…

'Ah yes, Mr Haynes. You have made your point quite clear,' interrupted Simon. 'I take it that somewhere along the line you will proclaim that you did not kill Robert Porter?'

'Chief Inspector,' replied Henry, throwing his hands out, palms upward in a c'est la vie gesture, 'I am sorry, but unfortunately you will have to continue this game of charades as you're perfectly correct, for once; I did not kill Robert Porter.'

Another disaster, Noel thought as he tried to melt further down in the dining chair. He could tell neither Paxton nor Fisher were overly impressed with the results of Simon's earlier declaration that the guilty person would be identified by the end of the night. However, Simon had the two Masons, Andy Crawford and Paul Stack to go, and it was still early.

SIMON HALTED his pacing in front of the fireplace, his left arm now held across his chest, his right on his chin, his index finger tapping his lips. He was deep in thought, still. 'Right,' he finally announced and, with hands clasped firmly behind his back, continued his patrol of the fireplace. 'Mr Crawford, it has come to our attention that you were touting for a hit-man to do a job on Robert Porter. Is there any reason why we should not think you were successful in your quest, the end result being your collusion and conspiracy to kill Mr Porter?'

Andre Crawford threw Paul Stack a very black look and said 'Well, thanks a heap, Judas. Hope you got your thirty pieces of silver.' He then turned his attention to Simon's question. 'I suppose you are referring to a conversation I had with Mr Stack, here. Yes, that conversation took place but there was never any mention of killing anyone. I think I may have suggested someone may want to talk to Porter to see if he would change his mind about his stupid casino Bill, but nothing more than that. Unfortunately, I can't be held responsible if Mr Stack lacks the subtleties of a Grammar school education and misinterpreted or misunderstood my meaning.'

'So, although you sincerely believed you had substantial justification for killing Porter, you refute the allegation that you conspired with person or persons unknown to do Porter in?' Simon demanded as he stopped his pacing and folded his arms in a confrontational manner.

'Of course I refute the allegation, and you've got no evidence to suggest otherwise or to back up your theory. And that's all it is, some deranged theory.'

'And Mr Stack, you stick to your story that Mr Crawford alluded to doing Porter in?'

Paul Stack squirmed on the settee. 'Well, he didn't come straight out and say anything about killing anybody, but he did say the options were running out. My understanding is that once you have no options, you're at the crisis point and have to start to look at the final solution.'

'Which is?' Simon enquired.

'Elimination, murder, assassination. You know, you get rid of the problem. It's like having a mosquito buzzing around you in the middle of the night annoying the tripe out of you. What do you do? You kill the bloody thing. Problem solved. Final solution. Simple,' replied Mr Stack.

'Yeah, that's all very interesting but we ain't talking about a flamin' mosquito. We're talking about the deceased Robert Porter, God rest his sole,' returned Simon.

'Okay, but the final outcome is the same. They're both dead. The mosquito and Porter.'

God help me, another yo-yo from the cabbage patch, Simon thought. So, who have I got left; the Mason and Buckmaster, and I suppose I should have a chat with Wally, seeing it's his house.

Simon sighed and decided to press on resolutely, irrespective of the monumental devastation he had already brought down on his career. A glance at Chief Superintendent Paxton confirmed his assessment of the situation, the Chief in the process of tossing back an extremely large glass of whisky appropriated from the cocktail cabinet where he now stood. Before Simon could continue, Paxton beckoned to Simon with his index finger before making a similar gesture to Superintendent Fisher, Ron Lange and Noel.

Having conferred with those from the blue corner, Paxton made a short announcement to the red corner. 'You'll have to excuse us but we believe it an appropriate time for a short break. I have no doubt the Deputy Premier won't mind should you wish to avail yourself of refreshment from his well-stocked cocktail cabinet if you haven't done so already. In fact, even if you have already done so, feel free to do so again as the night isn't proving to be the most exhilarating way to waste your time. Now, gentlemen,' addressing the blue team, 'outside.'

Chief Superintendent Paxton led the way into a

hallway where the group assembled themselves into something of a circle, Paxton in the middle. 'Okay, Webster. You aroused my curiosity by stating you will name the guilty party by the end of the night. Unfortunately, the way in which you are going about the naming of whoever, gives me the distinct impression you're guessing and, in all truth, haven't a clue who killed Porter. Now, if I am correct, you have seven possible suspects in there without counting the Deputy Premier who is obviously beyond reproach. You've spent half the bloody evening telling us who the guilty bugger isn't, so could you please get on with it and tell us who the guilty bugger is. And if you think I'm fed up with proceedings, even the paparazzi outside the front door has called it quits and gone home.'

Simon's face turned a distinct shade of red. 'Sir, I'm aware that proceedings have become a little protracted. However, we are dealing with the assassination of a politician, probably the first of its type in Australian history, and hopefully the last. Our investigation has revealed a number of what we might call "shonkies", or at least corruption, fraud, swindles, and cheating to name a few, within the parliamentary system. The majority of those people sitting in there, if not all of them, are guilty of crimes, some criminal, some moral, some ethical and some that come without a label.

'I apologise for the time taken to get to the point of tonight's entertainment. However, three of our guests are politicians, as was our assassinated victim and that tends to suggest the murder was politically motivated. I therefore hope I may be able to provide both you and Superintendent Fisher a bit of an insight into the activities of our illustrious squeaky clean, democratically elected assembly of politicians.

'Now, sir, I have three other potential suspects in there that I wish to cross-examine, not counting the Deputy Premier, two of those being politicians and one the wife of a politician, poor girl. Despite the current standing, I still believe that by the end of the night we will have identified the killer of Robert Porter.'

Paxton looked at Fisher and said, 'Ten bucks says he won't.'

Fisher purser his lips and contemplated for no more than a second. 'You're on,' Fisher replied. It wasn't as though Fisher thought Simon would be able to identify the culprit; he at least felt compelled to support his chief inspector.

Chapter 35

On re-entry to the lounge room it was found that Wally's cocktail cabinet had become the centre of attention with members of the red corner taking full advantage of the kind invitation extended by CS Paxton to imbibe in Walter's not so cheap alcoholic beverages. In view of the circumstances, it appeared that most of the guests, if not all, had developed an unquenchable thirst while Wally regarded his rapidly diminishing stock with some dismay.

'Okay people, if you could please take your seats, we'll get this debacle over with,' Simon declared as he punched his right fist into the palm of his left hand. 'First up, Cheryl Mason.' Cheryl, looking quite alluring in a pair of navy blue jeans and a white crew neck jumper that highlighted her short black hair, glared at Simon. You tell anyone about my little problem and Robert Porter won't be the only person to be carved up, she thought before she gulped the remains of her gin and tonic.

Simon ceased his hand punching, clasped his hands behind his back and started to pace to and from in front of the fireplace - again. 'Cheryl, it is generally known you had an affair with Robert Porter before he was murdered, correct?'

'Well, damned as hell I wasn't going to have an affair with him after he'd been murdered. What a bloody stupid question.'

'Well, I don't care just how stupid you think it is, so please answer the question, Cheryl. Did you, or did you not have an affair with Robert Porter?'

'Yes I did, but so did half the women in Macquarie Street, and those who didn't were too old or too smart to be bothered.'

'But I believe the affair ended in some acrimonious feelings between you and Porter?' Simon asked as he continued his pacing, his hands still locked behind his back in the Hercule Poirot manner.

'Yeah, you'd have acrimonious feelings too if your mistress gave you a dose of the clap.' Bugger, thought Cheryl as she banged her glass on the armrest of the chair, her face contorted with frustration, her eyes screwed shut. A ripple of uncontrolled giggles filled the room while Louisa Porter buried her head into Graham Lee's shoulder in a convulsive snigger.

'And your husband knew of this little dalliance, Madam Mason?'

'Of course he knew. He was going to find out one way or the other, wasn't he?'

'Aah yes, of course,' Simon said as he stopped his pacing and turned to face Cheryl Mason. 'Mrs Mason, I put it to you that you were unaware of Porter's exploits within the female population, and you only became aware of this after he had…'

'You don't have to say it, Chief Inspector, but you're right.'

'And this, Mrs Mason, was a total embarrassment to both you and your husband, sufficient embarrassment for you to go to Bondi Beach where you knew Robert Porter engaged in his morning exercise routine. Being aware that the Ackermans were overseas, or supposedly overseas, you broke into their home via an open window and stole the kris that was mounted on the plaque you see here above the fire place. You then drove to Bondi Beach where you did feloniously and maliciously hack Robert Porter to death. Am I not right, Mrs Mason?'

'Yes.'

'So, you admit to the killing of Robert Porter.'

'No, I certainly did not kill Robert Porter.'

'But you just answered "yes" to my accusation.'

'No. I answered "yes" to your question "am I not right" to which, if I had answered "no", would mean your assertion would have been correct. I answered "yes" because your assertion was wrong in the first place and I answered the "am I not right" question, which conversely means "am I wrong" question by answering in the affirmative, which you are.'

'Are what?'

'Wrong.'

'Aah yes. Maybe I should have framed the question a little bit more succinctly,' conceded Simon, totally unaware he had just taught Noel a very good lesson in the art of questioning techniques. Undeterred, Simon returned to the clasped hands behind the back posture and commenced his toing and froing, his head down.

'And you, Mr Mason. The actions of your wife left you in a pretty precarious position,' Simon said, without raising his head. 'I am sure the Premier would not wish to have two of his ministers fighting over the redoubtable Mrs Mason, irrespective of her medical condition.'

'See, that just goes to show how much you don't know,' proclaimed Mr Porter. 'If there were only two ministers fighting over a woman, I'm sure the Premier would be ecstatic. Cheryl wasn't the only one to have the occasional tryst with Porter.'

'And you didn't mind?' Simon asked as he stopped his pacing and looked at Mr Mason.

'I'd be a hypocrite if I did. It would be a case of the pot calling the kettle black as I admit I've strayed within the hallowed halls of parliament more than a few times. Hell, when you get so many men and women together in the one place with stuff-all to do most of the day, you have to expect a bit of hanky-panky. The only difference between Porter and me is that I didn't pass on any…'

'Yes, we quite understand. So, this sort of behavior, together with your wife's involvement gave you a good reason to kill Porter?'

'Yes but no.'

'Yes but no?'

'Yes, it gave me good reason to kill Porter, but no, I didn't, although I bet there are a few other members who wanted him dead, apart from me. You don't think Cheryl was the only one Porter weaseled into bed to spread more than his wild oats? My only fear was that the Premier mightn't take too kindly to the situation you expressed earlier with everyone fighting over the spoils.'

'Hey, hang about,' Cheryl fumed. 'And just how long have you been referring to me as "the spoils", Peter. That's grounds for divorce.'

'Yeah, well so is screwing around and you're in no position to deny the fact, so just shut it,' came Peter Mason's emphatic response.

'Tut tut, Cheryl, no interruptions although I'll concede it does sound all very spicy. Now, Mr Buckmaster, you were aware of what was going on?' Simon, his hands now in his trouser pockets, and looking quietly confident, asked. Needless to say, there were three members of the blue corner who didn't share Simon's apparent confidence with only Superintendent Fisher in support, probably more out of concern for his ten dollar bet.

'You know what's going on, Chief Inspector,' Gavin Buckmaster replied as he crushed an empty beer can. 'I have explained quite thoroughly the ins and outs of social behaviour within Parliament House, along with a few other activities which would, no doubt, be frowned upon should the plebs out there ever got wind of them.'

'I take it you mean the general public?'

'Yes, that's what I said, the plebs.'

'We are talking about overseas junkets and the selective awarding of government contracts to companies, irrespective of whether they've tendered or not, along with a host of other shonkies, including kick-backs to ministers for favourable consideration, such as redevelopment proposals?'

Buckmaster shifted uncomfortably in his seat. 'Look, Chief Inspector. I don't refer to these anomalies as shonkies. They're part and parcel of fringe benefits available to the democratically elected members of parliament and have been available, in one form of another, since time immemorial. Hell, if they hadn't been sanctioned by someone they would never have published "Lurks, Perks Shonkies and Scams" a copy of which everyone gets, along with regular updates.'

'And Mr Porter was an avid reader of "Lurks, Perk, Shonkies and Scams?"' Simon asked.

'Must have been,' Buckmaster replied with a giggle. 'His parliamentary pay went on women and he still had a bank account you couldn't jump over. He used to brag about how much he was being paid.'

'By whom?'

'Chief Inspector, as far as I know Robert may have been receiving money from Humpty Dumpty. How the hell should I know where his money was coming from?'

'Mr Buckmaster, I don't think you realise the position you are in. If our further investigations reveal you had knowledge of just where such payments were originating, you would be liable to a host of criminal charges being laid against you. And you still claim you don't know the origins of such payments?'

'I refuse to answer that question on the grounds of incrimination, but I suppose Monica Ackerman, in her capacity as head of Eastern Development, might have been the instigator. After all, any person appointed Minister for Development and Infrastructure receives bribes from developers; it's all perfectly normal.'

'Yes, we're well aware that you had intimate knowledge of the association between Mrs Ackerman and Mr Porter, both in their financial and social arrangements. And how did you feel about that, Mr Buckmaster? You, having put in so much time and effort in assisting Mr Porter in his ministerial roles, believed you deserved a few steps up the slippery pole from the obscurity of the backbenches. Quite apart from the prestige a ministerial position would provide, such a promotion in the pecking order would, at the same time, present you with a far more rewarding seat on the gravy train.

'Unfortunately for ministerial aspirants, these positions are hard to come by as there are only a finite number of ministerial portfolios available. Sadly, for the backbencher at least, such positions only become available when a minister throws in the towel to accept a quango in some exotic place, like head of the trade delegation to Tahiti, he retires or gets himself expelled from parliament on the grounds of misconduct. And am I correct in assuming there's a promotion for someone when a minister gets themselves hacked to death on Bondi Beach?'

'Yes, I suppose someone might, not that that's an every day event.'

'And you, Mr Buckmaster, were well aware of the bucket loads of money Mr Porter was making while you worked your fingers to the bone making sure Mr Porter's ministerial work was up to scratch. You felt cheated and angry being left by the wayside while Mr Porter was able to get away with doing very little parliamentary work, if any, while reaping the benefits. However, with your extensive knowledge of "Lurks, Perks, Shonkies and Scams", you couldn't wait to inherit the opportunities available to a minister over and above those available to a backbencher.

'The Premier was unlikely to sack a minister for some banal activity, such as that perpetrated by Mr Porter, Mr and Mrs Mason, along with a host of other sexually inebriated paragons of virtue. At the same time, why would anyone want to resign and give up a job offering so many fringe benefits for so little work? For you to make it to ministerial level, someone had to go.

'Mr Buckmaster,' Simon said, having reached the climactic, 'you were, and are, the eyes and ears of the Deputy Premier. It is you who provides him information on what's going on in the backbenches, such as plots, murmurings, scandals and conspiracies. The price Mr Ackerman offered you for this service was the promise to hoist you to a ministerial position, albeit in the unlikely event of a position becoming available. I have no doubt that as you were aware of the scams Wally, I mean Mr Ackerman, was perpetrating, such as the travel rorts, the thought of reaching your goal by a little blackmail may have been considered.

'However, your seat in parliament is on very shaky ground with you just scraping home in the last election and your chances of re-election as a backbencher Buckley's. However, your chance of re-election would be far greater if, by some serendipitous quirk of fate, you held a ministerial position. Unfortunately, the only way you could ensure a vacancy became available on the front bench within your expected elected lifetime was to make sure someone moved on. Mr Buckmaster, I put it to you that that someone who had to move on just happened to be Robert Porter whom you hacked to death on Bondi Beach.'

'Crap and garbage, Chief Inspector, although I will admit that some of what you say is true. Any piece of gossip I hear from the backbenches I pass on to Mr Ackerman. And yes, he did say that whenever a front bench position becomes available, he could think of no reason why I shouldn't be promoted. But no, I didn't kill Robert Porter although he was a sleaze and will probably be stoking the fires of hell right now. I've already told you, I knew he was on the take from a property developer, but so did the Deputy Premier.'

'Well, I think it would be extraordinary if he didn't know, the property developer in question being your wife, isn't that right, Mr Ackerman?'

'Okay, so I might have thought something was going on, but thinking something doesn't make it illegal,' a very smug and self-assured Walter replied. 'Well, Detective Chief Inspector, it looks like your evening has been a complete disaster. I appreciate you may have stumbled across some alleged fraudulent activities, but I have an idea that was not the aim of the exercise. At the beginning of the night you said the perpetrator of Robert's murder would be identified. So far, all we've done is sit here and watch you going around pointing the finger at anyone who may, in your opinion, be abusing the system. So, Detective Inspector, just who is the killer?'

Simon shook his head, one hand on his hip, the other scratching the back of his head for, through Paxton's stated process of elimination, Simon was getting close to the bottom of the barrel. 'Just hang on to your horses, Mr Ackerman, the murderer will be revealed all in good time. Okay, a lot has been said about Monica, so let's have a look,' Simon said addressing the gathering.

'Monica, who can't speak for herself because she's wandering around the Amazon jungle somewhere, was paying kickbacks to Robert Porter. At the same time Walter, who has no officially recognized interest in her Company, was perfectly happy for Monica to pay bucket loads of money to Porter as the government was paying bigger buckets of money to Eastern Development and Investment for government contracts approved by Robert Porter. While I'm no mathematical genius, I have no doubt Monica was making a not insignificant net profit when all the payoffs and kickbacks had been completed. We now know Porter had upped the ante on Monica, demanding a bigger slice of the profits in the form of kickbacks. But as Porter wanted more, that would mean less for Monica. And who knows just where Porter's demands would have ended.

'While he was happy with the status quo for a time, he

was ready to see how far he could push his luck by upping his price for favourable considerations. Obviously, he enjoyed the wicket he was on, but he was also receiving the same fringe benefit Monica was providing from three or four other women. Now, Mr Ackerman, irrespective of your assertion, we maintain you were well aware of the pecuniary arrangement Monica had with Mr Porter. Further, it beggars belief that you were ignorant of their physical relationship as everyone within Parliament House seemed to know what was going on.'

'What do you mean, physical relationship? Monica and Porter had a business arrangement and it was nothing more than that.' Walter stated indignantly.

Simon raised his hands, palms forward in a placatory manner. 'I'm sorry, Wally, but I was hoping to have a more discrete discussion with you. But now you ask, Monica was one of Robert Porter's conquests, although from what I hear she gave in pretty easily. They had both a business arrangement and an extra marital arrangement.'

'Balderdash. What a preposterous allegation.'

'You must have been aware something was going on between the two?'

'Of course there was something going on and it was totally business like. Monica, in her role as boss of Eastern Development, had a lot going on with Porter,' Walter Ackerman replied.

'Aah yes. They obviously entered into consultations and deliberations resulting in an amicable agreement by both parties as to the amount of kickback Mr Porter would receive quantum meruit,' Simon said. 'And these services rendered included the cancellation of contracts already in the system and the reallocation to Eastern Development, all signed off by you, Mr Ackerman.'

'Probably, but I can't recall everything that comes across my table. Look, Monica ran her business and I ran mine.'

'And what exactly is your business? Wally.'

'Good God, man. I'm the Deputy Premier and I have a State to run. And my name is Walter not Wally.'

'Okay, keep your shirt on and let's have a look at Monica's business seeing we now know what your business is. Monica, as boss of Eastern Development, was paying Porter for contracts that normally could have gone to any one of a dozen other developers. Apart from Porter and Monica having a little fling on the side, Porter was getting ahead of himself by trying to up the price paid by Monica for these jobs, or to be more precise, kickbacks. Initially he was happy to receive far less cash from Monica than that willing to be paid by other developers. However, Monica was providing Porter with fringe bene-fits, benefits other developers might baulk at. Come to think of it, I wonder how the Tax Department imposes a tax on such benefits.

'At a guess, and despite your rebuttal, I'd say you were aware that Monica and Porter were shagging like a pair of sex-starved rabbits. It would be very surprising if this situa-tion didn't create a certain amount of ill feeling between you and Porter. At the same time Porter, who couldn't care less who knew what he was up to, was blackmailing you.'

'He was doing no such thing,' roared Wally, kicking over an empty beer can on the floor as he jumped to his feet. 'I have done absolutely nothing that could compromise my integrity, honesty and principles for the duties I have been democratically elected to perform. Blackmail, be buggered.'

'I take it then you repudiate my statement?' Simon asked, quite unruffled by Wally's tirade.

'Of course I repudiate it. The whole idea is a scandalous lie and I'm going to sue you for every penny you have.'

'Aren't you the least interested as to why I make the claim Porter was blackmailing you?'

'No, not in the least.'

'Now, why does that not surprise me, Wally? Sure, go ahead and sue me, for slander I suppose. But all I have said was that Porter was blackmailing you. I haven't said anything about the reasons, but I'm sure everyone can add two and two together.'

The Deputy Premier sank back onto his chair. 'So, no matter what I do now, I'm stuffed.'

'Yep, Wally, although I can't anticipate what action your colleagues in the Party will take. Everyone at Macquarie Street may be on the fiddle but Porter didn't care if he exposed the whole affair to the unsuspecting plebs in the electorate. You're sunk either way. So, for the benefit of Chief Superintendent Paxton and Superintendent Fisher who will, no doubt, convey the information on to the press, I shall press on with the grim details.'

SIMON RETURNED his hands to his trouser pockets and started pacing back and forwards in from of the fireplace, his gaze fixed on the floor in front of him. 'To start with, it was inconsequential if you knew about Porter's relationship with your wife as everyone else in Macquarie Street seemed to be having some sort of relationship with someone else's spouse. It was also common knowledge of the rorts being perpetrated. Every so often some poor unsuspecting back-bencher would be hauled over the coals, vilified, and his crime, usually something so trivial no-one gives a damn about, would be subjected to criminal action, along with his immediate expulsion from parliament. This selective action is designed specifically to inform the unenlightened general public that politicians, on both sides of the House, will not tolerate any activity, real or imagined, that might cast aspersion on the integrity, honour and trust of those elected to parliament.

'However, along comes Mr Porter who's raking in the money hand over fist with kickbacks from Mrs Sainsbury Ackerman, on top of his parliamentary salary. With a little bit of luck he thinks maybe he can scrape in more money with a little blackmail. Armed with the knowledge he has, he threatens you; pay up or I go to the press and reveal your corruption and the waste of tax payer's money.'

'Yeah well, no-one would have ever believed Porter,' Walter sputtered. 'Don't forget, he was still married to a woman who's currently shacked up with a thug who just happens to be the owner of an illegal gambling casino.'

'Yes, that is so,' replied Simon. 'But as you are well aware, Porter held another ace up his sleeve quite apart from the overseas travel rorts, and that was your failure to disclose your interest in Eastern Development. Just because the company is in your wife's name, Monica Sainsbury, you are still required to divulge your pecuniary interest, which you have failed to do. If that little piece of information ever got to the press, your credibility would be shot to the proverbial.'

'Okay, I'll admit Porter and I didn't see eye to eye, but I didn't kill him.'

'I find that hard to believe, Mr Ackerman, as you had motive, means and opportunity. You were being blackmailed by Porter and he was screwing your wife. Surely that is sufficient motive for any self-respecting man to eliminate Porter. You were aware that Porter's exercise regimen included an early morning jog along Bondi Beach which presented you with an ideal opportunity. I also have no doubt that the kris we currently hold as evidence, and according to forensics is the murder weapon, came from the presentation made to you while you were in Malaysia some years ago.'

'Look, Chief Inspector Webster, you're way off course,' responded Walter. 'There are very few politicians from both sides of the House who haven't been guests in this house. There must be literally dozens of people who knew about the kris. Anyone could have stolen it with the aim of setting either Monica or myself up for a murder charge.'

'Ahh yes, the kris,' returned Simon, now addressing members of the red corner with an unconcealed confidence. 'Anyone wishing to frame Walter or Monica Ackerman could have broken into the place and stolen any item that could be trace back to the Ackermans. In this case the kris was a unique item and readily traceable back to the plaque above the fireplace here in this room, a clear piece of evidence pointing straight back to the Ackermans.'

Chief Superintendent Paxton shook his head. 'Yes, I can believe other politicians may have known about the kris. But what about people like Mr Crawford, and Mr Haynes? I'm sure they've never set foot in the place and wouldn't have known about the hatchet.'

'Yes sir, that's very true,' Simon replied, 'and that's one of the reasons why I view the chances of Porter's murderer being perpetrated by a politician as far greater than by one who's not. But surely no-one wishing to frame either of the Ackermans would have disposed of the kris the way it was as it would have been essential for the kris to be found. However, the kris was disposed of with the specific intent that it would not be found. It was just a million to one chance that it was. This suggests that the killer must have been someone who was not out to cast suspicion on either Monica or Walter. And just who had no intention of casting suspicion on the Ackermans? None other than the Ackermans themselves. As a consequence, Mr Walter Ackerman, I arrest you for the murder of Robert Porter. You are not obliged to…'

Paxton jumped to his feet, utterly beside himself. 'Chief Inspector Webster, have you gone completely nuts? This bloke is our Deputy Premier and you're accusing him of murder?'

Wally slouched forward in his chair, rested his elbow on his knees and held his head in his hands. The tension in the room froze as everyone waited expectantly. The silence seemed to drag on before Walter suddenly raised his head and held up his hands to shoulder height in a gesture of surrender. There were those in the red corner who gave a heavy sigh of relief, the murderer finally identified, while Paxton and Fisher looked at each other in sheer amazement. 'I told you, Chief Inspector,' Wally said as he slowly shook his head, 'I did not kill Robert Porter. Monica did.'

Chapter 36

Detective Chief Inspector Simon Webster stopped his pacing, folded his arms and stared intently at Walter Ackerman. If Simon's arrest of Walter Ackerman had caused a ripple of consternation throughout the gathering, this latest revelation created nothing short of a tidal wave. Of all the people gathered in the Ackermans' lounge room, it was Noel who appeared unruffled by Wally's disclosure. After sidling up to Simon, Noel and Simon had a short conversation before Simon addressed the gathering. 'In view of the Deputy Premier's little bombshell, we will take a ten minute break before we continue. I'm sure Mr Ackerman will maintain his hospitality by making the cocktail cabinet available to those who wish to imbibe and I've no doubts there will be a few who do so.'

With the quiet murmur of conversation filtering throughout the room, Chief Superintendent Paxton, Superintendent Fisher and Simon took the opportunity to converse with Walter who had just completed pouring himself a substantial Glenfiddich, his pallid face etched with a look of forlorn dejection. The four men moved to a quiet corner of the room where CS Paxton opened the discussion. 'I hope you know that if what you say is correct, you have just confessed to being an accessory to murder which is an indictable offence?' he asked in a very serious tone.

'Yeah, yeah. So, what are you going to do about it? Lock me away?' Walter responded carelessly.

Simon pursed his lips and raised his eyebrows. 'You know, Chief Superintendent, I'm just a humble policeman who doesn't think too far down the line, but in common law, is Walter obliged to divulge information that would expose his spouse to a criminal charge?'

'It's a bit late for that now as Wally, Walter, has already claimed Monica killed Porter,' Paxton replied. 'I've no idea whether he would be obliged to testify against her, in criminal law, as anything he said would probably incriminate himself.'

'But you've said he's already confessed to being an accessory which is rather incriminating, apart from being an indictable offence in itself,' Simon pointed out.

'Yes, but whoever Wallyter says is the killer, we don't know that that person actually is the killer. Hell, you've got me calling him Wally now. But Walter could say it was his mother-in-law who killed Porter. We'd have to prove it *was* his mother-in-law, and until then Wally can claim Monica, or anybody else he likes to name, is the killer. The operative word here is "claimed" despite the context in which he says it.

'You can't make him tell us another thing about the murder as I think a person is not obliged to expose his spouse to criminal charges, which is what he appears to have already done. Now, if we can prove his wife did kill Porter, it's obvious Wally was aware of the murder, and that would make him an accessory after the fact, if not before as well, which is rather incriminating for Wally. Obviously, we would have to prove Monica did kill Porter before we could charge Wally.' After a moment's thought as to what he had just said, Paxton shrugged as he struggled to come to terms with the legalities of Wally's confession.

'But what if Wally's wrong and she didn't do it? To prove Wally is guilty of being an accessory to murder, we have to prove she is the guilty bugger. Obviously if we can prove someone else is the guilty person, that will let Wally off the accessory hook and we can nail him for a number of other things, including perverting the course of justice and interfering with a police investigation. Despite Wally's assertion, Monica Sainsbury Ackerman doesn't appear to be available to charge her with jay walking, let alone stabbing Robert Porter to death,' Simon said, totally lost as to where the discussion was headed.'

Having listened to Simon and CS Paxton debate the fate of Monica and Walter, it was Walter who lost his patience. 'Look you two, how about I tell you what I know about Porter's death and then you can go away and play around with the technicalities?' he proposed as he finished his drink.

Simon looked at Chief Superintendent Paxton who gave a shrug, as did Superintendent Fisher. 'Alright, but I don't see any reason why we should keep everyone hanging around when it seems we're getting down to the nuts and bolts of this crime,' Simon suggested.

'No, that's fine. You can dismiss them,' replied Paxton.

It came as no surprise following Simon's dismissal that the remaining members of the red corner, each member having already been accused of murder, remained seated in expectation of the gruesome and sordid tale Wally Ackerman was, evidently, about to reveal. The only movement in the room was that of Henry Haynes and Ralph Glover who proceeded to the cocktail cabinet for refills and subject the cabinet to a rigorous search by Henry for peanuts or popcorn.

The members of the blue corner returned to their seats leaving Walter standing alone in front of the fireplace. 'Okay, Wally, let's have your side of the story,' Simon said as he took a seat and crossed his legs while Noel extracted his notebook, expectant of forthcoming copious note taking.

'Alright, but I'll précis it down to the significant facts. First off, Monica and Robert Porter had a thing going; well, obviously lots of things. As you know, Monica was the boss of Eastern Development and Investment, which is a pretty good achievement in such an industry. But Monica was tough and would get what she wanted, and she wanted the plum government contracts. While I was able to help in her acquisition of such contracts, we felt it would look far more kosher if she had the support of someone else in government, apart from the Deputy Premier who just happened to be her husband. As a consequence, I introduced her to the Minister of Planning and Infrastructure, Robert Porter. For his support in the allocation of contracts, Monica agreed to pay him a percentage of the contracted price; the bigger the contract the bigger the kickback.

'Everything was rosy until they, Monica and Porter, decided to have more than just a business arrangement. That's when they started what was referred to around Macquarie Street as The Grand Shagathon. Of course, everyone thought it a bit of a joke, but as everyone else was up to something or other, no-one said a word. Unfortunately for Monica it became a bit more than a physical thing, which meant it was time for Porter to head for the hills as the last thing he wanted was to get emotionally involved. In the meantime, Porter had started to get greedy and wanted a higher percentage of the contract kickback. Eventually it came to a head when Porter told Monica to pay up or no more government contracts, and that their personal relationship was over. Monica was devastated, despite her being the hard-nosed company executive. She apparently really liked the bloke, stupid woman. After giving the matter some thought she approached me with an idea. If Porter could be removed from his position as Minister for Planning, we could replace him with someone more conciliatory, like me.

'I told Monica that it would be difficult to dismiss Porter without a good reason. Unfortunately, both of us already had the reason but neither of us could do anything about it. I might have jokingly said something about whacking him but …'

Yep, Simon thought. Wally is getting a bit peeved. 'And have you any idea as to when your wife will choose to return to Australia?'

'She said she'd be back in a few days but knowing Monica that could be a few months,' Wally replied.

'And your departure was amicable, despite your assertion your wife had butchered one of your parliamentary colleagues?' Simon asked with raised eyebrows.

'Of course it was amicable as there was nothing to fight about. What did you expect it would be, a domestic slinging match?'

Simon left his seat, placed his hands in his pockets and

started his fireplace stroll, head down. After what seemed to be an inordinate time of deep deliberation, he stopped his pacing and looked at his attentive audience. 'Okay, people, I'm stuck with a bit of a conundrum. Wally has pointed out the motive his wife had for killing Porter. She knew when Porter was available to get himself stabbed to death, and she had access to the weapon that stabbed him. By the same token, some of these points so painstakingly alluded to by Wally can just as well apply to himself. Now, while we haven't heard a whisper from Monica Sainsbury Ackerman, I believe there are always two sides to a story. Do we therefore take it on face value and accept what Wally has said and that Monica did feloniously and brutally hack Robert Porter to death, or do we chase after Monica and hear her side of the story?'

'String him up now,' yelled Henry. 'If Wally says she's guilty, then so is he. And don't forget, he's a politician and when's the last time you believed what a polly had to say.'

'It's got to be one or the other,' stormed Buckmaster, eager to see the demise of the Deputy Premier; two parliamentary vacancies on the horizon.

'No, his old woman did it. She's the brains behind the Ackermans' fortune. She'd do anything for a buck and she saw a way of getting more buckets of money by getting rid of Porter,' put in Peter Mason in the hope his support for the Deputy Premier would not go unnoticed.

'Well, I reckon whoever did him in should get a medal,' interjected Andrew Crawford. 'To carry on with his stupid Bill to legalise gambling casinos was nothing but hypocrisy and just plain bloody stupid. And this is one time where Paul and I agree. Isn't that right, Paul?'

'Yeah, Andy's right,' Paul agreed. 'Who cares who crossed him off their Christmas mailing list?'

Simon removed his right hand from his pocket and held it up in the universal "stop" sign. 'Okay, okay, let's not get carried away. There are ten of you, including Wally. Hands up those who think Wally's right and that Monica did away with Robert Porter.'

Chief Superintendent Paxton couldn't believe what he was hearing. 'Hey, have I missed something? This is the most idiotic thing I've ever seen and certainly not the way to go about conducting a murder investigation, Chief Inspector Webster. And just how often do you conduct a survey to determine who the guilty person is?'

'What else can I do, sir?' Simon appealed. 'Either Wally or Monica killed Porter, or maybe they both did. And right at the moment I haven't a clue as to exactly what happened. I just know they were both involved.'

'Okay,' replied Paxton. 'Just for interest sake, let's find out what the general consensus of opinion is.'

'Right, those in favour of Monica being guilty, raise your hand. And not you, Ron. You're in the blue corner,' Simon directed.

Ron reluctantly pulled his hand down. 'Yeah, well only a crazed woman could hack up a body the way Porter was hacked up. Blokes are more circumspect about wielding the hatchet,' Ron added, disgruntled that his vote was invalid.

It was easy for Simon to take the count; four of the ten red corner members for Monica's guilt. 'And those who think Wally is the murderer.' Another four hands went up. 'Okay, I take it the two abstainers, Andy and Paul, couldn't care less who did Porter in as long as he was done in. Right, Sergeant Elliott, do you have anything to offer seeing we have a hung jury?'

'Oh, yes,' Noel replied eagerly. 'I have a bit of information that may warrant another vote being taken by the time

I'm finished. You have no objections, Chief Commissioner?'

'No, not at all. I'm a little intrigued to hear what you have to say.'

Chapter 37

As Simon drew up a chair next to the cocktail cabinet, Noel took centre stage in front of the fireplace. Dressed in a charcoal grey suit, white shirt and light blue tie, impeccably tied for a change, he looked the epitome of correctness and efficiency and ready to throw the case of the murder of Robert Porter wide open. 'Ladies and gentlemen, before I start, I would remind you that there will be no interruptions. Any points you wish to make may be made at the end of my disclosure.

'Now, Detective Chief Inspector Webster has already covered some of the possible motives for the murder of Robert Porter. Monica Sainsbury Ackerman had just been given the flick by her boyfriend, Robert Porter, while the same boyfriend was in the process of trying to extort a bigger slice of the kickback pie from Monica. On the other hand, we have Walter Ackerman being blackmailed by the same Robert Porter, the grounds for this blackmail being the systematic abuse of the parliamentary system and the failure to disclose pecuniary interests.

'We have heard from Wally of the events both leading up to the murder and the subsequent events, including the hasty departure of both Monica and Wally for greener pastures, notably the Amazon jungle. We will not muddy the waters by delving into matters of parliamentary fraud and scams perpetrated by the Honourable Member, Walter Ackerman, but will concentrate on the events following Monica and Walter's arrival in those greener pastures. Just one point, Walter. You didn't tell us Monica was born in the UK and holds a British passport.'

'Why should I? It's none of your bloody business what she holds.'

'Ooh, Touchy bugger. Okay, I won't labour the point right now so let's kick on. On the fifteenth of March, Wally and Monica took the afternoon flight from Sydney to Buenos Aires. After spending three nights at the Hilton Buenos Aires they travelled to Manaus by air where they stayed at the Intercity Premium before taking a four day trip up the River Negro on the luxury cruise boat, "Grand Amazon". Both Walter and Monica have been confirmed as passengers on the vessel when it departed Manaus. Members of the crew of the "Grand Amazon" can recall having seen Monica for the first two days of the cruise when, according to Wally, Monica felt unwell and remained in her cabin for the rest of the cruise.

'Now this is where we start to have a problem. According to Manaus police, there is no record of Monica ever having left the vessel on its return. At the same time, the police have confirmed that on the return of the "Grand Amazon" to Manaus, Wally immediately bought a ticket on the ferry for downstream Santarem. Once there he checked in, alone, into the El Dorado for two nights before flying back to Buenos Aires and on to Sydney. While information is readily available on Wally, nothing has been seen or heard of Monica since the second day of the trip up the River Negro.

'Wally says Monica, who had miraculously recovered from her bout of whatever it was, caught the ferry from Manaus to Santarem with him. While staff on the ferry can remember seeing Wally, they cannot recall having ever seen Monica. It seems strange that no-one saw Wally in the company of a woman on board the ferry, and even stranger that Monica didn't check into the hotel in Santarem with Wally. But there again, he checked into a single room which prompts the question; just where was Monica?'

Simon rose from his chair and joined Noel centre stage. 'Thanks, Sergeant Elliott, I'll take it from here as I think you may have opened up a can of worms. There are ten people in this room who had motive for killing Robert Porter and there are ten people in this room who have professed their innocence. Alright, as there isn't anyone willing to confess, let's assume for a moment that Monica Ackerman is the murderer. She had motive, means and opportunity. On top of that, it seems Monica fled, or should I say departed, the country on the day of the murder. But it could be said Wally did too. However, Monica's disappearance in the middle of the Amazon jungle might be viewed by some as an admission of guilt and that she will lie low until the heat is off, so to speak.

'But what if Monica is innocent? I will present a scenario of what I believe happened and remember, it is only a scenario based on fact, innuendo and ridiculous claims. To begin with, it must be remembered that Robert Porter was no paragon of virtue or integrity so, in effect, he was no different from any other member of parliament, but with one exception. While Porter had enough ammunition to blow the whistle on every politician in Macquarie Street for their corrupt shenanigans, there must be a host of other members who could probably do the same thing. Irrespective of who could, or couldn't, Porter was the only one who seemed to have the guts to try it on, with Mr Ackerman being the target.

'Porter was well aware of the scams, especially those relating to fact finding tours being perpetrated by all and sundry. In fact, Porter was blackmailing Ackerman with his knowledge of these scams, together with Ackerman's failure to declare his pecuniary interest in his wife's company. I won't go into the details as you are well aware of what was going on. However, things were getting pretty tacky for both Walter and Monica, the situation all brought about by Robert Porter.

'Having discussed the matter, Mr Ackerman and Monica came to the conclusion Porter had to go, his position as Minister for Planning and Infrastructure to be taken over by someone else. The fact that Monica had decided Porter had to go was made all the more easy after Porter told Monica their intimate relationship was over. Needless to say, Wally considered himself to be the logical replacement for Porter while Monica had someone else in mind. Now, who actually did the carving up of Porter is open to speculation, although psychological profiling would suggest Monica was the murderer. We're all aware that the female of the species is the more dangerous and beware the rage of the woman scorned, and Monica had definitely been scorned by Porter.'

'Hey Simon, just how long is this going to go on for? It's

getting late and Louisa and I haven't had dinner,' Graham Lee asked with an annoyed look.

'Sorry, Graham, no-one is obliged to hang around, but I'll let you know we're just getting to the juicy bit. Feel free to leave although I think you might like to hear my theory of what happened,' Simon replied. No-one departed. 'Okay, so now we're at Manaus and Wally and Monica decide to take a four day trip up the Negro which enters the Amazon at Manaus. Everything is rosy until Monica drops the bombshell. She tells Wally that the next Minister for Planning and Infrastructure will be Gavin Buckmaster. Okay, so Wally has no idea that Monica even knows Buckmaster and he suddenly has the thought that Monica and Buckmaster have to know each other pretty well for Monica to say what she just said.

'It's here that things get a bit complicated. Monica was involved with Porter emotionally, although I doubt her feelings were reciprocated. Porter wanted more money from Monica and less of the fringe benefits; he had amble supply of that commodity as it was. Monica now wanted Porter out of the picture altogether as she had found a new bedmate, Buckmaster, who was willing to provide support for Monica's development plans. All she had to do was convince Walter to get rid of Porter, metaphorically, and she could have her cake and eat it as well.

'After her patience ran out waiting for Walter to do something, Monica probably took things into her own hands and got rid of Porter, literally as she was in no position to get rid of him metaphorically. If Monica was present tonight I have no doubt she would claim that it had been Wally who killed Porter. I can only speculate that when Buckmaster's name entered the equation, with all the ramifications that presented, Wally flew off the handle and dispatched Monica over the side of the good ship "Grand Amazon". Needless to say, the chances of finding her body floating down the Amazon are pretty remote, even if the piranhas haven't already disposed of the body. The police in Manaus have been very helpful but there is little they can do. They claim it would be a pointless exercise to go running off down the Amazon looking for a human body even in the dry season; and it's the wet season there now. They'll keep a watching brief on the subject but unless something comes up and bites them on the bum, that's all they can do.'

'And what role do you claim I had in the murder of Robert Porter?' Gavin Buckmaster enquired nervously.

'Oh, I think there may have been some pillow talk between you and Monica, you know, hypothetical stuff and the "what if" questions,' Simon suggested. 'Now, correct me if I'm wrong, but I wouldn't mind betting the idea of doing away with Porter literally must have been mentioned at some point.'

Gavin Buckmaster shook his head in vehement disapproval. 'No, no, no. It was not like that at all. Sure, I wanted a ministerial position so I could get a more rewarding seat on the gravy train. Monica suggested I might like to become the Minister of Planning and Infrastructure which is the best unofficially paid job in parliament and one you don't normally get as your first ministry. I told Monica what a great idea and that I would be willing to forego the kickbacks she was paying to Porter. Provided I received certain fringe benefits, we had a deal. Needless to say, Monica agreed enthusiastically. Even without the kickbacks, Monica would get my support in the allocation of government contracts and I would be happy just with the better rorts that are only available to ministers, and receive Monica's fringe benefits, of course. But as far as my involvement in the Porter killing goes, I had nothing to do with it.'

'Okay,' Simon said, 'you have always maintained your innocence, Mr Buckmaster, so if you are telling the truth, that leads us back to Walter's statement. But as it happens, there is no-one to refute Walter's claim that Monica killed Porter. We can only speculate what Monica might say on the matter if she were here, and alive, that is.'

'Hey, hang about. Who says Monica is dead and what makes you think I chucked her overboard from some stupid boat up some stupid river?' Walter sneered. 'She was the one most likely to go around killing people, not me.'

Simon, in response to Walter's aggrieved comments turned to Wally Ackerman. 'Mr Ackerman, right from the beginning of tonight's little soiree you have alluded to Monica in the past tense; Monica *was* the boss of Eastern Development; Monica *was* tough. It's as if Monica is a part of history and no longer exists. You also mentioned earlier that if it was proved she was guilty of killing Porter, and to use your exact words, she would be viewed as the deranged homicidal wife of the Deputy Premier, a title that would be somewhat detrimental to your position.

'Apart from that, we have only your word that she killed Porter. It's a case of "he says, she says", but in this instance there's no "she says". Maybe you are the killing type.'

'So, what now?' Wally asked contemptuously. 'I claim Monica killed Porter and you claim I killed Monica and might have even killed Porter. There's a hell of a lot of "mights" being bandied about, including the one that Monica might be dead. You haven't any proof of who did what to who.'

'To whom,' interjected Noel.

'To whom what?' Walter responded somewhat bewildered.

'Who did what to whom. Grammar, Wally. You know, the Queen's English stuff.'

'Christ, of all the time to give me an English lesson. Look, you plods, Monica killed Porter and right at this moment she's shacked up in some plush hotel sippin' a pina colada in downtown Manaus,' responded Walter, his dander again rising to extreme levels.

'Okay,' Simon replied, 'let's have another vote on the subject of who killed Porter. All those in favour of Wally being guilty?' After some time one hand was slowly raised and, following some furtive glances around the room, another three followed. 'Okay, those in favour of Monica?' Six hands went up almost instantaneously. 'Well, well, well. Andy Crawford and Paul Stack have changed their minds. What was it that made you change your mind, Andy?'

Andy Crawford shrugged and pursed his lips. 'Wally's story was good but really, Simon, I think you've hit the nail on the head. Monica killed Porter, with or without Wally's help or approval. But as Wally himself said, Monica's little enterprise in ridding herself of the cursed politician would probably be viewed as a career inhibiting factor for himself. To clean up the mess, he did Monica in as you have described. And to be honest, Noel's information does seem to cast a teeny bit of doubt on Walter's story.'

'And you, Paul?'

'Well, I look at it this way. If you knew your misses had just hacked up a bloke with all the finesse of a Jack the Ripper look alike, there must be a pretty good reason to jump on the same plane and travel to some out of the way place halfway up the bloody Amazon. I'd say Wally must have been a little irritated when Monica revealed to him her exploits of what had happened on Bondi Beach. Monica sealed her own fate by killing Porter as she immediately became the albatross around Wally's political neck. As a consequence, he decided to get rid of her and the middle of the Amazon jungle seemed like a good place to do it. Right now you'll probably find Monica Ackerman floating off down the Amazon on her way to the Atlantic Ocean.'

Simon looked at Paxton and gave a shrug which was duly reciprocated. What now? Simon thought. 'Okay people, I know what I said at the beginning of the night regarding the exposure of the person responsible for the death of the Honourable Robert Porter, MP. I am under no illusion that the killer of Robert Porter must be either Walter or Monica Ackerman.' Although the investigation, at least to this point of time, has failed to positively identify the killer, you may be sure the truth of the matter will eventually be revealed. The other person of considerable interest with whom we would like to interview is Monica Ackerman who appears to have vanished somewhere in the Amazon rainforest. Despite whatever I may think regarding Walter's involvement in her disappearance, there is nothing to support my theory; a non corpus delicti situation. With that in mind, and the assertion by Walter Ackerman that his wife is guilty of murder, Monica Ackerman will have to be considered both a suspect and a possible victim.'

Reluctantly Superintendent Fisher extracted a ten dollar note from his wallet and offered it to CS Paxton. In a display of gracious magnanimity, Paxton smiled and rejected the note. 'No, Nigel, let's call this a draw as Simon has given us the name of the murderer, albeit in a round-about sort of way. May I suggest you play the diplomatic role and simply tell the press that investigations are continuing? I'll let the Commissioner know what's going on and he'll, no doubt, tell the Minister.'

'Well, I suppose that means we can go home now?' Cheryl Mason asked pointedly.

'Yes, I suppose it does, Mrs Mason,' Simon agreed, 'I suppose it does.'

Chapter 38

A bright, sunny winter's morning, a cloudless sky and a gently sou'wester creating nothing more than a gentle ripple on the harbour; what could be better, thought Simon as he and Georgie headed hand in hand along the pontoon. On reaching their destination, Charlie Chambers helped the couple onto the deck of the fifty five foot flybridge cruiser, "Gemini". Moored at Rushcutter Bay, the "Gemini" was owned by Graham Lee and had been the object of past episodes of intrigue and police curiosity. The last episode had occurred some twelve months earlier when Charlie, the "Gemini's" fulltime deck hand, found a body attached to the anchor. After Simon and Noel had conducted an extensive investigation, it had been determined that the body, by sheer coincidence or a quirk of fate, belonged to Bruce Glover, brother of Ralph Glover.

'Well, this is a pleasant change,' Simon announced as he and Georgie entered the saloon. 'Sun shining and not a cloud in the sky.'

Noel, who had arrived earlier, was sitting with Sue on a

lounge running along the port side of the saloon. He absently scratched the back of his neck, frowned and slowly shook his head. Simon, having noticed Noel's facial expression take on a new dimension, knew something moronic was forthcoming; he wasn't wrong.

Addressing Simon, Noel asked, 'Simon, is that an example of tautology or is it a pleonasm?'

'Is which what?' Simon replied somewhat mystified.

'Sun shining and not a cloud in the sky.'

'Well, what about it? That's what we have at the moment.'

'Just wishing to improve my grammar, purely for my report writing skills, but "not a cloud in the sky"; isn't that using unnecessary words? Like, if a cloud wasn't in the sky, where else should we expect it to be? In fact, I don't think I have ever seen a cloud that wasn't.'

'Wasn't what,' Simon asked, totally ruffled by Noel's asinine questions.

'In the sky, where else? So, you see what I mean then?'

'God damn. Someone get me a beer.' That boy just has to go, Simon thought as he shook his head. Graham Lee, aware of Simon's discomfort, handed him a can of beer along with a look of pity.

After relaxing back into a comfortable chair, Simon took a long draught of the amber fluid. 'It's been far too long since we've all got together and I do miss our little back lawn gatherings, even if it has only been a month or so. And I must admit, Graham, "Gemini" is a bit more modern than "Chez Anne" although both of them seem to be predisposed to murder and mayhem; good times and bad.'

Graham Lee only smiled on the odd occasion but when he did it was a pleasant, whole hearted smile augmented by his smiling eyes. He was smiling now. 'Yes, good times and bad although I'm not sure whether the body on the end of the anchor was good or bad, but I will admit, it was different. Anyway, what's the verdict?' Graham asked as Louisa took Simon's empty can and handed him a glass of beer and Georgie a wine.

Simon settled himself and gave a deep sigh. 'What a bloody shambles this one turned out to be. But first off, my apologies for claiming you and Louisa were suspects. I had to do that to shy away from any bias or conflict of interest other people may have considered existed.'

'No, that's perfectly understood. Louisa and I do plan to marry and with Robert out of the way there's no impediment to that marriage.'

Simon smiled. 'Yes, we can't have you and Louisa living in sin just because Louisa's husband was playing silly buggers, can we?'

'Well, I don't care who did it, but when you find the person, you can thank whoever from both of us,' Graham said as he took Louisa's hand. 'Come on Simon, you can tell us. Just who did do it and what's the current situation?'

'Yeah, and what did Paxton have to say?' Noel asked. 'He made it quite clear he didn't want me around at the time.'

'Okay, okay. One at a time, please. First off, Graham. Your question as to who did kill Robert Porter. I don't know is the short answer.'

'But you had ten suspects there the other night. Does that mean no-one there was the killer?' Louisa asked, mystified.

Simon took a long draught of his beer before replying. 'Eight suspects,' he corrected. 'Let's go through them and see what you think. 'We'll eliminate the Mason' as I don't think Peter wants to climb the parliamentary ladder with all its back stabbing, disloyalty and corruption. He's an ex foot-baller and played by the rules. I think politics and the dubious antics of politicians have been something of a cultural shock for him. As for Cheryl, Porter did her wrong and she had good cause to be annoyed with him. But if everyone infected with a dreaded social disease decided to kick the infectee off the planet, we'd have a population implosion.'

'Ooh, I wouldn't say that. If she did kill Porter for that reason, I'd say it would be a case of justifiable homicide,' interrupted Judy.

'Now, now Judy. Just calm yourself and have another wine,' Ron said as he poured Judy another glass of Chardonnay.

Simon gulped the last of his beer, took another can offered by Graham, pulled the ring tab and filled his glass; not a garbage can in sight; such decorum. 'Right, next two on the list are Ralph Glover and Henry Haynes. I list these two together as they basically have the same problem; Eastern Development and Investment. Porter...Sorry Louisa, you don't mind if I refer to Robert as "Porter"?'

'No, that's fine. You can refer to him however you like, but not as a gentleman, thank you,' replied Louisa with more than a hint of apathy.

Simon continued. 'As I was saying, Porter was in a posi-tion to obtain government contracts for specific property developers, more notably Eastern Development. In fact, he was in a position to reverse some decisions already passed by local councils, as Henry Haynes found out, to his loss. Porter had no scruples and considered a property developer as nothing more than a money-making android. For him people didn't exist, just the company. He never considered the personal disruption and angst created when his actions sent a company to the wall, such as when Dayman Brothers collapsed. I suppose that's only to be expected as only a few, if any, politicians have ever lived in the real world.

'Fortunately for Henry, Ralph Glover was aware of Henry's animosity, or more likely hatred of Porter. At the same time, Ralph could see the writing on the wall for Glover Property Development which would mean Henry would be soon out of a job, again. But Ralph could placate Henry's rage by the mere fact that he is a pragmatist. Despite Porter being more destructive than a wrecking ball, Ralph realised that Porter's time as the wrecker were finite; no position is eternal. Glover Property Development was just hanging on in the belief that something had to happen and it did; Porter got himself murdered.

'With Porter dead and the position of Minister for Planning and Infrastructure vacant, every politician on the government side of the House will be scrambling over the dead body to get the position. The government hasn't indicated one way or the other what the future of Wally is although I suspect Buckmaster is now hoping he stays on as Deputy Premier.

'Although everyone knows that everyone else knows, there's a tacit acknowledgement that the Minister for Planning's position is substantially subsidized by cashed up developers prepared to pay mega bucks for favourable consideration, commonly referred to as kickbacks. Really, nothing changes with Porter's death and the status quo remains, even if Buckmaster does get the job. So, in the words of Ralph himself, they can only tender for contracts no bigger than the construction of an outside dunny in the schoolyard.'

'Okay,' Ron exclaimed, 'that leaves us with two politicians, Ackerman and Buckmaster, and two...' Ron screwed up his face in intense concentration. 'I don't know how you refer to them; gangsters, thugs, casino operators.'

'Don't worry about it as we all know to whom you are referring; Crawford and Stack,' Simon replied. 'Crawford was concerned as to the future of his establishment once Porter's Bill for the legalisation of casinos was passed. Stack was far more open minded and was quite indifferent as to the outcome of the Bill. Crawford was the more outspoken of the two and had often considered his options, including the elimination of Porter. I think both Crawford and Stack finally realised the Bill would be introduced into parliament irrespective of whether Porter was alive or dead. Ergo, it would have been a complete waste of time for Crawford to kill Porter, and Stack couldn't have cared less.'

AFTER ABOUT THREE quarters of an hour's cruising at a leisurely pace, Charlie engaged neutral and let "Gemini" slowly drift to a halt before letting loose the automatically driven anchor. In view of the light westerly breeze Charlie had decided to park off Forty Baskets Beach, on the Manly side of the harbour, a small, quiet, out of the way spot generally free from noisy and uncivilized boaties.

'Since Simon's down to the last two remaining suspects of the Porter case, it might be a good time for lunch which will be held on the afterdeck' Graham suggested, 'it should keep you all a quiver with anticipation.'

It was during this pleasant luncheon that Noel turned to Judy and asked, 'I hear you had a bit of a problem with your house at Collaroy?'

Judy nodded and finished off a mouthful of salad before replying. 'You could say that, but everything seems to be turning out for the better. The police have called it arson by persons unknown, and the insurance company has called it arson by persons unknown and has already settled my claim, bless their little heart. I've been to see a builder and work should start on the new place pretty soon. All hunky-dory, really.'

'And have you seen Jacko since the fire?' Noel asked tentatively.

Judy slowly shook her head and replied, 'No, I don't think anyone has but I seem to recall someone saying he'd left town. I really feel sorry for Jacko as he's a nice bloke and was only trying to help me out. We were all wrong about the neighbours, or at least I'll concede, all us girls were. But at the same time, we were right in that they were into growing stuff using hydroponics, and they did give any reasonable thinking person the idea of what it was they were growing. It just that the stuff turned out to be toma-toes, not marijuana.' Noel pause to considered the phrase "reasonable thinking person" and decided, with discretion being the better part of valor, not to go there.

Following an enjoyable lunch everyone returned to the saloon eager to hear Simon's conclusion to the sordid tale of bureaucratic swindles and murders. Well, at least one murder. Standing at the forward end of the saloon, Simon folded his arms and waited until everyone was seated and relaxed. 'Now, although the debacle at the Deputy Premier's home has given us cause to think we just about know who Porter's murderer is, I have not totally exoner-ated all the suspects of the crime.'

'Graham Lee looked troubled. 'Okay, if that is the case, can you give us some idea as to the extent of your suspicions?'

'Yes, I think so. As we are all betting people here, the

best way to illustrate the situation might be by framing a betting market based on probabilities. As a consequence, I would have Andy Crawford at eight to one; Stack at fifties; Glover and Haynes at tens; the Masons at twenty to one and Graham and Louisa at one hundred to one.' Before he could continue with the remaining suspects, Charlie Chambers interrupted the proceedings.

'Excuse me, Mr Lee. Mind if I join you?' Charlie asked having torn himself away from his favourite position high on the flybridge. 'I am a voter and a tax payer and I'd like to see just what sort of person I get for my money.'

'No problems with me. Simon?'

'No, not at all. Come on in Charlie. We're just about to have an inquisition into the life and times of our illustrious Deputy Premier, Walter Ackerman, MP, and his wife, Monica, or at least into their involvement in the death of Robert Porter, MP. As you might not be aware, the end result of the meeting at the Ackerman's house the other night ended in a bit of a fiasco although I honestly believed Walter Ackerman to be guilty of Porter's death. Just as I'm about to caution him, he stuffs everything up by saying it was Monica who killed him. Now, it seems Monica has done a bunk and nobody can find her, although you are probably aware of my ideas on that score. For Charlie's benefit, I reckon Wally chucked her off some Amazon River cruise boat. Needless to say, we can't say for sure if she was dumped overboard but if she was, the chances of finding her body are pretty slim.

'As far as the Porter case goes, the only evidence we have against Walter is circumstantial, as is the evidence against Monica. With Monica we have both circumstantial and a hell of a lot of hearsay evidence which, as you probably know, is inadmissible, especially as long as

Monica continues to deny us the pleasure of her company. Monica's situation is more problematic as neither we, nor the Brazilian police, have any evidence of a crime being perpetrated. I don't know how the Brazilian legal system works, but I think they would need a body before they would investigate. And to be honest, if I was a policeman stuck half way up the Amazon and someone rang me from the other side of the world saying there might be a body in your lagoon, I'd tell them to get stuffed.'

'So that means you don't know who killed Porter; you don't know if Monica is dead; you don't know if it was Monica who killed Porter; you don't know if Walter killed Porter; you don't know if Walter murdered Monica, if Monica has been murdered. It seems like there's a hell of a lot you don't know,' Charlie remarked.

Simon shrugged. 'Doesn't make us look good, does it? Fortunately, Paxton is sympathetic to the problem and appreciates there's not much we can do about it. I'm just glad it was Superintendent Fisher and not me who had to face the press meeting. Fortunately, the press believes there is far greater news around now the football season has started. They're too busy chasing up idiotic events, like which footballer got drunk last night, to worry about the murder of a Minister of the Crown. I suppose the only get out of jail card we have is that we have sent the investigation report, for what it's worth, to the Director of Public Prosecution. It'll be up to him to determine whether there's enough evidence to establish a prima facie case against Walter and whether that evidence is sufficient to stand up in court.'

'And what about Monica?' Louisa asked. 'All you have is Walter's claim that she's the killer.'

'Together with a bit of circumstantial stuff,' Noel broke in.

Charlie handed Simon a can of beer, already opened, which Simon gladly accepted choosing to dispense with the glass. 'As I said, the Brazilian police will let us know if her body turns up, not that there's much chance of that, at which point they'll start an investigation. If she does happen to be still alive, contrary to popular belief, they'll let us know if and when she tries to leave the country. Trouble is, Monica has dual nationality; apart from her Australian passport, she also holds a British passport as she was born in Bradford, a fact we were unaware of until Noel had talks with the Immigration Department. That in itself could help her disappear, although as far as we know she hasn't left Brazil, yet. Problem is, no-one seems to know where she is. Maybe she's already in Argentina, or the USA, or anywhere, if she's not dead that is. If Monica is guilty of Porter's murder, as claimed by Walter, my guess is she'll head for some country that doesn't have an extradition treaty with Australia. Mind you, there are a few countries close handy to Manaus, such as Costa Rica and Honduras, or even Guyana. But who would choose to live in any of those countries unless you had a substantial income from somewhere?'

'So, what's the betting market on the Ackermans?' Noel enquired.

Simon pursed his lips and thought for a moment. 'With Crawford at eights I'd say Walter is at fours and, with injuries inflicted on Porter's body that only an enraged woman could make, Monica has to come in as favourite at three to one.'

'Okay, in view of the fact you think we're a bunch of

bimbos, the girls will put twenty dollars on no-one going to trial,' taunted Judy.

'At even money?' replied Simon.

'No way. Two to one at least,' replied Judy.

Ron looked at Graham before casting a searching glance at Charlie who appeared somewhat disillusioned by the whole affair. 'You mean to tell me this is the way our elected representatives behave, like a bunch of yahoos?' Charlie asked anyone who cared to answer.

'No, not all of them, I think,' Simon replied. 'There must be some good ones in there somewhere. But let's look at it. This case started off with a simple murder which progressed to the uncovering of rampant scams being perpetrated by politicians who are legally entitled to a host of benefits us plebs couldn't begin to imagine ever existed. Then along comes the gravy train stacked full of little under-the-counter goodies and shonkies that the pollies would never admit to being available.'

'So, this is what I vote for,' Charlie said, now thoroughly dejected by Simon's revelation. 'Next time I'll remember just what our illustrious representatives in parliament get up to; murder, scams and gravy trains.'

About the Author

John Henderson was born in Singleton, New South Wales. The family moved to the town of Yass soon afterwards where he spent his younger days before a further move, this time, to Sydney. John went to Manly Boys High School, represented the District in cricket and spent time surfing. He joined the army in 1968 and toured Vietnam in 1969-70.

After a brief stint in the Commonwealth Public Service, and with his dry, cynical sense of humour, John chose to write crime satire. A Blind Eye, Anchor Man and Murder, Scams and the Gravy Train in the Simon Webster Fiascos Series, represent an amusing and skeptical view of life and bureaucratic nonsense as view by the author.

 twitter.com/JohnHenderson07

www.ingramcontent.com/pod-product-compliance
Lightning Source LLC
Chambersburg PA
CBHW071257170626
46809CB00001B/257